Hannah had the str
the answer to her h **hope**
was near.

She took a step forward. Then the doors swung open and out walked the man she'd come to find. Why hadn't she prepared better for this first glimpse of the rebel preacher? Hannah stared as the tall, powerful figure stalked across the street. His dark blond mane hung a little too long and she was enthralled by his bold, chiseled features.

He suddenly turned his head and their stares connected. Locked.

Hannah couldn't move. Couldn't breathe.

She quickly tore her gaze away. She had to remember why she'd come all this way to find this particular man.

"Reverend O'Toole?" Hannah called out. "May I have a word with you?"

"Do I know you, miss? What can I do for you?"

"I've come from Chicago to enlist your help. I must find your brother Tyler, before it is too late."

Books by Renee Ryan

Love Inspired Historical

*The Marshal Takes a Bride
*Hannah's Beau

*Charity House

RENEE RYAN

grew up in a small Florida beach town. To entertain herself during countless hours of "laying-out" she read all the classics. It wasn't until the summer between her sophomore and junior years at Florida State University that she read her first romance novel. Hooked from page one, she spent hours consuming one book after another while working on the best (and last!) tan of her life.

Two years later, armed with a degree in economics and religion, she explored various career opportunities, including stints at a Florida theme park, a modeling agency and a cosmetic conglomerate. She moved on to teach high school economics, American government and Latin while coaching award-winning cheerleading teams. Several years later, with an eclectic cast of characters swimming around in her head, she began seriously pursuing a writing career.

She lives with her husband, two children and one ornery cat in Georgia.

RENEE RYAN

Hannah's Beau

Steeple
Hill®

Published by Steeple Hill Books™

STEEPLE HILL BOOKS

Steeple
Hill®

Recycling programs
for this product may
not exist in your area.

ISBN-13: 978-0-373-82816-6

HANNAH'S BEAU

www.SteepleHill.com

Printed in U.S.A.

Wherefore receive ye one another, as Christ also received us to the glory of God.

—*Romans* 15:7

To my fabulous editor, Melissa Endlich.
Your suggestions, support and overall guidance
were invaluable in the process of writing this book.
Thank you for taking a chance on me.
You are, quite simply, the best!

Chapter One

The Grand Opera House, Chicago, Illinois, 1883

Shakespeare's delightful comedy *Twelfth Night* progressed toward its dramatic conclusion as planned. Lies were exposed with the perfect blend of surprise, satisfaction and charm. Truths unfolded at a precise, believable pace.

Usually, Hannah Southerland loved the challenge of translating every nuance and plot twist found on paper into a memorable performance onstage. But as tonight's final act drew to a close she found herself wondering if art didn't imitate life a bit too closely, at least in her case.

Mistaken identity? Twins separated by misfortune? A woman in disguise from her true nature?

Uncanny, really. Peculiar.

Eerie.

With nothing left to do but take her bows, Hannah stood poised in the shadows, watching the last moments of the play. The only sign of her growing unease came in the rhythmic tick-tick of her pulse and the slight shake of her hands. Otherwise, she held herself rock still, letting the sound of actors reciting their lines, and the rustle of patrons shifting in their seats, echo in her ears and pulse through her blood.

These moments, when fantasy blurred into reality, were why she'd first pursued the stage five years ago. She'd craved the escape. Needed it as much as breath itself. In the end, she had found a new home with a large family to love her as her own had never been able to do.

Unwanted memories slid into her mind, playing out as strangely real as the last moments of the play. She'd been so afraid that dark, wintry night when her father had banished her from his home. All because she had played a well-rehearsed role, one she would never take on again.

In the ensuing years since her exile, Hannah had discovered a more powerful force than fear. *Faith.*

Now, if only her twin sister could find the same peace in Christ that she had.

With that thought, Hannah leaned slightly forward, her eyes searching for the woman positioned off the opposite end of the stage. There she stood, a mirror image of Hannah, yet profoundly different. It was the look in her eyes that set Rachel apart from Hannah, the startling combination of purity and audacity that had turned the heads of many unsuspecting men.

Rachel's presence at the theater tonight evoked a myriad of emotions—happiness that Rachel had left her fiancé barely a month before the wedding for the sole purpose of reconnecting with her estranged sister. Disappointment that Hannah's father had chosen not to come with Rachel. Hannah had hoped that after five years the venerable Reverend Thomas Southerland could find it in his heart to forgive her.

As Hannah had forgiven Rachel.

If, during her sister's brief stay, Hannah could teach Rachel about true accountability, maybe, *maybe,* Hannah could move on with her life. Without the guilt. Without the burden.

Without the shame.

Her hands started to shake harder, threatening her outward calm. A deep, driving urge to run away washed through her. Instead of giving in to the cowardice, Hannah threaded her fingers together and clutched her palms tightly against one another. In this mood she could feel the edgy nerves of her fellow actors, the underlying desperation to deliver the perfect performance.

Unable to bear their emotions along with her own unsettled ones, she shifted her gaze toward the audience. Flickering light illuminated the theater, casting a golden glow over tonight's patrons.

Hannah squinted deep into the shadows until her gaze focused. Countless faces stared at the stage with the kind of rapt attention that widened the eyes and slackened the jaw.

As expensive and wealthy went, the affluent men and women viewing tonight's closing performance had no rivals. Except, perhaps, in London. And like those patrons of the British theater, they fully accepted the illusion of true love found in the midst of deception.

Hannah took a deep breath and turned her attention back to the stage.

At last, the actor playing the clown recited his final line and made his exit. A hushed pause filled the theater. Like waking from a lovely dream, eyes slowly blinked and then...

The applause thundered, passing through shadow, to light, to empty stage.

The curtain began its slow descent, but not before the audience played its own part in the production and surged to its feet. The sound of their approval rumbled past the velvet folds as the soft thud of the thick, heavy material landed on the stage floor.

Chaos instantly erupted behind the delicate veil between audience and actor.

"Places, everyone," yelled the director. He turned to Hannah and motioned her forward.

Hannah wove her way through the labyrinth of rushing humanity, gliding toward her spot in the center of the troupe. She pushed back an unexpected flash of trepidation—one she hadn't felt since that terrible night of her banishment—and moved with the liquid grace born from tedious hours of practice, practice, practice. Each step required concentration, control and commitment. The kind that set Hannah apart from her other, more talented contemporaries.

Once in place, Hannah allowed the soft buzz of excited chatter to drift around her as she waited for her fellow players to join her. She rubbed her tongue across her teeth, a nervous gesture left over from childhood, before turning her head to seek out her sister once more.

Rachel stood watching the commotion with the wide-eyed innocence that had led her to be termed the "good" twin. But as with the play just performed, the outward impression was pure illusion.

Hannah was suddenly jostled by the actor on her left,

jerking her attention back to the drawn curtain. Her hair swung out with the swift gesture, curved under her chin, then settled.

With a flick of her wrist, Hannah shifted the ebony mass of curls behind her back. Thoughts of her sister were not so easily set aside. However, right now, Hannah needed to concentrate on the other, equally disturbing emotions warring inside her.

Lord, fill me with a humble heart.

How easy it would be to fall for the adoration displayed inside the deafening applause seeping through the velvet barrier. To believe the praise was for her alone. To give in to the temptation of accepting glory for a gift that was merely on loan to her from her heavenly Father.

Blessed are the poor in spirit, for theirs is the kingdom of heaven.

Hannah pressed her lips together. Her mentor, Patience O'Toole, had taught her how to focus on being a light in the dark world of theater—a modern-day Babylon that required the resolve of Daniel and the courage of Shadrach, Meshach and Abednego to keep selfish ambition at bay.

How she missed the grounding influence of Patience and her flamboyant husband, Reginald. The surrogate parents who, with the perfect blend of Christian grace and earthly truth, had helped boost Hannah's broken confidence and heal her battered heart.

With a shake of her head, Hannah forced her mind on the present and smiled at her astonishingly handsome costar as he swept into view.

Golden, spectacular, larger than life, Tyler O'Toole— Patience and Reginald's youngest son—never missed an opportunity to make an entrance. Although likable and charming, Tyler had his own agenda in life. Three priorities ruled his actions. Amusement. Pleasure. And, lest she forget, merriment. Unlike the rest of his siblings, Tyler would always be a selfish boy at heart.

"You were breathtaking tonight, my dear." His voice was as dramatic as the rest of him, a husky baritone that carried to the last row in any theater.

Prepared to offer her own congratulations, Hannah looked up at his chiseled, beautiful face. He was the brother she'd never had, the one member of the troupe—other than his mother and father—who had worked tirelessly with Hannah to perfect her stage presence. In spite of his many faults, and there were *many,* Hannah couldn't help but admire the man. Tyler O'Toole was a brilliant performer.

Tonight had been no exception.

But before she could compliment his performance, he reached for her hand, bent at the waist and dropped a kiss onto her knuckles. The gesture was pure Tyler Bartholomew O'Toole, sincerity wrapped inside an insincere, theatrical flourish.

He rose slowly, deliberately, and then sent her a suave, half smile that seemed to say, *But, truly, wasn't I equally brilliant?*

Hannah lifted a single eyebrow. "Tyler, you—" She broke off, realizing she'd already lost his wavering attention.

Against her better judgment, she followed his gaze with her own—across the stage, past the rest of the hurrying cast, straight to the spot where her twin sister stood a little off to one side.

Rachel stared back at Tyler, giving him the serene, artful smile that had brought several men to their knees. Standing separate from the cast and crew, with a single beam of light casting a soft glow around her, Rachel looked like a beautiful, mysterious siren calling to any man willing to fall for her fantasy.

Tyler's answering sigh came out pitiful, a tiny bit miserable and yet, somehow…calculating. In the next moment he unleashed his own secret weapon, the careless wink that had been practiced and perfected over the years. And had left its own destructive wake along the way.

Hannah stared at the two in disbelief, a knot of anxiety tightening her stomach.

Different man. Same sister.

One perfect disaster in the making.

And somehow, some way, Hannah would be the one to bear the consequences. Just like last time. Just like *every* time.

She should have realized when she'd introduced the two yesterday she'd been putting an open flame to a haystack.

No. No, no, no. Hannah had spent too many years taking the blame for her twin sister's indiscretions, and too many months watching Tyler break women's hearts, to hold her tongue now. "Tyler, stay away from my sister. Neither of you has any idea what sort of trouble you're flirting with."

Her words came out flat, hard and—unfortunately for them all—fell on unhearing ears.

"Stay away from that gorgeous, stunning creature? You demand the impossible, Hannah darling," Tyler said. "Rachel's smiles slay me, and her voice is sweeter than any angel's."

Clearly oblivious to the tension growing between their two leads, the other actors continued scrambling into place.

"Don't, Tyler." Pressure built in Hannah's chest, stealing her breath and drying out her throat. "Just… *don't.*"

"Why, my dear girl, you sound quite discouraging. One might start to think you disapprove."

A familiar, albeit unwanted, affection broke past Hannah's annoyance. Tyler had the kind of droll humor that reared at the most inappropriate of times and invariably took the sting out of an uncomfortable situation. It was hard to dislike a man who was as fully aware of his faults as his talents. Even if he used both to his full advantage whenever the occasion suited him.

Well, tonight, where too many lives might be harmed, Hannah could not—*would not*—allow a budding flirtation to turn into something more destructive. "Tyler, you must listen and take heed. She's—"

A groan from the rigging stopped Hannah in midsentence and had both Tyler and her turning toward the curtain to fulfill their final duty of the night.

Conversation among the rest of the cast halted, as well.

A few more seconds of rope grinding to metal and the curtain began to rise. The audience leaned forward, eager to get a better look at the actors. With every inch of the curtain's ascent, their palms pounded wildly together, again and again and again. Louder and louder and louder.

Hannah slid a glance at Tyler. With a sly grin lifting the corners of his lips, he reached out and twined his fingers through hers. Together they raised their joined hands in the air then bent into a well-rehearsed bow.

Rising first, Hannah shot a quick slash of teeth at Tyler, and then leaned forward again. They repeated the process until the applause died to a mere spattering.

As the curtain made its final descent on the Chicago production of Shakespeare's delicious comedy, Hannah feared a tragedy far worse than any fictional tale was already in the making.

With another warning perched on her lips, Hannah turned to Tyler, but she only caught the wild flourish of coattails as he spun in the direction where Rachel stood.

"Tyler, wait. She's—"

He dismissed her with a careless flick of his wrist.

Hannah lifted onto her toes to see past the other actors. "Rachel," she called out. "You can't. You're—"

But her sister shifted to her left, literally turning her deaf ear in Hannah's direction. It was an old trick of Rachel's, a hard kick aimed straight at Hannah's guilt, an open defiance that did not bode well for a reasonable end to the escalating situation.

Nevertheless, Hannah set out after Rachel and Tyler. The two quickly disappeared behind a side curtain. The backstage area was already filled with commotion, making it difficult for Hannah to see precisely which direction they had taken.

After several long minutes of searching, Hannah thought she saw two shadowy figures leave the building, but prayed her riotous imagination had taken over her logic.

There was one dreadful hope left.

Shifting direction, Hannah turned toward Tyler's dressing room. She'd only taken two steps when one of the crew materialized in her path. "Hannah, your sister told me to give you this after tonight's production."

He pressed a piece of paper against her palm, then turned back to assist the stage manager in breaking down the set.

Hannah squinted toward the backstage door then looked down at the small, folded parchment in her hand. A foreboding filled her, and a hard knot formed in the pit of her stomach.

She unfolded the note with trembling fingers. Her sister's looping script flowed through a single sentence.

Be happy for us.

"Oh, please, *please,* not again."

Chapter Two

Denver, Colorado
Three days later

Harsh, irregular breaths wafted through the tiny room. The acrid smell of death filled the air. Both occupants sat wrapped in their own state of despair, each struggling for answers to unbearable questions. One had lost her will to live. The other had come to bring a final, eternal hope.

With the burden of his mission weighing heavy on his heart, Reverend Horatio Beauregard O'Toole swallowed his own sense of helplessness and looked at the haggard woman battling for each breath. There was little left of the vibrant creature Beau had met when he was but a boy. The gifted lead actress who had inspired a generation of aspiring young girls was now a broken shell of her former greatness.

She had no more faith. No more purpose.

No more hope.

Beau could barely reconcile this beaten woman with

the one who had played some of the greatest heroines onstage with such confidence and verve. Once her crowning glory, now her hair hung in blond, dirty strings. Her skin pulled taut across her thin face, while her eyes had sunk deep in their sockets. She was a mere apparition of the beautiful woman the public had adored with near obsession.

Beau dropped his chin to his chest and released a defeated sigh. No. He would not give up on the woman his mother had once called friend.

He lifted a skinny, limp hand into his, closed his fingers over the pale, graying skin. "Miss Jane, all is not lost."

She gave him a ragged, quivering sigh.

With his own answering sigh, he released her hand and brought a glass of water to her cracked lips. He lifted her shoulders with one hand and helped her navigate the glass with the other. "You may still survive if you turn from this life forever. We could leave for Colorado Springs this afternoon."

Jane took a slow, choking sip and then leaned back. "No." A slow, harsh breath wheezed out of her. "It's too late."

The words had barely slid off her tongue when she broke into a fit of coughs.

Beau pressed a white cloth against her mouth, afraid each cough wrenching through her fragile body would tear her flesh from the bone. After the bout ceased, Beau pulled back the cloth now filled with the red stain of blood.

Blood from her damaged lungs.

Another moment passed in utter silence.

Beau's heart pounded so hard with anguish for her, for what she'd become, he thought he might choke from it. Now that the stage was no longer a viable prospect, Jane Goodwin had chosen to earn her money in the most hideous way imaginable. It hurt to see how far she'd fallen.

A shudder racked through him. If only she would accept God's grace and Beau's charity.

"Dear, sweet Beau." Jane turned her head and blinked her dazed, drugged eyes up at him. "My sins are too many to wash clean now. Why else would I be here?"

She waved her hand in a gesture that seemed to say, *Look where we are.*

The heartsick tone of her voice took him aback. Beau glanced around the tiny room decorated purposely for sin. In the bright light of day, beneath the expensive silk and satin, hung a shabbiness that spoke of the years of hard, ugly work that had acquired the worldly trappings. And yet the room had a sad, unkempt feel. Once brilliant, now forgotten.

Just like this woman.

Just like the rest who shared residence in this... house.

Too many for one man to help.

He closed his eyes, once again praying for wisdom. A small, still voice inside said, *One at a time, Beau. Start with this one.*

All right. Yes.

Beau asked God for the words to convince her to leave, but behind his confident demeanor he was soulsick with the hollow feeling of defeat. "Miss Jane, please reconsider my offer. The sanatorium is only a day's train ride away."

He tried to capture her stare, but her gaze darted

around, eventually locking on to his left shoulder. "I...
No, it's impossible."

He reached out and cupped her hand in his, staring
fiercely into her eyes. "All things are possible through
Christ."

"Not for my kind." Her voice was uneven, shaky, the
underlying disgust at herself no longer hidden behind
false bravado.

She'd given up then, resigned herself to die thinking
she'd turned so far away from God that she could never
find her way back, had convinced herself she deserved
this sort of hell on earth.

"God forgives all sins, even the seemingly unforgivable ones." He spoke with the conviction of his heart.
"You need only to ask."

"You don't understand." Jane tugged her hand free,
the sharp gesture at odds with her infirmity. She struggled to speak, her lips moving frantically while words
seeped out in a soft wispy whoosh. "I have a daughter."

Beau studied Jane's vulnerable expression with
mingled pity and horror. He hadn't known. Hadn't
realized. But he should have. He'd seen it often enough.
The unbearable chain of sin continuing from one generation to another. "She is here? Living in the brothel?"

"Megan is at Charity House. If I leave, if I don't
work, I cannot continue to pay her board."

Charity House. Of course. Beau knew all about the
special home where children born to women of ill repute
were welcomed without question. Marc and Laney
Dupree, the owners, never turned a child away. No
matter the financial circumstances. Jane was worrying
over something that would not be a problem, ever.

"But if you don't leave, you will make your daughter an orphan. How is that any better?"

Another fit of coughing was her only response.

Beau shut his eyes for a moment. He must not quit on Jane. He must not. God had called him to minister to the ones with no more dignity, no identity, no...hope.

He knew firsthand what it meant to be an outcast, never fitting in the world around him. Although he adored his family, without their passion for acting, the constant years of traveling from stage to stage had left him feeling alone and separate from the rest of his siblings. Even in seminary his modern ideas of preaching and evangelizing had never truly meshed with the more traditional views of his professors.

He had yet to find his place in the world. Thus, he traveled from mining camp to saloon to brothel, ministering to the outcasts of this world. Outcasts such as women like Jane.

But soon, if the vote went his way, he would have his own church in Greeley, Colorado. It would be a place where he could put down roots and begin a normal family with a traditional wife by his side. Her soft, compassionate nature would temper his overly bold, often impudent personality. He hadn't found *her* yet, but he would and then his days of traveling across the territory and ministering to the forgotten would come to an end.

Well, not completely.

All would be welcomed in his new congregation. No matter their past sins or current ones. His church would be a safe haven for the lost. For the—

The door flung open with a bang. In swept a whirlwind of angry female and bad attitude. "Beauregard O'Toole, you know your kind isn't welcome in this establishment. To think. A minister, here, in *my* brothel." Her voice was incredulous. "It's just plain bad for business."

Beau rose and turned to face the new occupant of the room. With her outrageously buxom figure, unnaturally blond hair and overly painted face, Mattie Silks looked far older than her reported twenty-nine years of age.

She took two steps into the room, and then relaxed into a pose that spoke as much of her profession as her vanity.

Notorious. Legendary. With her own unique flair for the dramatic. Even without formal training, she could hold her own against any stage actress Beau knew. His lips pulled into a wry grin. Clearly, the woman had missed her calling.

Nevertheless…

If there was one thing his childhood had taught him, it was how to appease a dramatic woman in a fit of theatrics.

"Now, Miss Silks." He gave the surly madam a smile so filled with O'Toole charm that even his rogue brother, Tyler, would envy the result. "I am only here to visit my mother's dear friend."

"No." She switched poses, thrusting out one hip and slamming her fist onto the other. "You are here to talk my best girls into leaving."

Perhaps. But if Beau didn't try, who would? The Bible had taught him to look past the outer wrapping of a person and see into their heart. Well, Beau had done that sort of looking in the past weeks he'd held vigil by Jane's bedside. Not a single "girl" in Mattie Silks's employ wanted to be in the notorious madam's…well, *employ.* Not even one.

But without a concrete alternative, most had no other means of supporting themselves.

Beau considered the situation to be an opportunity straight from heaven. There were only two things humans could accomplish on earth that they would not be able to do in heaven: sin and evangelize. Beau truly believed God had brought him to this den of iniquity to be a light of hope. To plant a seed that might bring the lost back to Him.

One ill-tempered madam wasn't going to run Beau off that easily. "I simply offer to listen, and give advice accordingly."

"You mean preach."

Love the sinner, hate the sin.

Even Mattie Silks deserved his best efforts. "Preach, give advice. Semantics, Miss Silks, nothing more."

She gave him a hard look. "Thanks to you, two of my girls have already quit."

Beau sighed. He'd hoped for more. Shaking away his feelings of powerlessness, he continued holding Mattie's stare. "Only two?"

Her lips twitched before she pointed at him with a gnarled finger that revealed her true age. "You are an arrogant man."

Beau couldn't deny that one. He was, after all, an O'Toole. His natural arrogance was a character flaw he had to fight against daily. His professors at seminary had tried to break him because of it. His fellow students had shunned him. He'd been run out of countless churches. And even now, the Rocky Mountain Association of Churches still questioned his ability to shepherd the new congregation in Greeley. All because he was an arrogant son of…actors.

Beau dropped his gaze to Jane and watched her fight

for each breath of air. "I won't leave my mother's friend in the midst of her distress." He brushed a hand across her brow. "There is no changing my mind, Miss Silks. I am determined."

Mattie's eyes flashed. "And if I say otherwise?"

Beau couldn't fault the woman for her territorial reaction. This wasn't the first time he'd walked into a brothel since leaving seminary, only to be unceremoniously tossed out when the madam in charge discovered who he was. Or rather *what* he was.

Nothing like experiencing a little shunning of his own to help him better relate to his unusual flock. "You'd deny one of your girls a moment of peace in her final hours of life? Are you so cruel?"

Her gaze wavered, just a bit, revealing that Mattie Silks might have a heart beneath the tough businesswoman veneer. "You think she's that ill?"

"*Dr. Bartlett* thinks she's that ill."

Mattie shifted from one foot to the other then peered slowly down at Jane, who had finally fallen into a labored sleep. For several long heartbeats the madam merely stared at the near-lifeless form dragging ragged breaths into its injured lungs.

"I saw her perform once. Years ago, here in Denver. Such a talent. Such a waste." She shook her head and sighed. "You may stay, Reverend O'Toole. But I'm warning you. Keep yourself hidden."

Beau blinked at the sudden capitulation. Mattie Silks, hardened madam, had gone from outraged employer to saddened friend in a heartbeat. Talk about dramatic range.

"I have no plans of leaving her side," he said.

"Then we understand one another. Stay away from

my other girls. You *preach*—" she spat out the word "—and out you go."

Beau simply nodded.

Fanning herself with her hand, Mattie sighed again. "It's scandalous, really. A preacher taking up residence in a parlor house."

Beau gave her his best Sunday-school smile. "The Lord works in mysterious ways."

Three days of unsuccessful searching had brought Hannah to Denver, Colorado, feeling defeated and frustrated. Rachel and Tyler had completely vanished. The sheer gravity of their selfishness, the reality of the ensuing scandal, had nagged at Hannah during the entire journey from Chicago to Colorado.

Hannah lowered her head and sighed. Why would Rachel run off with Tyler when she was engaged to a man who had adored her since childhood? Why would her sister throw away the guaranteed devotion of a good, Christian man for the wavering affection of a fickle actor?

Well, this time Rachel would face the consequences of her actions. Hannah would make sure of it.

Of course, she had to find her sister first.

With Patience and Reginald O'Toole performing in London, and the rest of their acting brood in New York, Hannah had one potential ally left, a man who might be able to help her right this terrible wrong.

Exhausted from her travels, but resolved nonetheless, Hannah checked the return address on the letter, folded the paper at the well-worn creases and shoved it into the pocket of her coat. For several moments longer, she allowed her gaze to sweep up and down the street, taking note of the houses and rushing populace, before her attention came to rest on the building directly in front of her.

If houses had gender, this one was surely female. Elegant, whimsical, the two-story building was made of rose-colored stone. The bold lines of the roof and sharp angles were softened by rounded windows and sweeping vines. On closer inspection the house looked a bit neglected; the twisting wisteria covered a few sags and wrinkles that made the building look like a woman refusing to accept her age.

A swift kick of mountain air hit Hannah in the face. She pulled her coat more securely around her middle and shoved her hands into her pockets. As her gloved fingers brushed against the letter, a fresh wave of guilt threatened her earlier resolve. At first, she'd been reluctant to read the correspondence addressed to Tyler from his brother, but after that initial hesitation she'd been too desperate *not* to open the letter.

Unfortunately, all Hannah had gleaned was the deep affection one brother felt for the other, and Reverend O'Toole's last known address. Thus, here she stood outside one of the most notorious brothels in Colorado, shifting from foot to foot like a nervous schoolgirl and praying Reverend O'Toole was still here, ministering to his mother's friend.

Buck up, Hannah, she told herself. *God has protected you this far.* Even with the gravity of the situation weighing on her heart, it was hard to marshal the courage to walk across the street and pass through those heavy double doors.

But really, how did one go about entering such an establishment in the light of day?

She took a deep, soothing breath and prayed for the nerve needed to continue her quest. Contrary to the cold, stale air, the sun hung high in the middle of the sky, bleaching the street with a blinding white light.

Oh, please, Lord, he's my last hope now. Let him agree to help me.

If she found Rachel and dragged her home, would their father believe Hannah wasn't to blame, after she had carried the burden of Rachel's actions all these years? Ever since Hannah had refused to chase after Rachel when they'd fought over a neighbor boy, Hannah had faced the consequences of her selfishness. Rachel had lost her way in the woods that cold winter day. She'd caught a fever and ultimately had suffered permanent hearing loss in one ear. Out of guilt—the debilitating guilt of knowing she was to blame for Rachel's disability—Hannah had accepted responsibility for her sister's many transgressions.

The pattern had been set long ago, the roles so familiar, to the point where Rachel was now a master at using Hannah's guilt against her.

Tears pushed at the backs of Hannah's lids, bitter tears of frustration, of helplessness, of the sharp fear that she would once again bear the burden of shame because Rachel would not atone for her own sins.

Of course, no amount of feeling sorry for herself was going to bring her sister back. Squinting past the sunlight, Hannah was filled with the strangest notion that the answer to her heart's secret hope—one so personal she hadn't known it existed—was near. She took a step forward. And another one. On the third, she froze as the doors swung open and out walked the man she'd come to find.

Every rational thought receded at the sight of him. Why hadn't she prepared better for this first glimpse of the rebel preacher?

Hannah stared, riveted, as the tall, powerful figure stalked across the street. The bright daylight set off his sun-bronzed skin. His dark blond mane hung a little too long, artfully shaggy. She held her breath, enthralled by the bold, patrician face, the familiar square jaw and chiseled features that declared he was, indeed, an O'Toole.

So similar to Tyler, but even from this distance Hannah could see the lack of slyness in the eyes that defined his scoundrel brother. Oh, there was boldness there, confidence, too, but also…sadness.

Oddly attuned to him, this virtual stranger, Hannah could feel the barely controlled emotion in each step he took, as if he were about to burst from keeping some unknown pain inside too long. With his head tilted down and his eyes looking straight ahead, his face was a study in fierce sorrow.

She knew that feeling well. Had lived with it for years, ever since her mother had died and she'd taken on the burden of caring for her more fragile sister.

He turned his head and their stares connected. Locked.

Hannah couldn't move. Couldn't breathe. Everything Tyler O'Toole pretended to be was real in this man, his brother.

She quickly tore her gaze away from those haunted silver eyes and prayed for the bravery to approach him for his assistance. She had to remember why she'd taken a hiatus, why she'd come all this way to find this particular man.

"Reverend O'Toole?" Hannah called out. Her heart picked up speed, nearly stealing her breath, but she'd come too far to turn into a coward now. "May I have a word with you, please?"

He stopped and cocked his head. A strange expression crossed his face, a mixture of astonishment and wonder, much like a theatergoer suddenly surprised he'd enjoyed a moment in a play he hadn't been eager to attend.

He blinked, and the look was gone.

"Do I know you, miss?" His voice was the same smooth baritone of his brother, but held a softer, more compassionate timbre. A tone that reflected the patience needed to minister to the downtrodden, the people no one else would accept.

She brushed her fingers across his letter again, only now realizing how much she craved the tolerance and compassion she'd read in the scrawled words.

For the first time in the last three hideous days, Hannah understood her sister's motivation to run. But where Rachel was running away from her promises and commitments, Hannah wanted to run toward… something. Something kind. Something permanent and safe.

Is this what the woman at the well had felt, Jesus? This rush of hope that all would be different, perhaps bearable at last, after her encounter with You?

The thought left her feeling slightly off balance, but then she realized it didn't matter how she felt. This meeting wasn't about her. It was about ending a decade-old pattern of lies and deception.

Hannah squared her shoulders, tilted her chin up and silently vowed to put the past to rest at last.

Chapter Three

For an instant, maybe two, the grind of wagon wheels, bark of vendors and squeak of swinging doors tangled into one loud echo in Beau's ears. Sadness over Jane, coupled with a terrible sense of helplessness, made his steps unnaturally slow. He wanted to be alone to think through the awful situation, to determine what to do about Jane's daughter, but he knew he had to push aside the selfish feelings and focus.

"Miss," he repeated. "May I help you?"

He could barely look at her. Her refined beauty stood in stark contrast to the seedy backdrop of Market Street, making him want a reprieve from all the painful emotions of the last few weeks. If only for a moment.

Beau gave his head a hard shake and stepped in her direction. By the time he'd closed the distance between them, he'd drawn a few conclusions about the woman in the blue velvet coat.

Wounded, was his first thought. Fragile. Tragically beautiful. He'd always been drawn to the poignant and injured, as evidenced by his unusual ministry. But some-

thing about this woman, with her large, exotic eyes and
heart-shaped lips, put him on his guard. He'd seen many
like her living in hopeless desperation in Mattie's brothel.
Who else in this town could afford the silk gloves and
matching hat she wore to draw attention to herself?

The wind kicked up, whipping a strand of her pitch-
black hair free from its pins. She shoved the lock back
in place. There was such delicate grace and quiet dignity
in that tiny gesture that Beau, exhausted from his efforts
with Jane, felt something inside him snap.

On your guard, Beau. This one's trouble.

Beau couldn't shake the notion that no matter how
young this woman was now, no matter how outwardly
beautiful, she would end up just like Jane and the others
in Mattie's employ.

*I have set you an example that you should do as I
have done for you.* At the reminder from the Gospel of
John, Beau knew he owed this woman his full attention
and an open mind. Nevertheless, her mysterious allure
somehow added to his earlier sense of defeat.

He swallowed. Blinked. Swallowed again.

"Reverend O'Toole, are you ill?"

At the warm pitch of her voice, his confusion vanished, and the sound of horse hooves hitting gravel separated once more from the shouts of vendors yelling
over one another.

"No. Yes," he said. His stomach twisted at the hard
note he heard in his own voice, and he struggled to
soften his tone. "That is, no, I'm not ill. And, yes, I am
Reverend O'Toole."

She sketched a small nod then glanced into his eyes
again. He saw relief there. Determination. And some-

thing else. Fear? Desperation? "I've come from Chicago to find you."

Chicago? By herself? Without a chaperone? Beau could no longer hear the activity around him. He flicked his gaze behind her, searching the area to see if his suspicions were correct. Baffled, he shifted his eyes back to her face. "You came here alone?"

She clasped her hands in front of her, frowned, and then lifted her chin. "I'm on a desperate errand that could not wait to find an appropriate companion." She swallowed, locked her gaze to a spot on his shoulder. "I'm a friend of your parents'."

"Are my parents…" Beau's heart tightened and began to throb in his chest. A riot of emotions slashed through him—worry, fear, dread—too many to sort through. "Has something happened to them?"

Her eyes widened at his question. "No." She reached out to touch him and genuine kindness replaced her earlier agitation. "Indeed, they are quite well."

"Good." He gave her one solid nod. "Good." But his heart was still rattling in his chest. He took a slow, deep breath. "Then why are you searching for me?"

A shadow of some dark emotion tightened her features. Guilt? Shame? A mixture of both?

Beau felt something equally dark inside him come to life. He couldn't help but think of Jane again. The famous actress had once been beautiful, as well. She'd been a friend of his parents', too. And yet, that hadn't shielded her from making poor decisions.

"What made you travel so far, *alone?*" He knew his voice was too sharp, nothing like the way he spoke to Jane and the rest of the women in Mattie's brothel. But surely no errand was worth this delicate woman embarking on such a dangerous journey by herself.

"I must find your brother Tyler." Her eyes went turbulent and she drew her lower lip between her teeth. "Before it is too late."

That wasn't the whole truth. Beau knew it with the same instincts that kept him from falling for every lie he heard from the less reputable in his flock.

But, still, it was only an instinct. And she'd said she was a friend of his parents'. Calling on the patience he'd used with Jane, Beau commanded this woman's gaze with his. He saw a deep pain there, much like the look in the eyes of the women he'd met in Mattie's parlor house.

Despite knowing she couldn't possibly be one of them, not with her obvious connections to his parents, why could he not stop comparing them? Was it the way she dressed with the sort of expensive, flamboyant clothing that captured his attention?

"Please. You must help me find Tyler," she said. "It is a matter of grave importance."

Moved by the distress in her eyes, the somber tone in his voice, his breath turned cold in his lungs and ugly possibilities assaulted him. He touched her sleeve. But her arm seemed very fragile, too fragile for handling, and he let go gently. "Tell me what sort of trouble my brother has put you in? Miss…"

"Southerland. Hannah Southerland. But I think you've misunderstood me. That is—" she sighed and folded her hands in front of her "—*I* am not in trouble. It's my sister."

Southerland? Beau knew that name well. But the odds were too great that there could be a connection between this woman and the imposing reverend.

Thomas Southerland was many things, including a respected member of the Rocky Mountain Association of Churches. He was also a man who openly questioned Beau's dedication to Christ because of Beau's penchant for ministering to hard drinkers, gamblers, prostitutes and the like. Although the age of the two would make a father/daughter relationship possible, Beau could not imagine a situation where the man would allow his own girl to travel alone.

Besides, this woman was too delicate to be related to the stern, hard-faced reverend. Except...there was something about Miss Southerland that was familiar to him. A look, a fierce determination, perhaps?

"Miss Southerland, my mind has been occupied all morning with pressing concerns of my own. I'm afraid I'm not following you."

Her answering sigh was filled with impatience—at him—at herself—at them both? "I'm not making myself clear."

She blew out a miserable breath, and he realized her cheeks were growing red from the frigid air.

Where were his manners? Had he been so long out of polite society he'd forgotten the basics?

"Let's find another place to talk. Out of the wind and cold," he offered.

She nodded, but in the next instant she was jostled by a passing man. Beau reached out to steady her, quickly releasing her when she cast an odd look at his hand on her arm.

"I am staying at the Palace Hotel, several blocks in that direction." She pointed behind her. "There is a respectable restaurant on the ground floor."

"The Palace Hotel it is."

Beau fell into step beside her. A dull drumming started at the base of his skull. His brother, her sister...

The news couldn't be good. But he held his tongue as they crossed the street and continued forward. Two blocks later, as they entered Denver's business district, the seedier buildings of Market Street morphed into more respectable brick and granite structures.

Beau quickly noted how Miss Southerland drew sidelong looks and murmurs from some of the men they passed along the five-block trek. Did she not see their interested stares? The speculation in their eyes? Hoping to shield her from the predators, Beau shifted her slightly behind him as they walked.

Best not to take any chances.

Once they turned onto 16th Street, the Palace Hotel loomed large and impressive before them. The nine-story building was one of a kind in the West, viewed as the best in town for both its elegance and service. Built exclusively from red granite and sandstone, the hotel was fashionable, eye-catching and well-dressed. Beau hadn't seen so handsome a building since he'd left New York seven years ago to pursue his education.

Upon entering the large structure, Beau took note of the opulent decor of rich fabrics and expensive mahogany paneling as they crossed the marbled lobby.

In no mood to sit through the ordering of food and subsequent false pleasantries as they waited to be served, he stopped walking. "Perhaps we should conduct our business here." He indicated two chairs in the corner of the room.

They would be out of the common traffic area but still

visible enough to be considered decent. Potted plants in priceless urns lined the perimeter of the room. Several were grouped around the two chairs he'd pointed out and created an alcove of sorts.

Once she was settled, Beau began the conversation with complete honesty. "Miss Southerland. I must confess my imagination has been running wild. Tell me what has happened."

She placed her hands gently in her lap. Once again, Beau was struck by her refined movements. There was nothing hard about this woman, which was at odds with her boldness in coming in search of him.

"I don't know quite where to start," she said in a very low, very quiet voice. What sort of woman could look so fragile and yet travel hundreds of miles alone? She had a strange blend of polished confidence and naiveté about her that didn't mesh with his first impression of a woman seeking attention.

His interest was stirred, but his plan for the future did not include a beautiful woman who drew attention to herself by merely existing.

With that thought, Beau shut down any personal feelings and looked deep into her eyes again. He saw a vulnerability that she tried to cloak as tightly as she'd cinched the velvet coat around her tiny waist.

The woman stirred his compassion. Yes, that was it. His compassion.

Nothing more.

"Perhaps you should start at the beginning?" he said in a gentle tone.

"Yes. Of course. The beginning." She nodded, sat up

straighter and squared her shoulders. "I suppose I should first tell you how I know your brother."

He offered an encouraging smile.

"Until three days ago, I was on tour with the same company as Tyler."

Beau's heart sank at her words. She was an actress, just like Jane. Although in light of her connection to his parents he should have expected this. A cold, unreasonable anger began to stir inside him, outdistanced by a sense of dread. He held his odd fury in check. Barely. He had no doubt that audiences adored this woman— how could they not?—but he also knew the public had once adored Jane, as well.

A fresh image of the broken woman he'd left in Mattie's brothel shot through his mind. No longer able to fill theaters with her talent and youth, she'd turned to a life of prostitution.

And now this woman, this *actress* sitting before him, with her youth and beauty and painful vulnerability, could easily end up in the same predicament as Jane.

Alone. Dying. Destitute.

The temper he rarely acknowledged swirled up so fast, so unexpectedly, his throat ached from having to swallow back the emotion.

Lord, show mercy to this woman. Guide her path.

"Go on," he said in a remarkably calm voice.

She ran her tongue across her teeth and nodded. The words spilled out of her in a rush, her voice halting and emotionless as she told the story of Tyler running off with her sister.

With each detail Beau gripped his chair harder and harder, trying to ignore the shock and anger that rose within him as the sordid events unfolded before him. Amazingly, Beau remained silent throughout Hannah's incredible tale.

As she came to the end of her story, she tapped her fingers quickly against her thigh in a rapid staccato. "I pray I'm not too late. The last time anyone saw them was three days ago."

Needing a moment to process all the information, Beau punched out an angry breath and batted away a fern leaf dangling close to his head.

Too many thoughts collided inside his brain, making it pound from trying to sort through the particulars. Tyler had often been thoughtless, but he had never gone so far before. This time, Beau's rash, selfish brother had done the unthinkable. And now a young woman's reputation was all but ruined.

The pain their parents would feel when they discovered Tyler's indiscretion would destroy them. Patience and Reginald O'Toole were good, honest, moral people. They had created a brood of four boys and one girl. Each member of his beautiful family, other than Beau, had made a life for themselves in the theater in some form or another. All had continued to honor God as their parents had taught them. Except, apparently, Tyler.

"There's more." Hannah's words broke through Beau's thoughts and jerked his attention back to her.

The pattern on her dress blurred before him, and Beau found he had to lower his gaze to her shaking hands to gain control over his own emotions. "Go on."

"Rachel isn't free to run off like this. She's engaged to be married. Her fiancé is my father's protégé, of sorts. Although each will handle my sister's recklessness differently, neither will take this news well. My father, especially, is not a man prone to forgiving selfish acts of any kind."

Beau gave his head a hard shake, but dread consumed him. He breathed in the scent of expensive perfume and fresh soil from the potted plants. One thought stood out over the rest.

He had to ask the question. Had to know. "Is your father Thomas Southerland? *Reverend* Thomas Southerland?"

Her mouth dropped open. "You have heard of him?"

"I met him when I was in seminary." And to say they hadn't seen eye to eye was a gross understatement.

Worse, the good reverend now held Beau's future in his hands. His voice was strong among the other members of the Association. With a few well-chosen words, Reverend Southerland could decide Beau's future in Greeley, Colorado. Although the man didn't trust Beau's modern views, he had been coming around.

What would the reverend think when he found out what Beau's brother had done, with the man's own daughter no less?

Beau couldn't let it matter. *Trust in Him at all times, O people; pour out your hearts to Him.*

The Scripture gave him hope, and he lowered his head to pray. *Lord, tell me what to do. Give me wisdom to—*

Hannah's voice broke through his prayer. "If you've met my father, then you understand why I must find Rachel. If I can get to her before she…before they… Well, the point is—" Hannah closed her eyes and swallowed, looking as though she had to gather her courage for the rest. "Rachel must accept the consequences of her actions."

Beau sensed there was more to the story, a personal element Miss Southerland wasn't going to reveal to him just yet.

It would be wise to focus on the particulars. "Why do you think they've come west?"

"They were last seen boarding a train headed this way." Her words came out steady, suspiciously controlled. "With your mother and father in London and the rest of your siblings in New York, you are my only hope."

He opened his mouth to speak but clamped it shut as a couple strolled by, their heads bent toward one another in an intimate gesture that spoke of familiarity. Partners. Beau ignored the odd spasm in his throat at the sight and said, "How did you know where to find me?"

She gave him a sheepish grin and pulled a letter from her coat pocket that had his handwriting on it. "I apologize, but I read your latest letter to your brother. I was desperate. I had hoped to find out…something." She lifted her shoulders in a helpless gesture.

Before he could comment, she added, "Rachel's fiancé will be devastated at the news of her disappearance with Tyler. But, as you can imagine, it is my father who will find the whole scandalous affair unacceptable. He warned Rachel to stay away from me. I'm afraid he'll blame me for this."

Beau had a terrible, gut-jerking sensation at her words. "Does your father not approve of you? Of your career?"

She looked away from him, but not before he saw the same sad, vulnerable light in her eyes that he'd witnessed earlier. "No. He does not."

"Well, then. That's one thing your father and I would agree on."

Her face drained of color, the pale skin standing out in bold contrast to the dark slash of her eyebrows. "What... What did you say?"

Beau moved his shoulder, a gesture that communicated his own frustration. "Don't you realize what can happen to you?"

"To...*me?*" Her angry gaze slammed into him like a punch.

All right, yes. He knew he was speaking too boldly, but he had to make his point now that he'd begun. "Jane Goodwin, one of the premiere actresses of her day, and once a dear friend of my mother's, is dying of a terminal illness in a brothel."

Beau ignored the shock in her eyes and pressed on. "Is that the legacy you want?"

Chapter Four

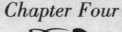

Hannah sat motionless under Reverend O'Toole's grim stare. Who did this preacher think he was to judge her, to heap her in guilt for a lifestyle someone else had chosen?

"You can't possibly believe every actress turns to..." She wound her hands tightly together in her lap. "Prostitution."

"Most do. Especially those without family support."

At his toneless response, bitter disappointment built inside her. In all things that mattered, Beauregard O'Toole was just like her father. Quick to judge. Unwilling to see past the exterior of a person to the heart that lay underneath.

"The point is this," he continued, his voice flat and emotionless and nothing like the rich baritone of earlier. "Once your looks are gone, there will be few options left to you."

My looks? Few options? The gall of the man!

He'd judged her before knowing all the facts. Her future plans were solid *and* well thought-out. The real estate in which she'd invested had already made her five times the money she'd earned on the stage. In a few years, she could retire a wealthy woman, free to offer her time and money to abandoned women and children in need.

She steeled herself as she'd done in her father's presence and ignored the hollow, shaking feeling of loneliness that took hold of her. "How can you talk like this? What about your mother and sister? They are actresses as well."

"They have family who love them, who accept them and will provide for them no matter what." He leaned forward and rested his elbows on his knees. "Can you say the same, Miss Southerland?"

She gave him a noncommittal sniff and focused her gaze on the plant behind him. As she absently counted the leaves, instant fear tripped along her spine. How could she face her father with this defeat? She'd failed to protect Rachel, again. And Thomas Southerland would never forgive her for it. Never.

But Hannah couldn't turn back now. She would not continue accepting blame for Rachel's bad choices. The time had come for Hannah to confront her father armed with the facts.

It would be up to him to decide if she spoke the truth.

Hannah fixed her gaze on Reverend O'Toole. She would confront her father with or without this man's help, with or without Rachel by her side. Hannah *would* break the cycle of sin in her life at last.

She had three weeks before Rachel's wedding. Three weeks to redeem them both. Three short weeks.

Yet here she sat with a man who saw her in the same ugly spotlight as her father did. Beauregard

O'Toole had let her down, to be sure, but Hannah would not hold a grudge against the man. The fault lay mostly with her. She'd been a fool to build him up in her mind. She had wrongfully put her hope in him, a mere man, and not the Lord.

That was one mistake she would never make again.

Disappointed with them both, Hannah stood.

The reverend unfolded his large frame and rose, as well.

"I was mistaken in asking for your help," she said. "I thank you for your time."

"Wait." He took a step to his right, effectively barring her exit. Although he stood close enough for her to smell the scent of lime on him, a deceptive calmness filled the moment.

But when he still didn't speak or move aside, Hannah's heartbeat picked up speed. Surely, he wasn't trying to trap her, to use his size to intimidate her?

Just as real panic began gnawing at her, he took a step back. She started to push around him, but he stopped her with a gentle touch to her arm.

"Don't leave," he said, surprising her with his mild tone. "I fear we've become sidetracked from the real issue here. Please, sit back down and we will discuss the next move together."

Hannah was tired. She was frustrated. But she was also out of options. With a reluctant sigh, she lowered herself back into the chair she'd occupied earlier.

Reverend O'Toole settled in his seat, as well. "You were right to come to me, Miss Southerland." He cleared his throat. "I have contacts all over the territory, in areas most wouldn't dream of going."

Hannah closed her eyes and pressed her fingertips to the bridge of her nose. Was he offering his help after all?

Did she still want his assistance knowing he'd already judged her and found her wanting? Should she risk the humiliation of spending hours, perhaps days, with a man who considered her one step away from prostitution?

She lowered her hands and slowly opened her eyes. "I don't believe I want your help." Her tone came out a little too spiteful, a little too high-pitched, and she regretted her rash words as soon as they left her mouth.

Where else could she go? Who else would assist a woman traveling alone, one who knew nothing of the surrounding territory? Certainly, no one with honorable intentions.

Feeling incredibly vulnerable, Hannah flattened a palm against her stomach. The twisting inside warned her she had little time left. But then she remembered what Patience O'Toole had always told her. "If you're unsure what to do, allow God to take the lead."

How do I do that, Lord?

As the silence between them continued, Reverend O'Toole rubbed a hand across his mouth and nodded as though he'd come to an important conclusion. "When we first met, outside the... That is, when we met on Market Street, I was on a special errand for Jane Goodwin, one I am afraid cannot be neglected much longer."

His odd change of subject took Hannah aback. Was this his way of dismissing her? Unexpected panic threaded through her. "I don't see how that is relevant to—"

"I want you to accompany me to Charity House. If after our errand you decide you want to continue your search for your sister, you won't go alone. I won't allow it."

"You won't *allow* it?"

His arrogance stunned her into silence.

She opened her mouth to speak. Closed it. Opened it again. But still no words came forth. Her fingers brushed across the letter folded neatly in her pocket. Was the compassionate man she'd found on the pages a complete fabrication?

As though reading her mind, regret flashed in Reverend O'Toole's eyes and his expression softened. "Forgive me, Miss Southerland, I spoke abruptly. What I meant to say is that this concerns my brother as well as your sister. I have a responsibility as much as you do to see matters restored."

Of course he had a stake in the outcome of this debacle. And yet…why did she sense his offer of assistance was more personal than he was admitting? He claimed he knew her father. Was there more of a connection than he was letting on?

A slow breath escaped from her lungs and she pressed farther back into her chair. What was keeping her from trusting Reverend O'Toole? Why couldn't she simply accept his assistance and proceed to the next step in finding Rachel?

All right, yes. She admitted that she'd come here hoping to find something special in this man, the admired son of her beloved mentor and friend. She'd hoped to find something more in him than she'd found in other men, something she hadn't been able to define.

But, *again,* Hannah reminded herself this wasn't about her. With nowhere else to turn, she needed Reverend O'Toole's help. She would trust God to take care of the rest.

The plans of the Lord stand firm forever, the purposes of His heart through all generations.

Yes. She would trust the Lord to guide her path.

"Thank you for your offer, Reverend O'Toole. I would very much like to accompany you on your errand." She pulled herself to her feet. "Please, direct the way."

Beau followed Miss Southerland's lead and stood, as well. But as his gaze captured her closed-lipped expression, something dark in him shifted and realigned itself. What had previously been anger and frustration now gave way to guilt.

Feeling like a fiend, he knotted his hand into a fist at his side, sucked in a harsh breath and then relaxed his fingers. Because of his own arrogance, Miss Southerland was wary of him.

Understandable, under the circumstances.

"Follow me," he said, accepting that he would get very little warmth from her now.

He'd unfairly judged Miss Southerland because of the hours he'd spent with Jane Goodwin. Setting aside his own prejudice now, he studied the woman walking beside him with fresh eyes. Her clothes were elegant and fashionable, her carriage graceful and refined. She was everything clean, unblemished…pure. No one in their right mind would mistake this woman for a prostitute.

Except, of course, a preacher too caught up in his own grief and frustration to see the truth standing before him.

Beau was reminded of a verse from the book of James. *The tongue is also a fire, a world of evil among the parts of the body.*

He'd spoken from the bias of his own circumstances,

not with the compassion of a minister. What sort of preacher did that make him?

Lord, forgive me my bold, outspoken words. Help me to make amends to this woman properly in a way that will bring You glory and her peace.

The moment they exited the hotel, cool mountain air slapped him in the face and shimmied under his collar. Beau immediately steered Miss Southerland back inside. "Wait in here, out of the wind, while I find us suitable transportation."

As he turned to go, he shot a quick glance at her over his shoulder. She stood gazing at him with a quiet, clear-eyed look that held far too much worry in it.

A muscle locked in his jaw, and he let out another quick hiss of air. Why hadn't he focused on easing her concern for her sister, instead of allowing his own worries to influence his behavior?

Returning to the curbside, Beau blew into his cupped palms and silently reviewed the harsh words he'd used with Miss Southerland.

His delivery had been insensitive, to be sure, but he didn't believe he'd been wrong in warning the actress of the life she could find herself leading if she didn't take care. She might be pure and innocent. Today. But she was only a few bad choices away from becoming another Jane. And then men would flock to her for all the wrong reasons.

Everything in Beau rebelled at the notion. The responding growl that came from his throat sounded almost primitive.

Men could become blind idiots, often treacherous, around the sort of devastating beauty Miss Southerland possessed. Although she believed otherwise, she wasn't safe traveling by herself in this part of the country.

Beau shouldn't have left her alone in the hotel.

Far too impatient to wait for a carriage to pass by, Beau informed the doorman of his transportation needs and went inside to retrieve Miss Southerland.

She stood along the edge of the lobby, hidden slightly in the shadows. As before on Market Street, he found himself no longer able to walk, to breathe, to...*move.* He simply stared at her like an idiot. The impact of her beauty hit Beau like a punch thrown straight to his heart.

Separate from the other patrons, Miss Southerland looked incredibly sad. And with her arms crossed over her waist, her eyes blinking rapidly to stave off tears, she captured the image of a tragic heroine. Beau had the sudden urge to wrap her in his arms, to protect her against the ugliness he knew was in the world.

If Miss Southerland's sister was half as beautiful and delicate as she was herself, it was no wonder Tyler had snatched her up and run away as fast as he could. Tyler was selfish, to be sure, but the man wasn't stupid.

No. That line of thinking was senseless and dangerous.

Beau could not start feeling compassion for his brother or the heinous act the man had committed. A stop at Charity House would restore his own priorities and remind Beau of the dangers both Miss Southerland and her sister faced if either ended up alone in this harsh land.

Lord, not that. Use me as Your instrument to prevent such a tragedy.

With his mission in mind, he forced his feet to move. "Ready?" he asked.

She nodded, the wary expression in her eyes cutting him straight to the bone.

Had he betrayed this woman's trust before he'd earned it?

Perhaps the damage wasn't permanent. Through Christ all things were possible. Yes. *Yes.* All was not lost.

His steps were lighter as he led her through the hotel's front door. Once outside, a burning cigar stump arced in the air and landed near Miss Southerland's feet with a thud. Beau took her elbow and circled her in a wide berth to avoid the glowing ember. Still holding her arm, he offered his other hand to assist her into the waiting carriage the doorman had summoned for them.

She looked at his outstretched palm as though she didn't want any further physical contact with him. He waited as a myriad of emotions ignited in her eyes. Finally, she relented with a soft sigh and placed her hand in his.

Palm pressed to palm, Beau liked how her warmth passed through her gloves and straight into him. With an odd sense of reluctance, he released her, gave the driver the address of their destination and climbed into the carriage, as well.

He settled on the bench opposite her. In the ensuing silence, he took the opportunity to study his surroundings. The blue upholstery had seen better days. It was faded in places, frayed at the edges and missing several buttons. The air hung thick and heavy, carrying a musty, unpleasant odor.

At least the wooden floor was clean.

Once the carriage began moving, Beau could no longer remain silent. "I apologize for the harsh tone I used earlier.

I have no excuse. My mind was on other concerns, but that doesn't mean I had the right to judge you so quickly."

She waved her hand in dismissal. "It's forgotten." But her guarded eyes and distant tone told him otherwise.

Accepting momentary defeat, Beau shifted the conversation to the reason Miss Southerland had sought his assistance in the first place. "Charity House has a school connected to it. The headmistress's husband is a U.S. Marshal."

"Do you think this man will help us?" she asked, her voice filled with a weariness Beau had missed until now.

Stunned at his own lack of insight, Beau took note of the purple circles under her eyes, the lines of fatigue surrounding her mouth. "When did you say Tyler and your sister left Chicago?"

She blinked at him, but kept her lips tightly clamped together.

He softened his tone and touched her gloved hand. "How long ago, Miss Southerland?"

"Three days," she said, pushing out of his reach.

"How much sleep have you had since then?"

Sighing, she turned her head to look out the carriage window. "I've had enough."

"Miss Southerland—"

"I'm fine. Truly." She returned her gaze to his. "Tell me about this U.S. Marshal you mentioned."

Beau let her switch the topic—for now—and called to mind the last time he had been in Denver. Trey Scott had helped him find a miner who'd run out on his wife and five children. Clearly an advocate for abandoned women and their families, the lawman had been ruthless in his search.

"He's a good man," Beau said with sincerity. "He'll

do all he can to locate your sister, or, barring that, he'll find someone who can."

"Thank you."

Relief glittered in her eyes. Still, she sat with her shoulders stiff and unmoving.

Time, he told himself. In time she would learn to trust him, perhaps even forgive him.

Uncomfortable on the bench that was far too small for his large frame, Beau shifted and rearranged his legs. "While we have a moment, I should tell you about Charity House so as to avoid any confusion once we arrive."

She nodded slowly, her eyes searching his as though she wasn't sure why his voice had changed but had decided to hold on to her curiosity while he explained himself.

What sort of woman had that kind of controlled patience?

"Charity House," he began, "is an orphanage—"

"Orphanage?" Her eyes lit up, and she tilted her head forward. "How many children are housed there?"

"Forty."

"So many." She relaxed her head against the cushions and blinked up at the ceiling. Her eyes took on a faraway expression, as though she was calculating what forty orphans would look like.

"I should warn you," he said, pulling at a loose thread in the upholstery. "When I say orphanage, I don't mean it in the strictest sense."

She cocked her head at him. "I don't understand."

He tugged on the string, the gesture releasing three more strands. "It's a baby farm."

She lifted a shoulder and shook her head in obvious confusion.

Releasing the thread entwined in his fingers, he boldly pressed on. "A baby farm is a home for prostitutes' illegitimate children."

Her eyes widened. "I've never heard of such a thing."

"The children aren't accepted in other, more traditional homes because of their mothers' profession. They can't live in the brothels, so Marc and Laney Dupree take them in without question." Beau kept his voice even, but the passion he felt for the orphanage sounded in his tone despite his efforts. "If not for Charity House, most of the children would have nowhere else to go. The cycle of sin and crime would continue in their lives."

"How—" Tears filled her eyes, skimming along her dark lashes like tiny ice crystals. They disappeared with a single swipe of her wrist. *"Marvelous."*

Beau hadn't expected such a positive, heartfelt response from her.

Why not? he wondered. Why had he expected her to show immediate prejudice?

Because you were so quick to judge, yourself. You saw her from your own failings, not hers.

"Yes." Beau swallowed. "It is marvelous."

They shared a small smile between them, but then her forehead scrunched into a scowl, effectively dousing the moment with a dose of reality. "Didn't you say you were going there on an errand for Jane Goodwin?"

"Yes, to pay the board for her daughter."

Surprising him once again, Miss Southerland looked at him with glowing respect, as though he'd transformed into something good and noble right before her eyes. "How very kind of you."

Unnerved by the change in her, he rolled his shoulders. "It's what I do."

"I know."

She really smiled at him then. It was nothing more than an attractive lifting of the corners of her mouth that revealed straight, white teeth, but the gesture carried a spectacular wallop.

Beau had thought her beautiful before, but now...

He had to cough to release the breath lodged in his throat.

He should start anew with this woman, here and now. He should find a way to earn back her trust, in degrees if not all at once. He should do a lot of things that involved words and a healthy dose of groveling on his part.

Instead, he repositioned his weight on the bench and released his own grin.

Her smile widened in response. And for the first time in years, a sense of utter peace settled over him.

Words, Beau decided, were highly overrated.

Chapter Five

Hannah sank back against the seat cushion and studied the pastor from beneath her lowered lashes. His eyes crinkled at the edges when he smiled. She hadn't expected that. Although she should have.

There was something familiar about this man's masculine good looks, a charming vibrancy that was one hundred percent O'Toole. And yet the tilt of his head, the slash of his cheekbones, the bewildering sorrow in his eyes were all profoundly his own.

Hannah released a slow sigh. After the last three days, she should be immune to any man with the last name O'Toole. She certainly didn't want to be attracted to the one sitting across from her. Anger and distrust were much more manageable emotions, certainly easier to define.

But he'd thrown her off balance with his passionate description of Charity House and the home's special mission.

The carriage bumped, jostling her forward then back again. Another bump. Another jostle, and Hannah had to place her palms on either side of her to prevent an unfortunate incident—oh, say, like diving headfirst to the floor.

As she struggled, Reverend O'Toole's smile dipped into a frown. "Can I assist you?"

She made a noncommittal sound in her throat.

He lifted a hand toward her.

"No." She glided smoothly out of his reach. "I'm steady now."

"We're nearly there," he said in a soft, understanding voice.

Oh. Perfect. *Now* his tone and manner held the compassion she'd hoped to find in him earlier.

At the genuine show of concern in his gaze, she had to work to catch her breath. His silver eyes held such depth, such consideration. He was worried. *About her.* Which made him infinitely more likable.

The cad.

The carriage suddenly felt too small, too confining.

Hannah reached for her collar. Cleared her throat. Forced a smile. Cleared her throat again. "It's hot in here."

His teeth flashed white, and the crinkles deepened around his eyes. "It is."

Careful, Hannah, she warned herself. *He's far too charming when he smiles.*

She had to keep her mind on the task she'd set before her. *Not* on the beautiful gray eyes of a rebel preacher who unfairly judged her one moment and showed genuine contrition the next.

A surge of impatience had her tapping her fingers against the seat cushion. Time was running out. The longer Rachel and Tyler remained hidden, the harder it would be to uncover their location.

Hannah reached up and fiddled with the top button of her coat again. As much as she wanted to rush to the next town, she had to trust this small interruption in her search was part of God's plan. Just as Jesus had stopped unexpectedly to heal the bleeding woman on his way to save Jarius's daughter, this detour had to mean something important, something significant Hannah didn't yet understand.

Hadn't good already come from this slight change in plans? An introduction to a U.S. Marshal was imminent. Certainly, seeking the expertise of a trained lawman was better than chasing around the territory with no real direction.

Not to mention, they were headed to an orphanage for abandoned children. *Go where God leads...*

The carriage slowed and stopped with a shudder, jarring her out of her thoughts.

"We're here," he said unnecessarily.

Hannah craned her neck to look out the window, but the reverend's shuffling of legs and arms captured her attention before she could focus on the scenery. He was so tall. She hadn't realized how confining the carriage must have been for him.

Rearranging his position one last time, he stooped forward and exited the carriage. Hannah clutched the seat tighter as the bench tilted from the sudden shift of weight.

Continuing the role of gentleman, the reverend reached back into the cabin to offer his assistance once again. Hannah stared at the outstretched palm, unsure whether to accept his help a second time or not. Even through her gloves, something strange had happened when their hands met.

Her reaction worried her, of course, but not enough to be rude. Bracing for the jolt, she slowly placed her hand in his. The expected tingle started in her finger-tips and moved swiftly up her arm. In an effort to be free of the disturbing sensation, she scrambled out of the carriage and nearly pushed the wall of man and muscle away from her.

He looked at her strangely, dropped his gaze to his now-empty hand and sighed.

With a theatrical flourish reminiscent of his brother, he motioned to the home standing behind him. "I give you Charity House," he said, adding a shallow bow and a flick of his wrist to emphasize his point.

Hannah blinked at the massive structure. "*This* is an orphanage?"

"Spectacular, isn't it?"

She blinked again.

Despite the grubby clouds that rapidly swallowed the pristine sky above, the house, with its clinging vines, stylish brick and soft angles, captured her imagination and made her think of fairy tales…rescued damsels in distress…happily ever afters…

"It's quite lovely," she said at last.

Unable to say anything more, she craned her neck and looked to her left and then to her right. It was evident that they stood in the middle of an exclusive neighborhood. Modern gas lamps sat atop poles at every street corner. Large, brick homes similar to Charity House in their grandeur marched shoulder to shoulder in elegant formation along the lane.

Caught between surprise and puzzlement, Hannah slid a glance at the man looming large and silent beside her. He stood patiently, his hands linked behind his back.

She turned her attention back to the orphanage. The

sheer glamour of the home—or rather *mansion*—took her breath away.

Dragging cold air into her lungs, she said, "I've never seen an orphanage quite like this."

And she'd seen plenty in the last few years. The buildings were usually sterile and functional, never as inviting as this one was.

She focused on the sound of laughter and good-natured shrieks coming from somewhere in the near distance. The joyful noise of children hard at play made her ache with an unexpected sense of homesickness. It was an odd sensation that was part confusion, part longing, and she felt her shoulders stiffen in response.

"Marc and Laney have spared no expense," the reverend said. "Each child in his or her own way has suffered a great deal in their short lives. At Charity House they receive a little beauty in their previously barren worlds."

Hannah noted the manicured lawn scattered with blooming autumn plants. "It's wonderful."

"It is."

A sudden thought occurred to her. "The neighbors don't mind living this close to an orphanage?"

"Most tolerate it."

It was an acceptable answer, but something dark flashed in his eyes and made her press the issue. "What about the others?"

"As you can imagine, some don't approve. They file complaints occasionally, but don't worry." His voice took on a convicted edge. "The Lord's hand is on Charity House. The orphanage is here to stay."

"Praise God."

He gave her a heartening smile. "Couldn't have said it better myself."

"Is the inside as grand?" she asked.

"You'll find out soon enough. Here come Marc and Laney now." He tipped his head toward the front door.

Hannah turned her attention back to the house in time to see a young couple negotiating the front steps together. Both were as beautiful as their home.

The dark-haired, clean-shaven man was dressed in what Hannah would have thought more appropriate for a successful banker. He wore a gold and black brocade vest and a matching tie, while a shiny watch fob hooked to a middle button dangled toward a small pocket. The entire ensemble looked both expensive and elegant.

The woman was dressed more casually, in a simple blue dress with a white lace collar. Her mahogany hair was pulled into a fashionable bun and she walked with an inherent grace any actress would envy.

The couple held hands, as though they were newly married, madly in love, or both. Other than Patience and Reginald O'Toole, Hannah had never seen two people so finely attuned with one another.

A gnawing ache twisted in Hannah's stomach. Would she ever find that sort of connection with a man? Or was she destined to be alone, to serve other abandoned women and children without the benefit of a husband by her side?

Only God knew for sure.

As they drew closer, Hannah studied their faces. Compassion and strength of character were evident in their smiles and sparkling eyes. Eventually, the couple separated and the woman pushed slightly ahead.

"Pastor Beau, what a pleasant surprise." Beaming, she gripped both of the reverend's hands and squeezed. "We didn't expect you until Sunday."

He lifted one of her hands to his lips then released her. "The pleasure is mine."

"Beau." The man slapped him on the back in a friendly gesture. "It's always good to see you, no matter the day of the week."

"Marc and Laney Dupree, I would like to introduce Hannah Southerland." He turned and gestured to her. "She's a friend of my...parents'."

Marc nodded at her. The accompanying smile was so genuine and guileless Hannah found herself smiling back.

Laney, however, clearly wanted none of the distant politeness required of first meetings. She boldly yanked Hannah into a tight hug. "Any friend of our favorite pastor is certainly welcome in our home."

At the genuine warmth in Laney's words and the open acceptance in her embrace, Hannah's stomach curled inside itself. Feeling more than a little desperate, she clung to the other woman with a fierceness she hadn't known she possessed. Fear, frustration and terrifying hope braided together in a ball of awkward longing. Hannah hadn't realized how alone she'd felt these last three days as she'd searched for Rachel and Tyler with no leads, no help and no advice.

As though sensing her mood, Laney patted her on the back and whispered in a voice only Hannah could hear, "You're safe with us."

Unable to respond, Hannah simply gripped the other woman tighter.

"Tell me, Beau," Marc asked from behind her. "What brings you to our home, on a Wednesday no less?"

Feeling awkward, foolish even, Hannah stepped quickly out of Laney's embrace. She was too emotional to speak, not that the question had been directed at her. But still...

She gave the reverend a pleading look.

His questioning gaze was so serious, so concerned, she lost the tiny thread of her control and tears pricked the backs of her eyelids. It took everything in her not to reach up and wipe at her lashes.

He touched her arm. "Are you all right?"

She nodded her head, a little too quickly, a little too intensely.

His eyes softened. He squeezed her hand a moment, and then turned back to Marc. "I have a delivery from one of Mattie's girls. Miss Southerland was kind enough to accompany me."

"I'm glad," Marc said with a kind look directed at her.

"And while we're here," the reverend continued, "we thought you might have an idea where your brother-in-law is today."

Marc and Laney shared a look. "You're searching for Trey?" they asked in unison.

Beau nodded, but didn't divulge any of the particulars.

"Well, you're in luck. He's actually here today," Laney said. "Last I saw, he was out back playing baseball with some of the older children."

Marc looked like he was going to add to the explanation, but he was interrupted by a high-pitched squeal of delight. "Pastor Beau! Pastor Beau!"

All four adults turned toward the gleeful sound. A little girl about seven years old skipped down the steps. Her sky-blue eyes sparkled with delight. Her broad smile showed off a missing front tooth, while two long black braids bounced from side to side with each step she took.

The adorable little girl was filthy from braids to bare feet and, quite frankly, the happiest child Hannah had ever seen.

Skidding to a halt mere inches short of running into the pastor, she asked, "Are you here to play with us today?"

Unfazed by the near collision, *Pastor Beau* stooped to her level and plucked at one of the messy braids. "Hello to you, too, Miss Molly Taylor Scott. What sort of game are you playing?"

Rocking back and forth on her heels, Molly performed a perfect little-girl swish with her shoulders. "Baseball, of course. My daddy's pitching right now."

Grinning, the reverend rose and placed his palm on her head in a gesture that spoke of genuine affection.

Man and child continued smiling at each other as though they shared some humorous secret.

Charmed by them both, Hannah just stood watching the two interact.

"Her daddy is the man you're looking for," Laney whispered.

Surprised at the news, she turned to Laney. "Molly isn't one of the orphans?"

"Not anymore."

Their voices must have carried, because Molly noticed Hannah then. With the typical attention span of a child, she deserted the pastor and bounced over to Hannah. "You're very pretty."

Completely captivated by the precocious child, Hannah lowered to her knees. "You are, too."

Lifting her nose higher in the air, the little girl slapped her own shoulder. "My name's Molly."

"I'm Hannah."

"Oh." Big blue eyes widened. "Like Samuel's mama."

More surprises, Hannah thought. "You've heard of her?"

"Well, of course." Molly let out a sound of impatience. "Pastor Beau told us about her last Sunday. She's the one that prayed for a baby."

"That's right. I was named after her."

Molly jammed two tiny fists on her hips and narrowed her eyes in pitch-perfect seven-year-old concentration. "You don't look like anybody's mama to me. You're too fancy."

"I'm not anybody's mother. Yet." Hannah smiled at the child, even as something a little sad quivered through her. "But one day I hope to be a lot of somebodies' mother."

Molly giggled. "Me, too. Someday."

Hannah joined in the child's laughter, feeling the tension ease out of her with the gesture.

Just then, a clap of thunder sounded in the distance.

Molly looked to the heavens, scrunched her face into a frown and marched back to Pastor Beau. "Well?" Her fists returned to her hips and her foot started tapping on the ground. "Are you playing or not?"

"Molly, honey," Marc said in a practical voice. "I think you're going to get rained on very shortly."

The little girl's face fell. "But—"

"Not to worry." Hannah rose to her feet and tapped

Molly on the shoulder to get her attention. "I know several games we can play inside."

Molly's eyes lit up. "You do?"

Hannah nodded, then looked at the approaching clouds. The breeze had grown still, and the sharp, pungent odor of rain pulsated in the air. "I'll teach one of them to you later."

"That sounds nice."

But clearly, Molly Taylor Scott was made of very stern stuff. She wasn't relenting without a fight. "Come on, Pastor Beau." She grabbed his hand and tugged. "Before it rains."

Beau lifted an eyebrow at Hannah as though seeking her permission. He looked so sweet standing there with the child's hand gripped gently in his.

He'll make a great father.

Now where did that thought come from?

"Go on," she said, more than a little touched by the picture the two made. "We can talk to her father after the game."

"I'll make sure of it."

"I know." Her heart punched two solid thumps against her ribs. "Thank you for that."

Opening his mouth to speak, the pastor shifted his weight toward Hannah, but Molly tugged on him again. "Let's go."

"I think I'll join you," Marc said. Pausing a moment, he angled his head toward Hannah. "It was nice to meet you, Miss Southerland."

"You, too, Mr. Dupree."

As Marc followed behind the other two, Laney let out

a loud sigh. "Five years of marriage, and I never get tired of looking at that man."

"Sounds like love to me."

"That it is."

The other woman's face glowed as she spoke, and Hannah felt her earlier sense of yearning grow more powerful. Home. Safety. Permanence. Until now, Hannah hadn't realized how much she craved all three. The years of traveling from stage to stage were obviously taking their toll. Hopefully one day she would find her own place in the world.

"You're very fortunate to have found such love," Hannah said on a soft whisper choked with emotion.

"You have no idea. I'll tell you the story someday." She tilted her face toward the incoming clouds. "For now, let's head inside. I'm sure some new drama is unfolding as we speak. Children." Laney gave her an ironic grin. "I do so love their unpredictable ways."

"Bless their impertinent souls," Hannah said with a wink.

Laney burst out laughing. "My sentiments exactly." Fastening their arms together, Laney steered them both toward the front steps. "Whatever your story is, Miss Hannah Southerland, I've decided to like you."

Hannah smiled in mingled surprise and pleasure at the unexpected announcement. "Well, glory, because I've decided to like you right back."

Chapter Six

An hour later, Beau watched as dark, ominous clouds devoured the last patch of blue sky. Consecutive cracks of thunder traveled along the back end of a powerful wind. The earthy scent of rain filled the air. All of nature stood poised for the watery attack, while seventeen children and three grown men—Beau included—pretended nothing was amiss.

Another succession of thunder rumbled closer, the sound reverberating through the backyard ball game.

And still the contest continued. For three more seconds. Two. One…

The rain let loose.

Fat drops of icy water pummeled man and child alike. Feet pounded. Shouts lifted in the air. Childish giggles and adult commands wrapped inside one another. Orders to get out of the mud and into the house were barked in a masculine, authoritative tone. A flash of lightning highlighted the urgency.

When the bedlam continued, the order came again.

"Everybody inside the house," Marc shouted. This time his tone brooked no argument.

A chorus of groans and complaints rose up.

"*Now.*"

One by one the children scrambled onto the back porch. Bringing up the rear, Beau hoisted one of the smaller boys into his arms and dashed up the stairs. By the time he commandeered the last step, he had to shuffle his way through a maze of arms and legs vying for space, as well.

Marc made quick work of gathering equipment in one pile and wet shoes in another before herding the motley group inside.

From his vantage point, Beau watched the giggling horde poke and pull and elbow one another en route to the house. The children managed to arouse his amusement and sympathy all at the same time. There was a reserved nature to their movements, something sad and self-preserving that kept the boys and girls from fully engaging in the fun. It was as if they were holding back a part of themselves.

Understandable. Given their histories.

There was a lot of God's work to do at Charity House. The orphanage could use a full-time minister on staff. But it wouldn't be Beau. Even if he didn't have his own plans for the future, he was already committed to the church in Greeley. Of course, that didn't mean he couldn't help Marc and Laney find a preacher who would fit in with the ministry already started here at the orphanage.

Despite his efforts to mentally organize a list of potential candidates, his mind shifted to another, more urgent subject. Beau owed it to Miss Southerland to get down to the business of finding her sister.

Shaking water out of his hair, he waited until the last

of the children banged inside the house behind Marc. Only then did he pull Trey aside. "I need a word with you, Marshal."

Eyes never leaving Beau's face, the lawman removed his hat and set it on a nearby rocking chair. "Trouble again?"

A cold ball of dread settled heavily in Beau's belly. "You have no idea."

Hitching his hip against the porch railing, Trey rubbed his jaw. The day-old stubble and grim twist of his lips made the man look as fierce as his reputation. With the nickname Beelzebub's Cousin, it was no wonder Trey Scott was known as a ruthless lawman who hunted criminals with a vengeance.

However, when Beau looked into Trey's eyes, he saw past the U.S. Marshal and found the loyalty and integrity that had won the heart of Charity House's schoolteacher, Katherine Taylor, and her little sister, Molly.

"Another runaway husband?" Trey asked.

"Not precisely." Beau shook his head. "This time, it's personal."

To his credit, Trey's expression never changed. "I see. Tell me what I can do for you."

The wind chose that moment to kick harder, pelting razor-sharp needles of rain straight into Beau's eyes. He shifted slightly and set his shoulders against the storm. "I need you to help me find my brother."

Frowning, Trey stared up at the ceiling. He stood in that contemplative pose so long that Beau looked up, as well. But then Trey shoved away from the railing and lowered his gaze back to Beau's. "Let's finish this conversation in Marc's study."

Beau nodded. "That'll be fine."

As he followed the marshal through the back of the house, Beau had to fight the urge to rush his steps. Even the homey scent of baking bread couldn't pacify his impatience. Now that the initial shock of the situation was wearing off and the possible repercussions were settling in, he wanted Tyler found. Immediately.

As they strode through the house, the only sound in the hallway came from their heels pounding against the wood floor like hammers to nails. An uneasy feeling darted toward the surface before Beau tamped it down. So much time had passed. Tyler and Miss Southerland's sister could be anywhere by now.

Lord, Beau prayed, *I'm overwhelmed by this task You've brought before me. Please, give me strength, wisdom and clarity, so I may guide Miss Southerland in this search.*

At the end of the hallway, they rounded the corner and came across Marc, who was exiting a room on their left.

"We'd like to borrow your study awhile," Trey asked in explanation of their presence.

Marc looked from one man to the other, and then nodded. "Take your time."

Remembering his original mission, Beau reached into his pocket and pulled out an envelope with Marc's name scrawled on the outside. "This is from Jane. For Megan's care."

"Set it on my desk," Marc said, but then his gaze turned serious. "How is Jane?"

Beau's chest pinched tight as he called to mind the unnatural pallor of the former actress's skin and the lack of fight in her eyes. "Time's running out for her."

Marc released a resigned sigh. "I'll prepare Megan."

"At some point I'd like to speak with her, as well."

"I think that's a good idea." Marc turned to go. "Let me know if you need anything."

Trey answered for them both. "Will do."

While Marc disappeared in the opposite direction, Beau followed Trey into the empty office. Once inside, Beau's mind circled back to Miss Southerland. He wondered how she was faring. She'd looked so fragile earlier, practically dropping from exhaustion.

Yet she hadn't complained once. He told himself he appreciated that rare quality in her, but it wasn't true. If only she would lean on him, just a little. But that would require trust. Something Beau had destroyed with an ill-timed, harshly worded snap judgment.

"Have a seat." Trey waved his hand toward a matching pair of leather, wingback chairs facing a large mahogany desk.

Beau lowered himself into the one on his right and looked around. The dark furniture, with its bold, masculine lines, lacked all sign of feminine frills. A fire snapped in the hearth, giving the room a pleasant, smoky odor. One day Beau hoped to have a similar room, a place where he could write his sermons and conduct the business of his ministry.

A private refuge all his own. No women allowed.

It wasn't that Beau didn't like women. On the contrary. They fascinated him, intrigued him. He liked the way they took such care with their hair and clothing, liked how they found joy in silly things like a new bit of lace. But as a child he'd been unable to get away from the flounce and feminine scents that were commonplace backstage.

Even now, as an adult, his ministry brought him to places like Mattie's, places that held many of the same female sounds and smells of the theater.

At least the women in the theater kept their dignity when they conducted the business of their trade.

Beau thought of Jane then. He needed to return to her bedside as soon as possible. Perhaps he could still convince her to move into the sanatorium. Perhaps there was still time to save her. Perhaps...

Thunder rumbled overhead. The rain made a hard hissing sound as it scraped against the windows in the back of the room.

Undaunted by the commotion building outside, Trey settled into the chair behind the desk and pulled out a sheet of paper from the top drawer. "Let's start with the basics. Tell me about your brother."

Where to begin?

In an attempt to gather his thoughts, Beau rose from his chair and walked over to the hearth. The fire cracked and popped, radiating a strong blast of heat. Rubbing his hands together, Beau cast a sideways glance at Trey. How did he go about revealing his dark family secret, one he had only learned of a few hours ago? For all intents and purposes, the man was a stranger to Beau.

And yet, without revealing the full truth of the matter, the marshal wouldn't be able to help him. "Did you see the woman that came outside to watch part of the game with Laney?" Beau began.

Trey's face went carefully blank. "Couldn't avoid noticing her. Nor could most of the older boys." He chuckled softly. "Thought I was going to have to scrape a few of their chins off the ground so we could continue the game."

Smiling at the reminder, Beau rolled his shoulders and dug his toe into the stone hearth at his feet. There was no denying the fact that Miss Southerland turned heads, stopped baseball games in midinning and literally dropped the jaws of men and boys alike.

Of course, it wasn't the boys that bothered Beau. It was the men. What lengths would the less reputable go to in order to win Miss Southerland's affection?

A dozen of the uglier possibilities came to mind, and a hot surge of uneasiness made Beau's breath back up in his lungs. Unwilling to explore the new emotion too deeply, he tapped an angry rhythm against his thigh.

"Is she a friend of yours?" Trey asked at last.

"No." Beau assumed a neutral expression and turned to face the other man head-on. "I met her this afternoon for the first time. She's with the same acting company as my brother."

A single eyebrow shot up. "Would that be the same brother you want me to locate?"

"Yes. Unfortunately, the situation is complicated. The short version is that after a two-day acquaintance, Miss Southerland's sister and my brother ran off together." Beau gnashed his teeth. "The girl in question is engaged to be married to another man. Her father, not to mention her unsuspecting fiancé, will find the situation unacceptable, perhaps even unforgivable. Miss Southerland wishes to locate her sister before anyone discovers she's missing."

As he retold the story, Beau realized the situation

was indeed as dire as Miss Southerland had indicated. What could have induced Tyler to do something so devious, so selfish?

Love, perhaps? Hardly. Love was patient. Love was kind. It was *not* self-seeking. No. What Tyler had done wasn't about love. It was about Tyler.

"Am I to assume you want me to uncover the location of the fugitives?"

"Precisely."

Beau went on to explain how Miss Southerland knew the two had come west. He then laid out the rest of the details in order of importance, ending with a description of Tyler—a younger, slicker version of Beau—and Rachel—an identical replica of Miss Southerland.

When Beau finished, Trey set the pen down. "I'll start making inquiries at once."

"We have less than a month before Rachel's scheduled wedding. I can't stress enough how desperate Miss Southerland is to find her sister." *That was certainly an understatement.* "She won't wait long for trickles of information."

Trey pressed his lips into a flat line. "Nor can she go off without any clear direction."

"Understood." For a few painful seconds, the churning in Beau's stomach became unbearable.

He didn't envy the poor soul who had to tell Miss Southerland to sit tight and wait for concrete news about her sister. And since *he* was that poor soul, Beau had a mind to throttle his baby brother the moment he found him. Maybe then they would talk.

Or…maybe not.

* * *

Hannah finished drying her hands just as the sun peeked through a seam in the clouds. The rain had stopped, but if the black sky hovering above the distant mountains was any indication, the storm wasn't over yet.

Setting the rag down, she pivoted to study her handiwork of the last hour. Five loaves of bread sat in a straight row atop the counter, waiting their turn for baking. It had been years since Hannah had dug her hands into dough. The sensation had felt nice, soothing. *Distracting.*

Mrs. Smythe, the housekeeper and resident cook, beamed at her. "Such lovely work, Miss Southerland." She motioned to the rising loaves. "Simply wonderful."

A swift jolt of pleasure shot through Hannah at the compliment. "Thank you. I enjoyed helping."

As if she'd timed her cue to perfection, Laney glided into the room and immediately honed in on Hannah's efforts. "You've been busy."

"Can't stand idle hands." Hannah waggled her fingers to punctuate her statement.

"I see that."

"What's our status with the children?" Mrs. Smythe asked.

With her face scrunched in concentration, Laney ticked off the specifics on her fingers. "The older children are getting cleaned up after their latest adventure in the mud. Trey and the pastor are shut in behind closed doors in Marc's office."

She shot a questioning look at Hannah but didn't wait for an answer. Lifting a third finger, she continued with her inventory. "Katherine and Mavis are deep into bath time with the little ones. And Marc is coordinating the rest. That means we have approximately twenty minutes before mayhem erupts again."

Mrs. Smythe blew out a satisfied sigh and shuffled toward a side door in the corner of the kitchen. "Well, then, I think I'll take a few moments to put my feet up before I start supper."

"Sounds good. And you." Laney pointed a finger at Hannah. "Why don't you rest, as well? You look exhausted."

Without waiting for a response, Laney placed a hand on her shoulder and gently guided Hannah into a nearby chair.

Officially too exhausted to fight, Hannah relaxed into the wooden seat. "I *have* been traveling for three days now." She shook her head at the declaration. "I can't believe it's been that long since I left Chicago."

Three days. And every moment spent at Charity House was time lost on the trail. Her entire body trembled with impatience. But what could she do? Hannah squeezed her eyes shut and sighed. There was no point in rushing off. Yet.

Just thinking about the vast number of places Rachel and Tyler could have gone made Hannah want to cry. More than a little heartsick, she felt the beginnings of a headache build behind her eyes.

Laney touched her arm. Hannah opened her eyes and looked into a gaze filled with genuine sympathy.

"Want to talk about it?" Laney asked.

Breathing slowly, Hannah seriously considered the offer. There was something about Laney that made Hannah want to confide in her. And then she remembered the verses from Ecclesiastes. *Two are better than one, because they have a good return for their work...*

Perhaps it would help to have another person on her side.

Laney pulled two mugs out of a cabinet and began pouring coffee. "I find it often helps to confide in a third party, someone objective."

Hannah nodded.

Oh, Lord, give me the courage to be honest with this kind woman. Help me to trust her with the truth.

"First, you should know that I'm an actress," Hannah said, waiting for the condemnation she often received at such a declaration. When none came, she let out a sigh of relief and continued. "I travel in a Shakespearean company with Pastor Beau's brother Tyler."

Laney set one of the cups in front of Hannah and brought the other to her lips. Curiosity sparked in her eyes, but she simply said, "Go on."

"A few days ago my twin sister came to Chicago to watch me perform. We'd become estranged over the years, and I'd prayed her visit would end the bitterness between us."

Her hope had been overwhelming, daunting even, but Rachel had quickly demonstrated that Hannah had built her dreams of reconciliation on shifting sand.

"I can tell by your sadness that she disappointed you." Laney looked at her with soft, understanding eyes.

"After a two-day acquaintance, Rachel ran off with Tyler. They haven't been heard from since."

"Oh my." Laney's eyes widened. "That certainly puts you in a bad situation, especially since I'm assuming she met the man through you."

How had Laney assessed the situation so accurately? Was her guilt that transparent?

"You're correct, I did introduce the two. And now I'm afraid my father may never forgive me for it."

Laney placed her hand over Hannah's. "I'm so sorry."

"I have to bring Rachel home." A rush of emotion threatened to overwhelm her. Hannah rose and started pacing. "The sooner the better, because she is to be married in a month."

"Do you have any idea where they went?"

"No. I only know that they were seen boarding a train headed west."

"Then you'll have to let Trey do the hunting for a while."

"I can't just sit here and do nothing." Hannah pounded her fists against her thighs. "I feel so...so... helpless."

"Of course you do." Laney pulled Hannah into her arms. "But you can't go blindly chasing after them, either. You have good men on your side. Have a little faith."

Faith. Trust. Both came at such a high price. Could she let herself become that vulnerable? Should she take the risk? Did she dare not?

Leaning into the other woman, Hannah shut her eyes and let the tension drain out of her. "You're right, of course."

"I usually am."

Hannah smiled at the lack of guile in the high-and-mighty statement.

"So, it's settled. Until you get more information, you'll just have to keep yourself busy." Laney patted her on the back and released her. "Would you consider moving in here until you get some direction? I could use the extra hands, and I'm thinking you could use the diversion."

Surprised at the instant desire to accept Laney's offer, Hannah forced her mind to focus, to concentrate on the particulars. No matter how appealing she found the prospect of living at Charity House for a while, she didn't want to make any more hasty decisions. "Can I think about it?"

"Absolutely. For now, let's get you—"

Laney's words were interrupted by the pastor's entrance. "Miss Southerland, could I have a private word with you?"

Hannah spun around. Her breath caught in her throat at the sight of Pastor Beau standing in the doorway. His broad shoulders filled every available space. No man had the right to look that tall, that masculine and that in charge when she was so worn-out.

Worse, he looked so much like Tyler that Hannah had to lower her gaze in order to contain the sudden spasm of anger that shot through her. Taking a few slow breaths, she swallowed back her irrational temper and lifted her gaze once again. This time, she saw the sadness, the fierce sorrow he so carefully masked.

He's lonely was her first thought. But that was impossible. Wasn't it?

Laney cleared her throat and stepped toward the doorway. "I'll just leave you two alone."

And that seemed the most frightening prospect yet. At least with Laney in the room, Hannah had an ally.

Unfortunately, her new friend—the turncoat—deserted her without a backward glance.

Chapter Seven

The moment Laney disappeared down the hallway, the temperature in the kitchen dropped several degrees. As easy as it would be to hold on to her resentment, Hannah decided the time for anger and blame had passed. Now she needed to focus on the next step in the search for Rachel and Tyler.

"What did the marshal have to say?" she asked in what she hoped was a mild tone.

"He's agreed to help us. He'll begin making inquiries immediately." The obvious relief in his eyes was evident in his gaze.

"Good. Good." Her own sense of relief coated her voice. "How long do you think it will take for us to hear something?"

"Hard to say. A day, a week." His gaze slid to hers, dark, serious and apologetic now. "Perhaps longer."

A gasp flew from her lips, and her heart pounded hard against her ribs. "Longer than a week? But we don't have that much time."

"I know."

"There has to be something we can do." She slammed her fists against her thighs and circled the room again. "I can't stand this feeling of helplessness."

The reverend's patient gaze followed her movements, but he remained in his spot near the door. "It's hard, I know. We'll have to pray we get news soon."

She nodded. Prayer, yes. Always good.

"In the meantime, I have a favor to ask of you."

Slowing her pace, she glanced at him from over her shoulder. "And what would that be?"

"I'd like you to accept Laney's offer to move in here."

The question stopped her in midstride. "You heard that part of our conversation?"

"I did." He gave her an uncomfortable smile. "Your voices carried as I was making my way down the hallway to find you."

That seemed possible. Nevertheless, why would he want her to stay at the orphanage instead of the hotel? Unless he thought she needed a babysitter. She narrowed her eyes at him. "Are you afraid I'll set out on my own?"

"I can't say the thought didn't cross my mind." He raised his hand to keep her from speaking over him. "But the real reason is that I don't wish for you to be alone in a cold hotel room, fretting over something you can't do anything about."

"Are you saying you're worried about me?" Her pulse picked up speed at the notion.

"That's what I'm saying."

Hannah simply stared at him. What was she supposed to do with that startling declaration? And more to the point, what was she supposed to do with the jolt of pleasure spreading through her at the prospect that this man was actually concerned about her. Her! A virtual stranger. A woman whose own father had banished her from his home without a moment's remorse.

Hannah wasn't usually prone to self-doubt, not lately, anyway. But something about this man, something in the way he threw her off balance with a simple declaration of concern, made her question whether or not she'd truly dealt with the lasting repercussions of her banishment.

That last thought made her bristle.

"I'll tell you what I told Laney," she said, keeping a careful lid on her conflicting emotions. "I'll think about it."

He crossed his arms over his chest and leaned his weight against the doorjamb, looking as though he had all the time in the world. "I'll wait."

Hannah frowned at him. "You want me to make my decision *now?*"

"Within the next few minutes will do." He wound his wrist in the air between them. "Carry on with your thinking and pacing and whatever else you need to do to settle this in your mind."

Her mouth dropped open. "Has anybody ever mentioned your phenomenal arrogance?"

His eyes filled with amusement. "At least a dozen people, half of those just today."

A charming man was bad enough, but a charming O'Toole, Hannah decided, was downright dangerous. "So few?"

He put his unreadable pastor face on and continued to lean against the doorway. He wound his wrist in the air between them again. "Continue considering Laney's offer."

"You're not going to budge from that position until I say yes, are you?"

"Stubbornness is another one of my finer qualities."

"What about smugness, haughtiness and overconfidence?"

His eyes crinkled around the edges. "Those, too."

"You win," she said with a soft, feminine snarl that belied her growing amusement at his absurd attitude. "I'll check out of the hotel. But just so we're clear, I'd already decided to make the move *before* you asked it of me."

"Of course."

"Your suggestion carried no weight, none at all."

"Whatever you say."

"Did I mention you have an arrogant streak?"

A slow grin spread across his lips. "I seem to remember something along those lines."

"I stand by my assessment."

"I expected as much."

"Are you going to continue staring at me with that pompous smile on your lips?"

"There's a large possibility."

She sighed. Why, why, why did he have to be so utterly appealing when she so desperately wanted to hold on to her initial distrust of the man? There was just no winning when it came to combating an O'Toole. "Can we call a truce?"

It was her only hope of maintaining a portion of the control.

"Thought you'd never ask." He shoved from the doorway and covered her hand with both of his. "To new beginnings."

His tone was sincere. His gaze was genuine. His

grip was gentle. So why did she feel the battle had only just begun?

Because anointed pastor or not, the frustrating man was still an O'Toole through and through.

Several hours later, Hannah was officially a resident of Charity House. Ever the gentleman, Reverend O'Toole had left to care for Jane only after ensuring Hannah had everything she needed. For a moment, just before he'd turned to go, his eyes had held such grief, such painful sorrow, that Hannah had wanted to reach out and comfort him. But when she'd stepped toward him, his eyes had gone glassy and unreadable.

Sighing, Hannah now slipped out the back door for the express purpose of capturing a moment alone with her thoughts. The simple pleasure of the solitude made her smile.

Even curtained in shadows, the mountains stood like sentinels. There was a chill in the air tonight, made raw by the drizzling rain. Rubbing her arms for warmth, Hannah drew in a deep breath. The scent of stirred-up mud and pine reminded her of home.

Her *former* home, she corrected. She didn't have a home anymore.

Hannah shut her eyes and sighed again. Behind her, she could hear the chatter of the children as they filed into the dining room for their evening meal.

Tuning out the voices, Hannah allowed her thoughts to run to Pastor Beau and their odd encounters throughout the day. She recognized the curling in her stomach as confusion. In the matter of a few hours, he'd frustrated her, angered her and then had the nerve to make her laugh.

Oh, he'd woefully misjudged her—at first—but Hannah truly believed he felt remorse over his mistake.

Pressing her palms to the porch railing, she leaned into the night and sniffed the clean air. As her mind cleared and she traced the morning's events, Hannah realized that she had met the reverend mere seconds after he'd left the bedside of a lowly prostitute who had once been the premiere actress of her day. A woman who had called Patience O'Toole friend, as Hannah did now.

Given those facts, it was no wonder the man had judged her as he had. And if she was going to be completely honest in her thinking, she'd admit he'd had a point. It was no secret that many actresses ended up like Jane. How was Pastor Beau to know that Hannah had a plan for her future?

Her mind settled at last, Hannah pushed away from the railing and nodded to herself.

She would forgive and forget. And, of course, trust.

If Rachel and Tyler were meant to be found, they would be found. In the end, it all boiled down to who was in control.

Oh, Lord, Hannah prayed. *I surrender this seemingly impossible task into Your hands. Please bring us news of Rachel and Tyler soon. In the meantime, I pray You protect them both and keep them safe. Let them—*

A loud bang of the screen door cut into her prayer. Hannah jumped at the sound and spun quickly around. "Oh."

Two years of traveling with odd-looking characters prevented her mouth from gaping open. But, truly, standing before her was the strangest apparition Hannah had encountered in quite a while.

"You must be that pretty actress the pastor brought over from town," said a hard, raspy voice of uncertain gender.

The woman—and yes, it was a grown woman, Hannah assured herself—was very small, rail thin and stood eye to eye with Hannah's chin. She wore a bright red dress over a pair of what looked like—Hannah narrowed her eyes—men's denim pants? Her hair was white as snow and shot out in wild waves from every direction. Her age was indeterminate, anywhere from fifty to a hundred.

Hannah estimated closer to a hundred.

If she was casting a play, this woman would be perfect for the role of the nurse in *Romeo and Juliet.*

Realizing she was gaping after all, Hannah shook her head and said, "Yes, I'm Hannah Southerland. You must be Mavis."

The answering grin revealed an uneven row of teeth with a few gaps thrown in for added character. "That I am. Marc and Laney adopted me a few months back."

Playing along, Hannah asked, "How are you settling in? Are you getting along with the other children?"

Mavis let out a cackle that would have been better suited for a character in *Macbeth*—oh, say, one leaning over a cauldron. And Hannah meant that in the best possible way. "So, tell me, Mavis, what do you do around here?"

"What don't I do? I'm the official bath mistress, naptime general and all-around helping hand to forty-some-odd orphans." She shot a line of spit through the gap between her front teeth. "Give or take a toddler or two."

"I'm pleased to hear it."

Leaning forward, Mavis looked to her left, then to her right and back to her left again. "Are we alone?" she asked in a perfect imitation of a stage whisper.

Hannah looked to her left, then to her right and back to her left again. "It appears so."

Mavis released a slow, happy sigh. "What. A. Day." She parked her nonexistent behind on a rocking chair and started rifling through one of the pockets on her dress.

Enjoying herself immensely, Hannah sat, as well.

"Them little ones hate their bath time. Don't mean to complain myself, but that U.S. Marshal's gonna get an earful from his wife. He's been telling the kids that playtime is more important than a 'stinkin' bath'—his words, not mine."

Hannah kept a straight face. Barely. "That can't be helpful."

"There's mutiny afoot." Mavis pointed a scrawny finger at Hannah. "You mark my words, that marshal's gonna get his. His deputy, too, if it were up to me."

Annoyance hiked Mavis's chin up a notch or two, but she continued digging in her pocket.

"Not to sound contentious myself," Hannah said. "But I always thought children hating baths was pretty universal."

"Yeah, well, it certainly helps to have someone to blame." The spark of amusement in the older woman's eyes told its own story.

But just to be sure.

"Marshal Scott isn't a troublemaker by nature, is he?"

"No sirree, I love that boy, even if he tells them younguns to run for their very lives when it's bath time."

Hannah shared a grin with her new friend. Obviously, Mavis adored the man.

"Aha, there you are." Mavis pulled out a leather pouch from her pocket. Fingers working quickly, she dumped a generous amount of brown tobacco onto a thin piece of paper and began rolling.

Hannah blinked. "What are you doing?"

"Making myself a paper cigarette," she said without bothering to look up from her task. "You want one?"

Hannah shook her head. "I don't smoke."

Mavis wiggled her eyebrows at her. "Don't know what you're missing."

"I'll take the risk."

"You know, Miss Hannah," Mavis said, her eyes focused once more on her work. "I used to tread the old boards in my day."

This information should have shocked Hannah, but as she further studied the older woman, she saw the flair in her movements, the tendency toward the dramatic in the flourish she used to roll the tobacco. "How long were you on the stage?"

Seconds ticked by before Mavis answered. "Well, I can't really say I was an actress for long. At least not in the traditional sense. Oh, I've played some role or another all my life, but I weren't no good onstage."

Hannah doubted that. With her personality alone the woman would have fit in perfectly with any acting troupe, past or present.

"I ended up finding employment in the age-old profession," Mavis said, her eyes dark with emotion.

"Age-old profession?"

"You know." She released one side of the paper and

gave a vague gesture with her hand. "Like that girl in the Bible that done saved those Jewish spies in Jericho, the one that ended up in Jesus' lineage."

Hannah thought a moment. "You mean Rahab?" *The prostitute?*

"That's the one."

Mavis struck a match off the bottom of her shoe, lit the cigarette with a long inhale and then took her time exhaling. "Glad to be done with that nasty work. I like it here better. Who knew I'd love helping with them kids in there?"

Hannah reached out and squeezed Mavis's hand. "Children have a way of doing that." And if working at Charity House kept this woman from living a life of sin, what a heaven-sent blessing. As Pastor Beau had said, God's hand was truly on Charity House.

"Maybe in my small way I can prevent these kids from going down my same road." Her eyes turned sad, almost haunted. "Maybe I can atone for my—"

"Mavis Elizabeth Tierney," came a high-pitched, angry female voice from just inside the house. "You drop that death stick right now."

Mavis heaved a dramatic sigh. "Here comes the spoilsport now," she whispered behind her cupped hand.

Out walked a very angry, stiff-backed woman. The screen door shut behind her with a bang. Even with her face scrunched into a scowl, the woman was extraordinary. And with her dark hair and blue, blue eyes, she reminded Hannah of a grown-up version of the little girl, Molly.

This must be Katherine, the marshal's wife, Hannah thought.

"Hand it over, Mavis." She thrust her hand out between them. "I mean it."

Mavis treated the woman to a withering glare, which had no effect whatsoever.

The stalemate continued a few more seconds.

"You're just not tolerant no more, Katherine Scott. Not since you got in the motherly way." Mavis looked pointedly at the woman's rounded belly.

Reminiscent of Molly's mannerisms, Katherine parked fists to hips and narrowed her eyes. "Dr. Shane said you can't keep smoking those and continue living." Her frown deepened. "I, for one, won't stand by and watch you kill yourself."

Mavis rose, muttering the whole way up. With exaggerated slowness, she took a mutinous drag of the cigarette and then blew out a long, thin stream of smoke.

Katherine snorted in disgust.

Mavis grinned fiercely, but then heaved another big sigh and handed over the incriminating cigarette.

"Thank you," Katherine said, her shoulders still stiff and unmoving.

"Humph." With a dramatic flick of her wrist, Mavis whipped her hair over her shoulder and marched back into the house without another word.

Staring at the screen door, Katherine took several deep breaths before throwing the cigarette to the porch floor. She folded her arms across her chest and dug the toe of her shoe over the burning ember. "Honestly. That woman tries my soul."

Unsure what to say, Hannah rose.

It was Katherine's turn to sigh before clearing her expression. "You must be Hannah."

"And you're Marshal Scott's wife."

"I am." Katherine blinked rapidly, clearly fighting to gain control over her emotions. "I'm sorry you got caught in the middle of that."

"No, I'm sorry." Hannah swallowed back a surge of guilt. "I didn't realize she was under doctor's orders. I would have tried to stop her."

Katherine peered at her with troubled eyes. "You didn't know. But if you ever see her smoking again, I'd appreciate it if you would discourage her."

"You have my word."

A look of exasperation crossed the other woman's face. "Honestly, she's worse than the children."

"And just as lovable."

Their stares connected, a ripple of feminine understanding passing between them.

Katherine let out a soft laugh. "She is at that. It's why I'm so hard on her." She took another steadying breath. "Actually, I came in search of you. Supper is nearly over. Laney sent me to tell you she'd like to discuss the indoor games you mentioned earlier."

Hannah nodded. "I'd be delighted."

As she followed Katherine back inside the house, Hannah realized the moments she'd spent with Mavis were the first in days she hadn't worried about her sister. In fact, she hadn't thought of Rachel once.

Hannah didn't know whether to be glad for it or incredibly sad, but either way Mavis Tierney had been a colorful diversion.

Chapter Eight

The scent of death cloaked the tiny room like a thick, heavy blanket. The raw odor gripped Beau's throat and squeezed it shut. A soft moan of misery drifted out of Jane Goodwin as she lay limp on her bed.

Dejected, Beau crossed to the back corner of the room and gave the young doctor who had arrived hours before plenty of space to work.

The time has come, Beau thought in frustrated agony.

At the realization that he hadn't been able to save this lost lamb, a strong sense of helplessness pulled sweat onto his brow. Lowering chin to chest, he prayed that the Lord would give him the right words to bring reassurance to the dying woman.

An eerie silence fell over the room, broken only by Jane's ragged breathing and the doctor's soft murmurs of comfort. Out of respect for Jane, Beau cleared his face of any expression.

But it hurt deep in his soul to watch the poor woman struggle for air. Her breathing was different tonight, more labored. For about an hour now, she would suck in a breath, pause, and then wheeze out hard before pausing again. Just as Beau would give up hope for her next breath, the pattern would begin all over again.

The death rattle.

He'd heard it before, and his own breathing rasped in his lungs.

"Is she in as much pain as it appears?" he asked.

Working with efficient hands, Shane Bartlett lifted Jane's wrist and checked her pulse again. "No more than expected."

Beau offered up a prayer of thanksgiving for the competent young doctor. Shane was the only physician in town who would dare to step into a brothel—in an official capacity, that was.

Straightening, the other man clicked his black bag shut and let out a slow stream of air. His brown hair stuck out at the ends, looking as though he'd run his hands through it far too many times and now the thick mane was on permanent revolt.

"Doctor?"

Shane turned sad, tired eyes to Beau. The empty, resigned expression said it all.

Jane Goodwin's journey here on earth had come to an end. All that remained was her final curtain call.

Breaking eye contact, Beau lowered his head. *Heavenly Father, I pray You bring Miss Jane some peace in her final moments. Most of all, I pray for her salvation.*

Opening his eyes, Beau connected his gaze with the doctor's once more. "Is there anything I can do? Any thoughts on how I can make her more comfortable?"

Shane shook his head. "You've done all you can." He reached down and dragged his thumb across Jane's furrowed brow. "I'm sorry, Reverend. There are some things we humans can't control. It's simply her time."

"I understand." And yet, Beau's heart clenched at the news. For a moment, he stared at the pale, limp figure lying on the bed. The lines of fatigue around her eyes and the odd angle of her mouth were clear indicators of how ill she truly was.

Jane moaned, twisting and kicking until she'd wrenched one arm free of the covers.

"Beau?" Her frail hand lifted a mere inch off the bed.

Beau rushed to her side, knelt down and wrapped his fingers gently around hers. "I'm right here."

She rattled through several more breaths before her eyes blinked open and focused on him. He was surprised at how clear her gaze looked, clearer than he'd seen in weeks.

A relieved sigh lurched through him.

"My daughter, Megan, is she…" Her words trailed off, turning into a soft moaning in between quick pants. Apparently, her body couldn't keep up with her will.

Beau looked at Shane for direction. The other man nodded for him to proceed.

"Megan is happy and safe at Charity House." Beau lifted her hand and gently squeezed. "She will always have a home there."

A smile spread across Jane's lips, and she struggled to lift her head. Her gasping increased until Shane moved in behind her to support her shoulders. Thanks to his assistance, her breathing eased a bit.

"Lie back, Miss Jane," Shane urged. "You must reserve your energy."

Once he had her settled again, Shane nodded at Beau to continue.

"I gave Marc the envelope," Beau said. "You truly have nothing to worry about."

She shut her eyes and relaxed back against the pillow. "Tha... Thank you."

Her breathing grew strangely calm then, as though she'd been waiting to hear about her daughter before she could finally give up the unbearable fight.

It was time.

But the most important work was yet to be done. *Oh, Lord, God, please open her heart to You.*

"Miss Jane, you have a Savior ready to welcome you home," Beau began. "A place where you will receive a new body, where you will be free of pain."

Out of the corner of his eye, Beau noticed Mattie slipping into the room and shutting the door quickly behind her. The moment her gaze dropped to Jane, her lips parted in shock. She staggered back, flattened against the wall behind her and stared wide-eyed at Beau.

But Beau had more pressing matters to attend to.

Giving Mattie a quick nod of acknowledgment, he opened his Bible and began to read from Matthew 11. "Come to me, all you who are weary and burdened, and I will give you rest. Take my yoke upon you and learn from me, for I am gentle and humble in heart, and you will find rest for your souls. For my yoke is easy and my burden light."

A lump formed in his throat, and his voice shook.

Beau lowered his head and continued to pray softly over Jane. Her eyes fluttered shut and her breathing calmed, the gasps of air coming shorter and more softly.

The violence slowly slipped out of her, replaced by a sense of tranquillity.

With very little struggle now, she took a shallow breath. Paused. Took another breath. Paused again, continuing the pattern until there were simply no more breaths left.

A surreal silence spread through the room.

Beau shut his eyes in a moment of devastating grief. A muscle locked in his jaw while a lone tear escaped from his right eye.

"Is she...?" Mattie whispered.

"Yes," Shane said.

Beau looked over at the madam. Tears ran unbridled down her cheeks. Never had he seen such a vulnerable look of anguish on the woman's face.

Catching his gaze on her, Mattie hardened her expression and quickly escaped from the room without a word or a glance behind her.

Another moment passed before Shane moved forward and lifted Jane's flaccid wrist. He felt around and then moved his fingers to her neck. "She is at peace at last."

Beau nodded, sucked in a lungful of the room's hot, putrid air and blew out a sad sigh. Miss Jane had been young by most standards, not yet forty. Such a waste of a promising life.

"I'll leave you now and start making arrangements for removing her body," Shane said.

Unable to tear his gaze from the now-peaceful face of his mother's former friend, Beau simply nodded. "Thank you, Shane."

The other man gripped Beau's shoulder then dropped his hand. "You did your best."

"I'm not sure it was enough."

"Only God knows a person's heart, but she and I spoke on the matter of her salvation before you arrived." Shane angled his head to stare at Jane. "She made her peace with her Savior."

Beau knew he should feel relief at the doctor's words. But lying before him—in the slack repose of death—was the personification of the uglier side of the acting profession.

A burning throb of anger knotted in his chest, stiffening the muscles throughout his body.

While Shane gathered his things and left the room, Beau gently pulled the blanket up to Jane's chin.

Silent and brooding, he stared at her without really seeing her anymore.

How many women died in equal desolation and solitude every day? How many lived in condemnation, without experiencing Christ's love in their lives? How many lived without family or friends to care for them when times turned hard?

Far too many was the only answer that came to him.

If only he could stop the vicious cycle.

But the task was too large for one man. Overwhelmed with the magnitude of such a burden, Beau lifted his gaze toward heaven. *I can't do it, Lord.*

A memory from the last time he sat at Jane's bedside lurched forward in his mind, and Beau recalled what the still, small voice had said to him. "One at a time, Beau."

Beau thought of Miss Southerland then, and his confusion instantly cleared into a single purpose. *Yes, Lord, one at a time.*

He would start with her.

* * *

Fighting sleep a little while longer, Hannah sat at the dining room table with Laney. Laney had an inkwell on her right, a pen in her hand and a sheet of paper spread before her.

They were alone in their task.

With everyone else either in bed or back in their own home, the house had a nice, relaxed silence about it. As tired as she was, Hannah felt a strong sense of peace wash over her. Charity House was no mere institution. It was a home that had welcomed Hannah as though she'd belonged here all her life.

She had visited many orphanages, but had never been inside one so filled with love and compassion. And to think most of the children were born under unholy circumstances. In her mind, that made Charity House that much more special.

Hannah's unclear idea of a future ministry had taken form in this tiny world within the harsher world surrounding it. She was both humbled and inspired by all the possibilities before her.

Feeling lighthearted and energized, Hannah turned to her new friend and smiled. "We have our two spies, the king and Joshua. Now we need to pick our Rahab. It should be one of the older girls." Hannah tapped her fingers on the table. "Any suggestions?"

"Megan." Laney's eyes turned sad, haunted even, but very, very determined. "It *has* to be Megan."

"Jane Goodwin's daughter?"

"With Jane dying soon, it will do Megan some good, or at least take her mind off her mother's illness."

Hannah felt the jolt of understanding all the way

down to the soles of her feet. Her own mother had died around this same time of year. The memory shifted, materialized and then cleared just as quickly, leaving a sharp pain of loss whipping through her.

Hannah shuddered.

Death was an inevitable part of life. But for a young girl to lose her mother—well, that was something no child of any age should have to experience, especially not alone.

Unlike Hannah, Megan was not alone. And Hannah would do her part to help the girl through this tragedy.

"Yes," Hannah said once she had her own emotions under control. "Megan will be perfect in the role of Rahab."

Smiling, Laney rubbed a finger over her temple and bobbed her head up and down. "I love the idea of putting on a play from the Bible. You said you do this all over the country?"

"If I'm in a city long enough. I've found it's an effective way to teach the children about the Bible." She lifted a shoulder. "We could read the story to them, give them a short lesson and then ask them questions. But when they physically participate in the telling of the story, they remember it better."

Setting her elbow on the table, Laney rested her chin in her cupped palm and let her gaze drift over Hannah's shoulder. "I can't believe we never thought of this before. The story of Rahab is the perfect choice."

Normally, Hannah wouldn't start with such a powerful story, one filled with intrigue and an unconventional heroine. But if there was ever a group of children that needed to learn about God's glory and how He often chose flawed individuals to carry out His plan it was the Charity House orphans.

"I'm looking forward to putting it all together," Hannah said.

"What will the others do, the ones who aren't given a part in the play?"

Hannah gave Laney a heartening smile. This had always been a concern, but Hannah had long since found a way to include all the children. "Everyone will participate. Either in a small role or behind the scenes making the sets or getting together the costumes."

Clearly unwilling to let the matter go without concrete assurances, Laney lifted a perfectly arched eyebrow. "And the ones who want the parts that other children have?"

"Understudies." Hannah raised a hand before Laney could interrupt. The orphanage had a large number of children in residence. There was only one way to ensure every child that wanted to be in the play got a chance. "We'll make sure some of the adults can't make the first production, whereby we'll have to put on a second show with the understudies in their roles."

Laney leaned back in her chair, her eyes brimming with satisfaction. "You've thought of everything."

Uncomfortable under the praise, Hannah repositioned herself in her chair. "Well, these things never go without a hitch, but we'll do our best to minimize the worst of them."

Laney slapped her palms on the table and pushed out of her chair. "That's good enough for me." She stretched her arms over her head. "I'll leave the particulars to you. I'm going in search of my husband."

The obvious affection Hannah saw in Laney's eyes made Hannah's heart lurch against her ribs. "Sleep well."

"I always do." She reached across the table and squeezed Hannah's hand. "Do you have everything you need for tonight?"

Hannah nodded, tears pricking at the backs of her eyes. "You've been very kind. I owe you."

"Don't think I won't collect."

"I hope you will."

Laughing, Laney waved a hand over her head and left the room.

As she watched the other woman leave, a sense of belonging crept through Hannah. It was a feeling she hadn't experienced since her mother died twelve years ago. How was it she had a twin sister, a woman that should have been her best friend, her confidant and ally, and yet she felt closer to Laney Dupree after a half-day's acquaintance?

Guilt tapped a painful melody across her nerves.

Hannah had spent a lifetime failing her sister in one capacity or another, especially when there was a man involved. First had been the boy they'd fought over as children—a fight that had ultimately resulted in Rachel's hearing loss. Then there had been the married schoolteacher who had been Rachel's secret tryst and the reason for Hannah's banishment. Their father had never questioned Rachel's claim that Hannah had been the one dallying with Mr. Beamer. He'd thrown Hannah out of his home without hesitation.

Now, Tyler stood between the sisters.

Why hadn't Hannah seen the pattern before?

Well, no matter—she was through letting a man come between them. Whether Rachel agreed at first or not, Hannah was going to push all men aside and forge a true bond with her only sister.

A passing flirtation with a man would carry no more weight. It was time to put family loyalty and the love of sisters ahead of a man.

And now that Hannah had made up her mind, Tyler O'Toole didn't stand a chance.

Chapter Nine

Early the next morning, Beau strode across the grounds of the Arapahoe County Courthouse with a clipped, impatient pace. Marshal Scott had requested an urgent meeting at his office before the start of the day. Beau could only hope the lawman had good news.

Cold, dark clouds drifted overhead, casting a gray, depressing light over the morning sky. The manicured lawn and geometric angles of the sidewalks did nothing to soften the imposing architecture of the three-story courthouse. Made from solid stone and marble, the building brought to mind stability. The obvious statement being that no matter how corrupt any one individual became, the courthouse itself would remain steadfast and true.

Still locked inside his grief over Jane, Beau was too weighed down with sadness to notice the rest of his surroundings as he strode across the grounds.

As he continued toward the front steps, his mind shifted to Jane's daughter. Megan would have to be told about her mother. It would not be an easy conversation.

Oh, Lord, You promise to be with us always, to the

*very end of the age. I pray you are with Megan today
and always.*

A roll of thunder rippled loud and menacing in the
near distance. Beau darted up the marble steps and
shoved inside the building. At the same moment the
heavy brass door shuddered closed, another clap of
thunder shook the air.

Beau circled his gaze around the wood-paneled lobby.
Men and women of all ages milled about. With a resolute
frown pulling his eyebrows lower, he searched the sea of
faces and wondered how he would find Marshal Scott.
Thankfully, his search was short-lived. On the other side
of the cavernous room, Beau caught sight of Trey in deep
conversation with a younger man. Both were dressed in
solid black with a tin star pinned to their chests.

Picking up speed, Beau crossed in their direction.
"Marshal Scott," he called out.

Trey lifted his head. "Ah, Reverend O'Toole, we
were just discussing your…case." He gestured to the
other man. "This is my deputy, Logan Mitchell."

Beau nodded at the other man. Blond, lanky and with
an open, honest expression in his eyes, Deputy Mitchell
looked more like an inexperienced ranch hand than a
lawman. But Beau had heard the rumors. A year ago,
the young deputy had saved Trey's life during a gunfight
in Mattie's brothel, of all places.

"Do you have news of my brother?" Beau asked.

Before answering, Trey looked around the lobby, his
gaze landing on a few people slowing their pace as they
passed by. "Let's continue this discussion in the privacy
of my office."

Beau fell into step behind the other two men as they

wound their way through a labyrinth of marbled floors and paneled hallways. Taking a deep lungful of air, Beau breathed in the scent of important business, a spicy blend of leather, wood and tobacco.

Along the way, several men stopped their conversations to look at Marshal Scott. A unique mixture of awe and fear filled their eyes.

Rounding a final corner, Trey directed Beau across the threshold of a tiny room that contained one wooden chair, one functional desk and a thick layer of dust.

"I take it you don't use this office very often," Beau said, flashing a conspiratorial smile.

With one quick slash of his hand, Trey dismissed the small space. "Now that I have my own home, I complete most of my paperwork there."

Beau didn't blame the marshal for avoiding this austere room. The man had a beautiful wife, a lovable daughter and a baby on the way. It was no wonder he spent every free moment he could with his family.

Beau's own dreams of the future slid unexpectedly into focus. The images came so abruptly, so unyieldingly, he had to gulp for air. Perhaps grief and the subsequent reminder of his own mortality increased his sense of urgency, but Beau wanted what Trey Scott and Marc Dupree had. He wanted a wife, a houseful of children and a home filled with Christ's joy.

"Have a seat." Trey motioned to the lone chair in the room.

Trudging forward with heavy feet, Beau took note of the thick grime on the indicated chair. "I'll stand."

Trey gave him a wry smile. "Probably for the best," he said as he reached a hand toward Logan.

The deputy presented a small stack of papers Beau hadn't noticed him carrying before now.

Trey adjusted the pile in his grip. "I'll get straight to the point. We've received several telegraphs in response to our inquiries about your brother." He riffled through the papers, paused, riffled some more. "Two came in from the Springs area, one from San Francisco, another from Laramie and, finally, one from our office in Cheyenne."

Cheyenne?

At the mention of the booming frontier town, memories of lost hope and a failed relationship threatened to materialize in Beau's mind. One he had purposely worked to forget. Squaring his shoulders, Beau shoved the reminder aside. If the Lord meant for him to return to Cheyenne after that last disastrous trip, then Beau would go out of obedience. Even if he didn't relish the opportunity.

Heavenly Father, please, not that. Not *Cheyenne.*

Head still bent over the telegraphs, Trey continued. "Several actors have arrived in San Francisco this week, but none that meet the description of your brother."

A relieved sigh passed through Beau. Tyler and Rachel hadn't made it to the coast. Yet. At least not together. But if they'd separated and Rachel was traveling alone...

No, Beau didn't want to think about the ugly possibilities of such a disaster.

"Two female dancers showed up in Colorado Springs three days ago, but both are much older than Miss Southerland's sister."

Beau grimaced. "That leaves Laramie and Cheyenne."

"No arrivals in Laramie to date. However, Cheyenne is a different story." Placing the bottom piece of paper on top of the stack, Trey slanted a quick look at Beau. "A famous Shakespearean actor arrived just under a week ago. The man was accompanied by a beautiful young woman. The descriptions of the two match your brother and Miss Southerland's sister."

The jolt of disappointment took Beau by surprise. There had been a small part of him—the part where blood and family loyalty resided—that had hoped Miss Southerland had been wrong about his brother.

Now there could be no doubt. But to have his younger brother land in Cheyenne of all places.

Beau's breath tightened in his lungs, and he fought the urge to clench his hand into a fist.

Oh, Lord, I know Your plan is bigger than my understanding. I pray for Your guidance and Your steadfast courage to face her again.

"Are they still in Cheyenne?" he asked.

Trey's gaze cut to Logan, and he nodded at the younger man.

Taking over the conversation, Logan reached to the pile of papers and sorted through the stack until he came to one in particular. "According to Marshal Montgomery, their room at a local hotel is paid through the end of the month," Logan said.

"*Room?* As in singular?"

Logan fixed his gaze on the wall behind Beau's left shoulder. "One room. Two guests. Registered as—" he looked back at the telegraph in his hand "—a Mr. and Mrs. Duke Orsino."

Mr. and Mrs. Duke Orsino?

Annoyance, quick and hot, shot through Beau. Leave it to Tyler to pick an alias from the popular Shakespearean play *Twelfth Night,* where the main characters were twins separated by misfortune. It was as if his brother was hiding in plain sight and daring Beau to come after him.

Well, the gauntlet had been thrown.

And Beau had no problem accepting the arrogant challenge.

"I need to give Miss Southerland the news," he said. "I suspect she will want to leave right away."

But this time she would not travel alone.

Once Beau had assisted Megan through the initial stages of her grief, he would make arrangements for his and Miss Southerland's journey to Cheyenne.

They would, of course, need a chaperone. And perhaps a guide. Or at least a written introduction to the marshal in Cheyenne.

With his mind organizing, calculating, Beau paced toward the lone, dingy window at the back of the room. Seeing none of the scenery beyond, he continued thinking through the particulars.

Trey's voice interrupted Beau's mental list-making. "Ordinarily I would offer to accompany you on the journey. But I'm in the middle of an important trial, and I can't leave my wife now that she's carrying our child." His voice sounded slightly troubled yet very, very resolved.

Beau turned to look at Trey. Unasked questions hung in the room between them. Maintaining eye contact with the other man, Beau waited.

"I realize Miss Southerland will have questions," Trey said in a toneless voice. "But I won't be able to go to Charity House with you this morning." He opened a watch linked to a fob on his vest. "Today's proceedings begin in less than an hour."

Logan shifted into view. "I'll go in your stead, Marshal."

Beau looked from one man to the other. The two appeared to be communicating without words, an important message passing between them.

When neither man broke the silence, Beau said, "Thank you, Deputy Mitchell. I would appreciate your assistance."

Remaining silent, Logan unbuckled his gun belt and handed it to Trey, who then circled the desk and locked the weapons inside the bottom drawer.

Confused, Beau asked, "Why are you leaving your guns behind?"

Logan lifted a shoulder. "We never wear our weapons around the children at Charity House."

Even with all the conflicting thoughts scrambling for attention in Beau's head, one point drew into focus. The men and women of Charity House were beyond compare.

Hannah touched Megan's shoulder. The teenager turned a questioning look to her. An old soul. Wise beyond her years. Those had been Hannah's first thoughts when Laney had introduced her to the seventeen-year-old this morning. And they still held now. With thick, wheat-colored hair, green, intelligent eyes and clear, flawless skin, Jane Goodwin's daughter was nothing so benign as pretty. Nothing so ordinary as beautiful.

She was spectacular.

"Did I do something wrong?" Megan asked when Hannah didn't speak. Her eyes filled with worry, and she drew her bottom lip between her teeth.

"No, no," Hannah assured her. "You're wonderful. All I need is for you to turn slightly to the left when you say that last line and place your chin a little higher in the air. Remember, Rahab is a courageous woman, one who is instrumental in the Israelites' victory. She has no doubt Yahweh is the one, true God."

"But she's a prostitute." Megan shifted from one foot to the other, her brows slammed together in a frown. "Why do you speak about her with such, I don't know…reverence?"

Activity around them stopped and all eyes—all twelve curious pairs—turned and waited for Hannah's response to the question. Knowing who their mothers were and what sort of life they'd chosen to lead, she knew her response would be important. Perhaps life-changing for these children.

Before speaking, Hannah offered up a quick prayer. *Oh, Lord, please fill me with the right words.*

"That's the best part of the story," she began in a light tone. "At least in terms of seeing God's glory shine over man's."

"Huh?" one of the boys asked.

Hannah took a deep breath. She wanted to keep her explanation simple, yet profound. "If God had chosen a perfect woman to carry out His plan that day, then how could we know the Lord was in control all along?"

All twelve sets of eyes widened.

"How would we know to trust in God and not mere people? Understand?"

A few heads angled in confusion, while others bobbed up and down in agreement.

"You see—"

"What Miss Southerland is trying to say," a familiar voice said from behind her, "is that by using Rahab as His instrument for rescuing the Israelites, God showed us that even the most unexpected people have a place in the Lord's plan and, ultimately, His heart."

Catching a wisp of limes and pine that was uncomfortably appealing, Hannah spun around and faced the reverend head-on. "Exactly," she said, holding his gaze.

Leaning against the open doorway, he loomed large and masculine as always, but something in his off-kilter stance made her stop and study him more closely.

Hannah gasped at the unconscionable grief rimming his golden gaze. And for a split second, his wounded, grief-stricken eyes simply stared back at her.

Hannah gasped again. Glory. *Glory.*

Like many women, she was drawn to people who needed her. And she was *always* at her best when one of those people actually asked for her help.

Beauregard O'Toole, although he didn't know it yet, needed her. Of course, the question still remained.

What was she going to do about it?

Chapter Ten

Beau tried to think brotherly thoughts. But once again the impact of Miss Southerland's appeal overpowered his efforts. For one shocking moment, his future had a face. Panic surged so violently at the notion that he had to lean against the doorjamb to catch his balance.

Mentally, he forced himself to step back, to evaluate. To...*think*. Running a hand down his face, he organized his thoughts as best he could. One ultimate truth came into focus. Miss Southerland would never make a suitable wife for a preacher in a small, conservative community.

She was too flamboyant, too alluring, too...*conspicuous*. And with his own reputation already controversial enough, Beau needed an unassuming woman by his side.

Hannah Southerland was *not* that woman.

Yet, as she continued to stare at him with that sweet, understanding expression, Beau was struck by a wave of tenderness, and he had trouble remembering exactly why she could never fit into his life.

She was a friend of his parents', after all. No doubt, his mother loved her. The two women were cut from the same mold, all the way down to their clear understanding of Scripture and outer beauty.

But Beau was a preacher in search of a conventional wife. She would definitely need to be plain, traditional, and would reflect the sense of stability so many of his superiors questioned in him.

A tug on Beau's leg jerked him out of his disturbing thoughts. "Hey, Pastor Beau, are you here to help us with the play?"

Happy for the distraction, Beau angled his head to look at little Molly Scott grinning up at him. "Play?" Her words didn't quite register. "What play?"

"The one Miss Hannah is helping us put on. It's about Rahab. I get to be a merchant. Bobby and Mitch—" she pointed to the boys behind her "—are the spies."

"I...see." Which, of course, he didn't. Not fully.

Beau shook his head in confusion.

Molly scooted to her left, leaned forward and waved frantically. "Hi, Deputy Mitchell. Are you here to help us, too?"

Caught in his own confusion, Beau had completely forgotten about the young deputy. Shuffling to his right, Beau moved out of the doorway and allowed Logan to step forward.

"Hey, kitten," the other man said as he plucked at one of her braids. "Help with what?"

"The play," a soft, feminine voice announced from the interior of the room.

Lifting his gaze, Logan instantly straightened and stood gaping at a pretty girl of about seventeen.

The young beauty seemed equally enthralled with the deputy. There was something familiar about her. But before Beau could make the connection in his mind, Miss Southerland cleared her throat.

"We're putting on a play about the Israelites' defeat of Jericho," she said.

She extended her hand to Logan, smiling as though she had a private joke all her own when he completely ignored her.

Shoving her hand forward again, she wiggled her fingers. "I'm Hannah Southerland, and you are…"

"I…uh…I'm…" Logan blinked, blinked again, shook his head and very, very slowly turned his attention to Miss Southerland. "Deputy U.S. Marshal Logan Mitchell, Miss…uh…South-land?"

His voice held the absent note of someone merely going through the motions of the introduction. Beau held back a grin as Logan ignored her outstretched hand and returned his attention to the girl.

The little beauty fluttered her lashes in a gesture surprisingly without guile.

Logan swallowed, audibly sighed.

The battle was won and lost in that moment. And Logan Mitchell was a goner.

Grinning at the smitten pair, Miss Southerland made an exaggerated effort of looking from Logan to the girl and then over to Beau. With an ironic tilt of her chin, she fluttered her lashes in an gesture identical to Megan's.

The humor was there in her eyes, but Beau found himself feeling as stunned as the young deputy looked.

Molly tugged on his hand again. "So, are you joining us or not?"

Beau forced his mind back to the conversation. He wasn't usually so daft. "You're turning Bible stories into plays. I think that's…" Beau paused, searching for the right word. "Brilliant."

Clearly pleased with his approval, Miss Southerland sent him a quick, lovely smile.

Sensing he was a goner himself, Beau felt his stomach lurch.

"Everyone gets a chance to help," she continued with her explanation. "Either as actors or set designers or costume mistresses." Her eyes went serious as she offered her hand to the young girl still trapped inside Logan's gaze. "And Megan here is going to play our heroine, Rahab."

Megan. Beau's mind focused to pinpoint clarity. Of course the girl looked familiar. She was Jane Goodwin's daughter. And now that he looked, now that he *really looked,* the resemblance was uncanny.

His pulse thundered loudly in his head, and for a moment he was transported back in time to when the magnificent Jane Goodwin was in her prime. The hope that the generational cycle of sin would be broken in this younger, fresher version came abrupt and violent.

And he was here to break her heart.

But not yet. He couldn't do it just yet.

Beau shifted his gaze to Miss Southerland. "I need a private word with you."

Logan's brows knitted together, but before he could speak, Beau said, "I won't need you for this conversation, Deputy, but I ask that you stick around in case I need you to fill in details I might have forgotten."

Logan nodded. "Of course." He turned his attention back to Megan. "Would you care to take a walk with me?" he asked.

His softly uttered words were in direct conflict with the intense expression in his gaze.

Looking both mystified and pleased, Megan's eyes widened. "Do you suppose it would be all right, Miss Southerland?"

"Of course, but take Molly with you. And stay close to the house." She paused to give Logan a meaningful look. "I'm sure you understand my meaning, Deputy."

"Yes, ma'am," Logan said, his face a study of obedience and propriety. "I certainly do."

In spite of the other man's promise, Beau could feel the anticipation in Logan as he offered his hand to Megan. But as the young adults left, with Molly chattering away by their side, Beau couldn't help but smile in relief. Miss Southerland had known exactly what she was about when she'd sent the pair off with Molly, who was, unbeknownst to the child, doubling as a very attentive chaperone.

Well, well, well. The unconventional, flamboyant actress had a conservative streak.

And as he nursed the surprising thought, Beau was beginning to suspect he had no idea who Hannah Southerland truly was under all that fluff and lace. The woman confused him, to be sure. The sensation was a lot like standing in quicksand.

Hannah waited until Megan, Molly and Deputy Mitchell left the house before breaking eye contact with the pastor. She didn't especially like the intense look the man had been giving her since he'd arrived, studying her as though he was trying to see past her exterior and straight into her heart. She should feel glad, happy that at last he was trying to see her for who she was, not what she looked like on the outside.

But what if he looked deep enough to see beyond her good intentions, deep down to her core, where she feared there was nothing of worth?

If her own father could see past her facade and find something repulsive, how could this stranger not? If her own father found her wanting, wouldn't this fellow preacher do so, as well? Because of her bold attitude and outspoken nature, Thomas Southerland had chosen to believe there was only sin below the colorful exterior. He'd chosen to believe Hannah was the bad daughter, and Rachel the good.

He'd never doubted, never sought facts or details. And he certainly never questioned the validity of Rachel's stories, which had been filled with holes the size of the Royal Gorge.

Was there something lacking in Hannah that brought on his unfavorable judgment? Would Beauregard O'Toole see it, too, if he looked deeply enough?

No. She'd promised herself she wouldn't allow this minister, a mere man, to have such power over her. And thus she would *not*.

Annoyed with herself, she took a deep breath and focused on the two boys she'd chosen to play the Israelite spies. "Bobby and Mitch, while I'm talking with Pastor Beau, you two go with Mary to work on some ideas for costumes." She turned in a circle, taking in the other children in one quick glance. "The rest of you start thinking about what you want the sets to look like."

With a smoothness that blanketed her nerves, she cocked her head and directed the pastor to follow her outside. Head held high, she didn't dare speak until they were completely alone.

Under her lashes, though, she threw a quick glance at the pastor as he shut the door behind them and made his way along the side of the porch. Her heart did one long, slow dip against her ribs at what she saw. His guard had slipped. Much like the first time she'd met him, he held his shoulders stiff. And his eyes glittered with pain.

He looked so lonely, she thought, so hopeless.

And then she knew. He had bad news.

Oh, Lord, give me the courage to hear what he's come to tell me.

She leaned against the railing and waited for him to speak. But when he lowered his head and shoved his hands into his pockets, she touched his arm. "Has something happened to Jane?"

It was the only thing that made sense, given his sorrow.

His head shot up. "How did you know?"

She rubbed his arm in the same way she would when she was trying to soothe a young child. "It's in your eyes." She dropped her hand. "Tell me what's happened."

"Jane Goodwin lost the fight. She died early this morning."

Hannah's stomach lurched. His tone was so flat, so unemotional.

"I'm sorry," she said, knowing how inadequate her words sounded. "Was it a peaceful death?"

"Yes." His gaze burned with anguish as he placed his hands on the railing in front of him and breathed in. "Megan will have to be told. Soon."

Tears sprang to Hannah's eyes. "The news will devastate her. Oh, Beau." She placed her hand over his, only partly conscious of the fact that she had used his first name. "What will you say?"

Releasing another slow breath, he turned his palm to mold it against hers. "I have to trust the Holy Spirit will give me the words."

Hannah stared down at their joined hands, stunned at how soothed she felt by the contact. The sensation didn't last long. Sorrow rose up and tightened in her throat. Her heart wept for this godly man, for what he had to do. But most of all, her heart wept for Megan and her loss. "I want to be with you when you tell her."

"I think that's a good idea."

He pulled his hand free of hers then. The loss of the warmth of his fingers hit her like a physical blow. She felt her eyes sting and a hot fist of guilt grabbed at her stomach. How could she be thinking about this man, and what he was beginning to mean to her, when Megan was the one she should be worrying about?

She could because she saw how hard this was for Beau, the part of pastoring that no man could train enough for.

"I'll need to tell Laney and Marc, as well," he said.

"We'll tell them together, and we'll tell them first. That will give Megan some time with the deputy."

She turned to go back inside the house, but he stopped her with a hand to her shoulder. "Hannah."

She lifted her gaze to meet his.

"I have news of your sister, as well," he said.

The softly spoken words should have staggered her. But she felt nothing. Waiting for the expected relief to come, she stared at him. Resignation was the only emotion she could muster.

There was no more putting off the inevitable. Hannah would go after Rachel. It was time to end this contention between them, to settle the real issue underlying their estrangement. To move on with their lives, separate or together.

But then a frightening thought occurred to her. "Is she…safe?"

The fact that she hadn't worried about her sister's safety until now shamed her.

"Perfectly safe." He gave her a wry look and slipped his hands back into his pockets. "They're in Wyoming and will be there long enough for us to travel to them."

Surprised at the confidence in his voice, Hannah lifted her eyebrows. "How do you know they'll still be there?"

"Their hotel *room* is paid through the end of the month."

She heard his emphasis on the singular, and yet couldn't find it in her to be scandalized by the information. This was all so familiar. So typical. So much like the night of her own banishment five years ago.

"You don't seem surprised," he remarked.

Her heart stuttered. "I'm not."

Clearly sensing there was more to her answer, he leaned back against the railing. "Do you want to tell me why?"

"No." The word came out too harsh, too firm, and she wanted to mean it. *Desperately.*

Despite their rocky start, Hannah sensed Beauregard O'Toole would understand if she burdened him with the truth of that night. Torn between bravery and uncertainty, she lifted her hands, let out a weary sigh and gave in to cowardice.

"Now isn't the time," she said. "We must first focus on Megan."

"Of course."

His voice was kind, but his eyes told her that he badly wanted to push for more information. The fact that he restrained himself showed another layer of his patient nature.

And in that moment, she knew she would trust him with the facts of that horrific night. Just not quite yet.

Chapter Eleven

The mood in Marc's study was one of somber acceptance, as though the people gathered around Jane's daughter were used to hearing the devastating news of death. Head bent low, Megan sat in a mahogany armchair with her hands clasped tightly together in her lap.

Beau grimaced. The girl looked terribly young, terribly small. At least she didn't have to bear this burden alone. Marc and Laney stood in front of her chair, their faces drawn in identical expressions of concern. Miss Southerland held vigil next to them while Logan Mitchell leaned over Megan's lowered head.

The young deputy murmured soothing, unintelligible words to her. Beau wasn't sure she was fully listening to him, but every once in a while she would nod her head at something he said.

Logan had surprised Beau by refusing to leave Megan's side when Marc had asked her to join them in his study.

It was as if Logan had known.

Perhaps Megan had, as well, which explained why she'd all but begged the young deputy to accompany her.

Eventually, Logan's words trailed off. He rose and exchanged a resigned glance with Beau.

"I'm sorry, Megan," Beau said. "Dr. Shane did all he could."

She lifted her chin to look at him. Her large, round eyes were drowning in sorrow, but they were bone-dry. "I'm sure he did."

Her shoulders stooped forward and down went her head again.

Making a sound of distress in her throat, Laney pressed forward. "Oh, Megan, don't worry. Your mother is at peace with the Lord now."

Megan sighed. "Do you really think so?" she asked the room in general, her voice a study in doubt.

Biting her bottom lip, Laney shot Beau a silent appeal. He had trained for situations such these, and yet he never felt adequate when the time came to ease another's suffering. Death was always worse for the ones left behind. Beau stared at Megan's pale profile and prayed.

Lord, Lord, give me the words to ease her pain.

Beau slid a glance to Hannah. She nodded in encouragement, as though she understood how hard this was for him. In that moment a verse from the gospel of John came to mind and Beau moved into the young girl's line of vision.

"Megan," he began, "Jesus warned that we will have troubles in this world. But He also told us to take heart. Christ has overcome death. Death is not the end. It is only the beginning. Your mother has a new body and a pain-free existence now."

Beau stepped closer, but Logan moved more quickly, barring further approach with his entire body. Narrowed, wolflike eyes warned Beau to keep his distance. Beau tensed. If the lawman's concern wasn't so palpable *and* genuine, Beau would have answered the challenge. The kid was obviously confused in the face of Megan's grief, making him forget Beau was a minister here to *help*. So, instead of joining in Logan's ridiculous contest of wills, Beau nodded in acquiescence and took a step back.

"In spite of your mother's…profession," Beau continued from where he stood, "she knew who her Lord was and what He did for her on the Cross."

As Megan held his stare, confusion flitted across her gaze. Her shoulders jerked, but still she searched Beau's face.

He waited for her to look her fill.

At last, she caught her lip between her teeth and lowered her head to stare at her clasped hands again.

Before he could reach to her, Miss Southerland rushed ahead of him, nearly sideswiping Logan as she knelt in front of the girl.

"Megan, listen to me." She took the girl's hands in hers and pulled them close to her heart. "Your mother was a brilliant actress in her day. I will remember her fondly, as will many others."

"You knew my mother?" Megan's voice squeaked with the dry, raspy sound of grief not yet released.

Lowering their hands, Miss Southerland offered Megan a kind smile. "The first time I saw her perform was when I was about your age. I'd never seen such talent, such *presence,* on or off the stage. The audience adored her. *I* adored her."

"Was she very beautiful?" The eagerness and raw

vulnerability in the young woman's expression pierced Beau's heart. Clearly, Megan wanted to hear that her mother had once been more than the broken wretch she'd become in her last days of life.

Brushing a wisp of hair off the girl's forehead, Miss Southerland's smile brightened. "She was stunning, nearly as beautiful as you."

Megan's cheeks turned bright red. "Tell me more."

"I'm not ashamed to say your mother is the reason I'm an actress now. I had the privilege of meeting her backstage that night. She was very kind. She told me I could do anything I set my mind to. Years later, when I had to make a life for myself out of nothing—"

She broke off, looked past Megan with a glazed expression in her eyes, but then she shook her head and continued. "That is...when I had to make a change in my life, I remembered how glorious Jane Goodwin had been, and I wanted to be just like her. I was proud to have known her."

Miss Southerland rose then and opened her arms to Megan. Sucking in a huge gulp of air, Megan leaped into the offered embrace and collapsed into choking, heart-wrenching sobs.

Logan shuddered at the unbearable sound of Megan's grief, his face a study in masculine panic. Yet he found the courage to place his hand on the young girl's back and rub gently.

Megan sobbed louder. Logan's face crumbled.

Sighing, Laney gently pushed the poor man aside, gave all the men in the room a meaningful look and then cocked her head toward the door.

Beau took the hint.

"Megan, we'll leave you alone with Laney and Miss Southerland for now," he said. "Come on, boys. Let's give the women a chance to speak privately."

To Beau's surprise, especially after Logan had been so uncomfortable in the face of Megan's grief, the young deputy moved his chin in a sharp gesture of denial. "I'm staying."

"You can come back later," Marc said in an unrelenting tone. "For now, come with us."

Catching Beau's eye, Marc made a motion with his hand toward Logan. Beau moved to the other side of the deputy. In unison, they gripped Logan's arms and tugged.

Logan shrugged them off with ease.

Clearly at the end of his patience, Marc lurched forward, eyes gleaming, and caught Logan by the arm again. Beau moved in, as well. Together, they calmly escorted Logan out of the room. Sensing more distance was needed than a closed door, Beau silently directed Marc to keep pulling.

Once in the hallway, Logan complained and threatened and generally spoke ill of both men along the way.

They passed through the kitchen and down the porch steps without incident. However, the moment they hit the backyard, the deputy broke free. Swinging wildly, he attacked.

Beau ducked to his left.

Marc swiveled to his right.

The deputy stumbled forward, righted himself and shot forward again. "How dare you take me away from her like that? She needs me."

Anger made the young man's movements awkward. Of one accord, Beau and Marc shifted again. This time, when Logan struck, each man gripped a shoulder. With momentum on their side, they swiftly pinned the young deputy against the side of the house.

Spitting and muttering under his breath, Logan's muscles bunched, relaxed, bunched again.

Neither Marc nor Beau loosened their grip.

Logan fought harder.

"Calm yourself," Marc said. "You can't do anything to help her right now. And if you try to touch her again, even in the guise of helping her mourn, I'll do more than dodge your punches. I'll throw a few of my own."

"It's not like that." Logan fairly spit out the words.

Beau and Marc shared a knowing look.

"It's *always* like that," Beau said for them both.

Struggling under their grip, Logan's lip curled into a snarl. "I was just... She and I were... That is, she looked so...*lost*."

"She's too young for you," Marc snapped.

Logan looked shocked, then seriously offended. "She's seventeen."

"And you're twenty-two." To drive home his point, Marc shoved Logan harder against the house, lifting him several inches higher on his side. "In my book, that's too many years separating you."

Breathing hard, Logan's expression turned mutinous. "You're eight years older than Laney."

Beau tried not to smile. The deputy made a valid point.

"Granted," Marc said in a surprisingly reasonable tone. "But at seventeen Megan is still too young for you. Or any man, for that matter. And if I see you sniffing around her again I'll make sure you know exactly what I mean."

"I get it." Logan scowled. "But, just so *you* understand. There'll come a day when you will no longer have a say. And I'll be there. You can't keep us apart forever."

"Can't I?"

Logan struggled in response. Working together, Beau and Marc tightened their hold and slammed him back against the house.

"This isn't over," Logan snarled.

Marc grinned. "It is from where I'm standing."

"Yeah, well, you're standing too close."

As the verbal warfare heated up, Beau's patience drained out of him. "That's enough. Both of you." Beau dragged Marc off the deputy and placed a hand on each man's chest to keep them a good distance apart. "Now is not the time for this argument."

Completely ignoring him, both men glared at one another.

"Think of Megan," Beau said.

Both men slid a quick glance at him, but then resumed glaring and snarling at each other.

"Marc."

"What?"

"Go tell Mrs. Smythe to make Megan some tea." When Marc just stood there, Beau turned to the other man. "Logan, come with me back to the courthouse. We have to make arrangements for our journey to Cheyenne."

"Our journey?" Logan turned his head to Beau. Lines of confusion encircled his mouth. *"What* journey?"

Beau tamped down another wave of impatience and spoke as calmly as possible. "Miss Southerland and I will need help with the law in Cheyenne. Since Marshal Scott is in the middle of a trial, you're our man."

Logan continued to gape at him. "You can't decide that on your own."

"I just did."

"But—"

"It's settled. You know our case, the players and the various details. But most of all, you know the law in Cheyenne."

Grinning now, Marc nodded his head enthusiastically. "Certainly makes sense to me. And, while you're at it, feel free to stay as long as you like. You—"

"Marc." Beau cut off the other man before he said—or did—something they would all regret. "Miss Southerland cannot travel alone with two men. Do you have any suggestions of a suitable chaperone to accompany her?"

"Let's see." Marc rubbed his jaw between his thumb and forefinger. After a thoughtful pause, his expression turned downright gleeful and he smiled. Or rather, bared his teeth. "Mavis."

"Mavis Tierney?" Logan gasped the name, his eyes round with shock and horror. "That old woman hates me."

Marc folded his arms across his chest. "You don't say."

"You have a mean streak, Dupree," Logan ground out. "Bordering on cruel."

"That I do." Marc looked entirely too pleased with himself as he shoved his nose an inch short of Logan's. "You'd be wise not to forget it."

"How could I? You won't let me."

And so the verbal sparring began anew.

This time, Beau just shook his head at the pair. At least they weren't throwing punches. Yet. And with the way his day was going so far, Beau considered that quite a victory.

Quite a victory indeed.

Chapter Twelve

The mournful sound of the train's whistle rent the air, while the burning scent of coal wafted on a steady stream of smoke. Wrinkling her nose against the unpleasant odor, Hannah made her way to the steps leading into her designated compartment. She left the rest of her party arguing over the appropriate number of bags needed for a three-day journey.

Well, Logan Mitchell and Mavis argued. The reverend mediated.

Shaking her head at them all, Hannah switched her *one* very small satchel to her left hand and boarded the train. After taking a short inventory of available seats, she chose one at the back of the railway car.

As she worked her way through the crowd, she breathed in the rich aroma of pipe tobacco, women's perfume and lemon-seed oil. The interior of the compartment had an expensive, stylish feel to it. Red velvet upholstery covered rich, dark mahogany seats. Large, rectangular windows were framed with intricate crown molding. The carpeted flooring and brass fixtures completed the pretty picture.

But as beautiful as the compartment was, Hannah's heart wasn't in admiring the decor. For many reasons, she hadn't wanted to leave Charity House this morning. She'd found a kindred spirit in Laney Dupree. And thanks to her time with the orphans, her dream of serving abandoned women and children had morphed into something far more tangible than "someday."

Although she'd promised to return and produce the play about Rahab, the entire group of children had been unusually quiet at her departure.

Sighing, Hannah smoothed out a wrinkle on her skirt and thought of one girl in particular. Megan.

Poor, dejected Megan.

Hannah had felt an especially strong bond with Jane Goodwin's daughter. It was yet another glaring reminder of how lacking the relationship with her own sister had grown through the years. Well, this time, when Hannah stood face-to-face with Rachel, she would not let the same old patterns of behavior control their encounter.

Oh, Lord. Her eyes fluttered shut. *I pray for the courage to face my sister in truth. Give me the courage to end the lies between us.*

Sighing again, Hannah opened her eyes in time to catch sight of her chaperone waddling down the aisle. Or, rather, she suspected the moving bundle was her chaperone. The wild white hair peeking over three large carpet bags certainly indicated her assumption was correct.

Hannah immediately rose to help her new friend. "Let me take those for you."

"Don't touch." Mavis teetered to her left, then quickly righted herself. "I'm perfectly balanced."

Hannah raised her palms in the air and stepped back.

With a loud plunk, all three bags hit the floor. Drowning in satchels up to her knees, Mavis shot her a triumphant look. "There. You see."

Hannah made a noncommittal sound in her throat.

Kicking and muttering and kicking some more, Mavis broke free from the luggage carnage and dropped into the seat next to Hannah.

Mavis's outrageous outfit brought a smile to Hannah's lips. The older woman had chosen a purple tunic to wear over her men's denim pants today. She'd topped off the shocking ensemble with clashing red gloves and a floppy hat that had real flowers pressed along the edges. Real. Dead. Flowers. The pungent odor was astonishing. Astonishingly *awful*.

Hannah covered her nose and coughed delicately. Although there should have been generous room for both women on the two-passenger seat, Mavis squirmed and burrowed like a prairie dog fighting to get out of a windstorm. She huffed and kicked and hoisted until she eventually situated two of the bags on her left and the largest on her right—which happened to be the side where Hannah sat.

Hannah's left shoulder was pressed so tightly against the window that her breath fogged up the glass. If she could, she'd move to the empty seats facing them. But those were reserved for Logan Mitchell and Pastor Beau.

Grimacing, Hannah wiped away the condensation on the window and turned her head to study the loot Mavis had deemed appropriate for the short journey. No wonder the deputy had given her such a hard time.

"What do you have in there?" Hannah asked, more amused than miffed.

"Only the necessities, dearie." Mavis patted the bag she'd positioned on her lap. "Only the necessities."

Hannah didn't know any one person with that many necessities. "Such as?"

"Oh, this and that." She puckered her lips and started whistling a cheerful tune.

Mavis was certainly happy. A little too happy, especially after her heated argument with Logan Mitchell on the platform.

Hannah narrowed her eyes. "This and that wouldn't include tobacco, now, would it? Because I promised Laney and Katherine you wouldn't smoke while in my care."

"*Your* care?" Mavis snorted at her. "I'm the chaperone of you, missy, not the other way around."

Hannah had her doubts. In fact, she knew exactly how sneaky Mavis could be when in need of a smoke. Hannah and Katherine had caught her three separate times with a homemade cigarette in her hand. Hannah made a mental note to keep a close watch on Miss Mavis Tierney. Age indeterminate. Sneakiness a definite.

As people began filing into the compartment, Hannah lifted her gaze in time to catch the rest of their party entering the railcar. Moving with masculine grace, the reverend came into view first. His shoulders were set. His jaw tight. His expression unreadable. Something, or someone, had obviously upset him.

Hannah suspected that certain someone was Deputy Mitchell, especially since the young man lagged a good three feet behind the reverend, dragging his feet and looking like one of the orphans after a good scolding.

The moment the reverend stopped beside Mavis, he

lifted an ironic eyebrow at the booty jacketing every available piece of space on their seat and laps.

Hannah shrugged her shoulders in a helpless gesture.

Shaking his head, the reverend tossed a book on the seat across from her and moved to allow a passenger to pass him on the other side of the aisle. "I need to speak to the conductor."

But before he left, Hannah thought she heard him whisper to Logan, "Behave."

"Yeah. Yeah." Frowning, Logan plopped into the seat across from Mavis. He glared at the older woman, looking as though he was daring her to say something that would require a nasty response from him.

"Good morning, Deputy Mitchell," Mavis said in a singsong voice that brought to mind pure sugar. Dripping molasses.

Logan's gaze settled on the duffel bags, and his lips curled into a sneer. "What did you pack in there, old woman, your entire wardrobe?"

Leave it to Mavis to notice the offensive name and nothing else.

"Hey! You call me old woman again—" she shook her finger at him "—and I'll tan your hide."

"I'd like to see you try."

Mavis started to rise. Hannah stopped her with an arm across the bag cradled in her lap.

"What is it with you two?" she asked. "You've been at each other since we left Charity House. One might start to think you both just turned four years old."

As if to prove her right, Mavis snorted. Logan responded in kind. And then both crossed their arms over their chests and began to pout. Well, Mavis pouted.

Logan sulked. If Hannah didn't know how worried both were about Megan, she'd say more. Instead, she left them to their silence.

But when Logan stretched his legs in front of him, and Mavis kicked his foot in response, Hannah rose. "Oh, honestly, switch seats with me, Mavis."

"I think that's a grand idea," Beau said, returning to their happy little group just as Mavis started to argue over the suggestion.

Clamping her mouth shut, the older woman glowered.

Beau regarded her with a patient, albeit unbending, expression.

"Fine," Mavis huffed. "I'll move."

After a round of dodging bags and Mavis rearranging positions—four times—and Logan's refusal to move his feet—all four times—they eventually exchanged seats.

Just to be contrary, the moment Hannah sat across from Logan he gave Mavis an innocent smile and then made a grand show of moving his feet back to his side of the compartment.

Hannah had no idea what had caused such animosity between the two, but she was losing her patience with them both.

"This certainly promises to be an interesting trip," she said with a perfect mixture of sarcasm and distress.

"It does at that." To punctuate his remark, Beau performed an exaggerated wink in her direction.

The gesture had O'Toole written all over it, but there was a special flair in Beau's delivery that set him apart from the rest of his siblings—one in particular came to mind.

"We won't arrive in Cheyenne until tomorrow morning," Beau said to the group in general, but his eyes never left Hannah's.

Her heart did a soft flip in her chest then meandered into a rhythmic tap, tap against her ribs. Slow. Steady. Agonizing.

"The dining car isn't due to open for several more hours," he continued. "I suggest we try to get some sleep before then."

"Right." Logan shot a pointed glare at each of Mavis's three satchels. "I'm confident that'll happen with all this room at our feet."

Normally, Hannah would have been amused by the deputy's sarcastic quip, but her mind chose that moment to focus on the life-altering nature of this journey. Soon, her business with Rachel would be complete.

And then what?

Pain, hope, dread, fury—all four slammed into her, blinding her, making her dizzy and warning her that once she faced Rachel, *none* of them would go on as before. Not Hannah. Not Rachel. Not Tyler. Not even Beau.

The thought left her trembling.

As dusk settled over the land, Beau looked out the window and smiled in satisfaction. God's handiwork was evident everywhere—in the steep incline of crumbling rock and the glorious pine trees that peppered the mighty slopes.

Beau wasn't surprised he was moved by the obvious manifestation of God's majesty. He was surprised by the depth of his reaction.

He'd been ministering in Colorado for years now, and

he never grew tired of the rugged territory. He felt at home here, as he'd never felt in London, Paris or New York. He wanted to spend the rest of his life serving the people bold enough to settle this harsh part of the world. He wanted—

A loud snort followed by an equally loud moan jolted him out of his thoughts. He turned toward the noise. Smiled.

Mavis Tierney, bless her ornery soul, had set into snoring with remarkable gusto. The woman was well past her prime but she had a passion for living—and, apparently, sleeping—that most people half her age would never achieve.

Logan had long since left for the dining car, leaving Beau alone on his side of their tiny area. He stretched his arms overhead, careful not to disturb either woman across from him.

While Mavis slept, Hannah sat quietly reading her Bible. With her head bent over the book, she was oblivious to his scrutiny. He took his time watching her, trying to pinpoint precisely when he'd stopped considering her an adversary and more a partner in this fiasco he liked to call "Not My Brother's Keeper."

Today, she wore a soft pink dress with darker rose adornments. In the dull light of dusk, she looked feminine, fragile. She made a man want to protect her.

Beau felt a sudden, overwhelming urge to grind his teeth together. He could not allow himself to fall for Hannah Southerland. He ignored the whisper in his mind that said, *Too late.*

He gave his head a brief shake and swallowed, suddenly feeling as though he was choking. The woman represented everything he didn't—*couldn't*—want in a wife. Not that she'd applied for the position. But Beau couldn't get the notion out of his mind that she was the one he'd been waiting for God to bring to him.

Which was absurd.

Surely, God had led Hannah Southerland into his life merely to help prevent a tragedy in their respective families and for no other reason. Especially when Beau needed a less conspicuous woman to help minimize his own penchant for the outrageous. His preaching spoke of a radical acceptance of sinners. Not radical by Jesus' standards, but certainly radical by the Association's standards.

The West was still untamed. He'd learned the hard way that the people settling in the frontier towns wanted safety. They wanted comfort in rules. He would win their trust first. Only then would he challenge them to look beyond the law—to the compassion Jesus required in all His followers. He would never win the necessary respect with a flamboyant woman like Hannah Southerland by his side.

Look past the exterior, Beau. Look to her heart. She accepts the unacceptable.

The thought brought him up short. Was he once again judging her unfairly? Hadn't she stepped into Charity House and won over the adults and children alike?

And who said she even wanted to consider becoming his wife?

Confusion made his head spin. Frustration pulled sweat onto his brow. Regardless of how he felt about her, at first or now, he should have told her about his association with her father long before now.

As though she sensed his eyes on her, Miss Southerland looked up from her Bible.

"Miss Southerland, may I call you Hannah?"

She leaned back, cocked her head and then smiled. "I suppose it makes sense at this point in our acquaintance."

"I have something to tell you," he said, pushing slightly forward in his seat. Now that he'd made up his mind to confess the truth, he wanted this business done.

She simply stared at him, unblinking.

He stared back for only a split second. "Your father holds my future in his hands."

She stared at him some more.

He continued to hold her gaze, his pulse raging loudly in his ears and his shoulders tightening in a spot just below his neck. "Well, not completely," he corrected. "But he could."

"Go on." She eyed him with the same wary look in her eyes she'd had at their first meeting.

However tight his shoulders were now, he continued to gaze at her directly. "I have been given the opportunity to plant a new church in Greeley, Colorado. The Rocky Mountain Association of Churches is sponsoring my efforts."

Her eyes widened. "My father was the chairman of the Association."

"Still is."

"I see." She looked flustered and irritated and completely disappointed in him.

A little finger of panic curled in his chest. "You misunderstand. I'm not on this journey to please your father. I'm here because it's the right thing to do. Your sister must be found and brought back home."

It was the surprise in her eyes, surrounded by a note of genuine concern and understanding, that gave him hope she believed him.

"What if Rachel refuses to return with us and my father blames you for your part? Could he take away your church?"

Tension the size of a railroad tie roped around his chest like an iron band. But at this point Beau owed her the complete truth. "Yes."

Dread leaped into her eyes. "Then you can't—"

"Yes, I can." He reached out and touched her hand. "Like I said before, going after your sister is the right thing to do."

"Oh, Beau. I'm so sorry."

Still holding his gaze, she turned her wrist until their palms met. He instinctively twined his fingers through hers.

For a moment, sitting like that, with a simple holding of hands, they were a unit.

"Don't be sorry for me, Hannah. The risk is mine to take. To be quite frank, my brother owes all of us an explanation. It is my duty to make sure he gives us one that will satisfy all the injured parties."

A look storming with emotion settled into her eyes. Now that they'd come this far, he had a choice to make. He could leave the conversation alone, stop where they were and let everyone settle down. Or he could press the conversation in another, equally volatile direction and be finished with the secrets between them.

Beau chose the harder of two routes. "Tell me about the night you were sent from your father's home," he blurted out.

Counting the seconds until she spoke, Beau waited for her to respond. When he made it to ten and she still kept silent, he feared she might ignore his bold request.

But she surprised him by pulling her hand free and shutting her Bible with a smooth snap. "You're sure you want to hear this now?"

Beau recognized the bleakness in her eyes, the desire to avoid the conversation. He touched her hand gently. "I do."

She paused, blinked slowly and then nodded. "I suppose it started when my mother died. Rachel and I were only ten years old at the time. On her deathbed, Mama made me promise to take care of Rachel because she was small for her age, and fragile, much weaker than I ever was."

Beau couldn't imagine a more fragile woman than Hannah. With a sudden flash of insight, he wondered if her parents had mistaken her inner strength for physical strength. "And so you did as your mother requested."

She studied her hands a moment. "At first it was just picking up her chores when Rachel was too ill or too tired to complete them herself."

Beau shook his head at the notion. She couldn't be serious. His eyes lingered on her face a moment, and he saw that she was indeed serious.

She cleared her throat. "What started as small chores here and there turned into far more the night Rachel ran off after she and I had a fight over a boy." Her eyes became haunted. "It was a stupid argument, and I refused to go after her. Rachel lost her way that night. When she was eventually found the next morning, she had caught a bad cold and suffered permanent hearing loss in one ear."

"You blame yourself." A lump, hot and thick, stuck in Beau's throat at the realization.

She dropped her gaze to her hands again. "I should have gone after her."

"It wasn't your fault she ran off and got lost."

"Wasn't it?" she whispered.

Troubled by the stark guilt he heard in her voice, Beau opened his mouth to speak, but she talked over him. "I tried to make it up to her. And so I began taking the blame for bigger transgressions."

He didn't want to ask. How could he *not* ask? "Such as?"

"I don't know." She shrugged. "If Rachel broke a valuable item, I told our father I did it. If she said something mean to make a kid cry, I confessed I said it."

Beau could see the hurt Hannah was trying to hide. It was in the slump in her shoulders, in the shake of her voice. "How could he not know it wasn't always you? No child is all good or all bad. Surely your father could see the truth."

"My father has always thought the worst of me." The calm resignation in her voice startled him. "I was different from every other kid, more colorful, more dramatic. It was easy enough to assume I was bad. A rose is still a rose by any other name." She snorted. "Or in my case, a thorn is still a thorn by any other name."

He wanted to deny her words, but Beau understood those particular dynamics all too well. By preaching in "dens of iniquity," by associating with sinners, he was suspect among the more pious ministers of the Association. By answering God's calling for his life in the way he felt most productive, he'd been labeled a rebel.

But there was a difference between Hannah and him.

He was guilty of everything they claimed. She was not. "Those weren't your sins to bear," he said softly.

Her head shot up, and her eyes speared daggers at him. "You think I don't know that? That I haven't scolded myself over and over and over in the past five years? But what else was I supposed to do? I promised Mama. If it wasn't for me, if I had gone after her, Rachel would still be able to hear in both ears."

Beau recognized the conflicting emotions on her face. Guilt. Sorrow. Despair. Anger.

"Hannah, listen to me." He lowered his voice and allowed the compassion he felt for her situation to flow into his tone. "By taking the blame for your sister's actions, you played your own role in her ultimate selfishness."

She bowed her head. "I know that. It can't continue. No more will I accept responsibility for her actions." Her gaze held his, determination blazed in her eyes. *"No more."*

"Good. *Good.*" He tilted his head and studied her mutinous expression. "But none of this explains why your father banished you from his home."

She broke eye contact and looked out the window, gulped in a deep breath as though she was gathering her courage to finish her story.

Beau waited in silence, giving her the time she needed.

"As you can imagine, the pattern had been set. By the time we were eighteen, Rachel was a master of manipulation. She had a secret tryst with the young, newly hired schoolteacher in town."

He'd heard of worse. He'd *seen* worse in some of the mining camps. And yet, her words startled him. In an attempt to erase all expression from his gaze, Beau rubbed his hand across his face. "That couldn't have ended well."

"He was married."

An odd combination of shock and fury left him speechless. He blinked, noticed how the moonlight streamed through the window and cast her in a pale, eerie glow.

"There's more."

Too many secrets. Too many shadows. Too much pain. "I can't imagine anything worse than adultery."

She gave a short, bitter laugh. "During the entire liaison, Rachel pretended to be me."

He should have guessed, should have been emotionally prepared. But his temper snapped anyway. Rage, hot and uncontrollable, bubbled just below the surface.

Beau suddenly wanted to hit something. He swallowed back the emotion. Swallowed again. But still the urge to unleash his anger held him in a death grip. Alarmed at his violent reaction, he turned to scowl out the window.

"I could never understand Mr. Beamer's strange, inappropriate looks," she said. "Or the way he tried to touch me when no one was looking. I never understood, that is, until the night the truth of the affair came out. The town instantly assumed it was me. *He* thought it was me. He'd been given no reason to believe otherwise."

Beau had to force his words out slowly and carefully in order to contain his temper. "And your sister let you take the blame."

"Yes."

"She never spoke up?"

Hannah crossed her arms in front of her in a protective gesture and looked at him with her own anger and grief warring in her eyes. "No."

For once in his life, whether in the role of pastor or friend, he didn't know what to say.

"I thought I'd forgiven her. And when she came to visit me in Chicago, I thought all would be different between us. After all, she was set to marry Will, a boy who has adored her since they could walk."

A muscle locked in his jaw. "Then she ran off with Tyler."

The sound that came from her throat was a rumble of pain and humiliation.

"Hannah—"

"I want her to pay, Beau. And I want it to hurt her. I—" She gasped and her hand flew to her mouth. Hot color flooded her face. Tears welled in her eyes.

Beau's heart responded immediately, even as his head told him to remember where they were. He struggled to keep from pulling her into his arms. It wouldn't be right. It wouldn't be proper. Nevertheless, he had to let her know there wasn't something inherently wrong with her for thinking such ugly thoughts.

He hunkered down in front of her and grabbed her hands in his. "Hannah, it's only natural to feel anger at your sister over this."

She was shaking her head before he finished speaking. "No. Holding a grudge is a sin."

"Yes. But once you confess that sin, you must try to accept God's forgiveness and let go of the guilt. Don't allow this to turn into shame."

Her chin trembled. "What if it's too late?"

"It's never too late with Christ."

She stared at him, searching his face.

Beau held her stare. He'd never met a woman quite

like Hannah Southerland. Even in her anguished state, she recognized that her bitterness was wrong. And because she knew it was wrong, she agonized over it.

In that moment, he realized his own enormous mistake. At the start of their acquaintance he'd judged her because of her outward appearance. He hadn't looked deep enough to see her real beauty, the beauty inside. That made him no better than the men and women who judged him.

It wasn't Hannah's character in question. It was his. And now the truth hung heavy in the air between them.

She wasn't unworthy of him. *Beau* was unworthy of her.

Chapter Thirteen

Hannah slept.

Mavis slept.

Beau, however, did not.

He had too much to consider, too much to organize in his mind. Now that he'd begun to get a good sense of who Hannah Southerland really was, on the inside, he only wanted to know more.

The woman was clearly the worst thing that had ever happened to him. For all intents and purposes, she was everything he shouldn't want in his life. Everything he *couldn't* want. Yet he did want her in his life. And now that he knew her better, *knew himself better,* there was no way he would be able to walk away from her. Not without leaving a part of himself behind.

Merely sitting in the same compartment with her felt too confining, too constricting, too…personal.

There was no question he had to fight this secret attraction. No matter how kind, compassionate and merciful of heart, she wasn't the right woman for a man starting a church in the conservative Rocky Mountain

Association, even if her own father led the largest congregation in the organization.

And it wasn't for his sake, it was for hers. She wasn't conventional enough. The people in Greeley could easily ostracize her, judge her, perhaps even look down on her merely for her profession on the stage. Beau could never put Hannah in that vile situation. She was too full of life, too full of joy to suffer a moment of that kind of prejudice. Prejudice that he himself had held.

Surely these feelings he had for her would pass. They *had* to pass, for both their sakes. Then he could resume his search for a nice docile wife. Until that time, Beau would simply keep his distance from the appealing actress.

Starting now.

His jaw tight and teeth clenched, he rose and went in search of Logan in the dining car.

The young lawman sat at a table in a back corner, looking woefully out of place among the fine white linens, sterling silver utensils and crystal water goblets. He had a full plate in front of him, heaped with all sorts of rare delicacies. But instead of eating, he stared unblinking at the untouched food.

"Are you planning to eat any of that?" Beau asked.

"At some point," Logan said, keeping his head bent over his plate. With his fork, he drew a series of invisible geometric shapes on the tablecloth, repeating the same pattern over and over and over again.

Beau lowered himself into the seat opposite the deputy. "Want to talk about it?"

"No."

"Want me to leave you to your brooding?"

Logan snapped his head up and give Beau one long,

frustrated stare. "I'm not brooding, I'm just..." His voice trailed off.

"Thinking?" Beau supplied.

"Something like that."

Knowing precisely what was troubling the young man, Beau went straight for the crux of the matter. "Megan will be there when you get back."

Logan gave a nod, which might have been acknowledgment. "I hated leaving her," he said as he shoved the plate of untouched food away from him. "She was so...quiet."

"Her mother just died."

"Yeah, well, I wish I could have helped her with—" He broke off and shrugged. "I don't know. I wish I could have done something."

In spite of the seriousness of the situation, one side of Beau's mouth kicked up. "You'd risk Marc's wrath?"

Logan's face tightened into an angry knot. "He doesn't scare me."

"He should. Marc takes his guardianship very seriously," Beau pointed out in the smooth, patient tone that marked his occupation far more than the words themselves did.

"Yeah, yeah. I've faced down worse. One over-dressed dandy isn't going to put me off from something I know is meant to be." The words came out strong, but Logan's gaze showed hesitation. "What does he have against me, anyway?"

"Try to understand. It's not personal, Logan. In his mind, Marc is protecting Megan, as any good guardian would."

Logan made a noncommittal sound in his throat, but

the uncertain look in his eyes was enough to make Beau lean forward and speak in earnest.

"You're both young. There's plenty of time to be together. You just have to believe it will all work out in the end."

"In other words—" Logan blew out a disgusted snort and sneered "—trust in God's plan. Is that what you're saying, preacher man?"

"Yes." Resting his weight on his elbows, Beau commanded the young man's gaze with a hard one of his own. "That's what I'm saying."

"I'm supposed to do nothing? Just wait for everything to work out?"

Logan's expression was mutinous, frustrated. And very, very angry. Beau registered all three, and then noted the panic underneath the emotions.

"Faith," he said, choosing his words carefully. "*Real* faith requires patience."

"I thought the Bible said God helps those who help themselves?"

How many times had Beau heard that blatant misquoting of Scripture? "That's not precisely what the Bible says."

"No?"

"No. Have faith. Fear not. Trust God. Those are clear commands set out in the Bible. But for a man to forge ahead with his own purpose motivating his actions, and then to tell God to bless the outcome, well, that's not Biblical. It's dangerous. And selfish. And more often than not leads to destruction."

Logan opened his mouth to argue, his eyes continuing to blaze with confusion and a good dose of youthful rebellion. Beau held the other man's stare, knowing they'd come to a moment of truth for the deputy. At last, Logan clamped his lips into a hard, thin line and nodded. "You'd know better than me."

Ignoring the belligerent tone, Beau pressed on. "If you and Megan are meant to be together, you will be together."

And in that moment, Beau knew he should listen to his own advice, especially where Hannah Southerland was concerned.

Have faith. Fear not. Trust God.

It was time Beau started walking his talk.

"Even if we don't understand the 'why' behind our circumstances," he said, "we can always trust that God works them out for our own good."

"Words, Reverend O'Toole, fancy words filled with nothing but rhetoric."

"Not just words," Beau said in a firm, unrelenting voice. *"Truth."*

"Well, here's some truth for you." Logan nailed Beau with a hard warning in his glare. The look revealed the seasoned lawman inside the boyish face. "If I lose Megan, someone will pay."

Gauging Logan's frustration, Beau ignored the threat and switched the conversation to a less volatile topic. "Since we're on the subject, what's all the animosity between you and Mavis?"

Logan shoved at his hair and made a face. "We aren't talking about Mavis."

"We are now."

"I say we don't."

"I say we do."

Logan's scowl deepened. "The woman hates me."

"Want to tell me why?"

Logan lifted a shoulder. "I don't know, maybe because I call her *old woman*." Frowning, he slapped his palms on the table and pressed his weight forward. "But I don't mean any disrespect. She just takes it wrong."

Beau stared at the other man for a full ten seconds. The deputy couldn't possibly be that dense. Trey Scott would never hire a stupid man to cover his back. "Let me see if I heard you correctly. *You* call Mavis *old woman,* and yet *she* takes it wrong."

Logan sat back. His mild blue eyes flickered with a faraway expression. "I used to call my grandmother *old woman.* She fancied the nickname. And unlike a certain woman in our impromptu search party, Granny had a sense of humor."

Beau nodded in understanding. Every family, even his own, had its set of codes and pet names and forms of speech that outsiders never quite understood, and often considered odd.

Given that fundamental truth, Logan hadn't meant any disrespect when he'd called Mavis *old woman.* He'd been giving her a compliment. Of sorts.

Breaking the silence, Logan sighed. "Granny kind of looked like Mavis. Well, not really. *Nobody* looks quite like Mavis. But there's something about the old woman that reminds me of Granny. It's in the way her face scrunches up when she's mad. And how she gets all ornery when you cross her. I kind of like the old bird. There, I said it. Happy now?"

"Have you ever told Mavis how you feel?" Beau asked. "Tried to apologize for the misunderstanding?"

"Are you insane?"

Beau smiled at Logan's horrified expression. "Do I look or sound insane?"

"If I so much as hinted at an apology, Mavis would never let me live it down."

"Would that be a bad thing?"

Logan looked like one of the Charity House orphans, full of belligerence and bad attitude. "I'd rather face Armageddon."

Pride, Beau thought. It got a man every time.

Hannah unfolded her legs, maneuvered past the pile of luggage on the floor and tumbled into the empty aisle beyond. Righting herself with as much dignity as possible, she lifted her arms overhead and released a jaw-cracking yawn. Every muscle ached from hours of inactivity. But that would soon come to an end. According to the conductor, they were due to arrive in Cheyenne within the hour.

Instead of feeling joy that they were another step closer to Rachel, Hannah found herself dreading the confrontation all over again. The revelation of her own unresolved bitterness toward her sister was still too fresh, too strong, in her mind. How could she face her sister with so much anger still in her heart? How could she prevent herself from saying something they would all regret?

Perhaps with Beau by her side, everything would go smoothly.

Beau. *Ah, Beau.*

Just thinking how far they'd come since their disastrous introduction brought a smile to her lips.

There was no denying that the rebel preacher had disappointed her at their first meeting, proving he was nothing like the compassionate minister she'd dreamed of encountering when she'd read his letter to his brother. And yet, in the ensuing days, his behavior had been above reproach. He'd been accepting of the children of Charity House, an advocate for Jane, an instrument of hope for Megan and a rock for Hannah.

The truth was irrefutable. Hannah was starting to care for Beauregard O'Toole. In the way a woman cared for a man.

But what did that mean for her, for him, for the future? For—

Mavis snorted.

Grateful for the interruption, Hannah turned toward the sound. As she stared at her chaperone, a jolt of affection hitched Hannah's breath. Mavis Tierney was quite a character. The woman snored louder than the train wheels churned. She squirmed and burrowed like a rodent. Most of the time, she chose to be surly, mean, and spoke her mind without thinking of the consequences.

And yet, Hannah adored her.

Mavis mumbled, snorted again but continued to clutch the smallest of her three satchels against her. Hannah bit back a smile. The older woman seemed overly attached to that canvas bag. In the realm of obsession. A fixation. A…

"Now hold on just a moment," Hannah whispered to herself.

Using the soft steps earned from years of ballet training, Hannah edged closer to Mavis and narrowed her eyes at the woman's white-knuckled grip.

Understanding dawned.

"You little sneak."

With slow, measured moves, Hannah wrapped her fingers around the handle of the bag. Inch by careful inch, she tugged. To no avail. Mavis's death grip was a force all its own, which only dug Hannah's suspicions deeper.

Another yank, a quick snatch, and Hannah freed the bag from Mavis's hold.

The woman didn't stir.

"Thank you, Lord, for sound sleepers."

Gliding through the railcar on her toes, Hannah moved to an isolated corner and turned her back to the rest of the occupants. Relatively alone, she rummaged through the contents of the satchel until she found what she was looking for.

"I knew it."

She poked her hand into the bag, quickly palmed the objects in question and turned back around. Only to come face-to-face with an engaging preacher.

"Oh," she said.

He smiled.

"I... Oh!"

He smiled some more. "You said that already."

"I...I..." Her heart stopped beating altogether, held a full five seconds, gave a slow pitch and then picked up speed. "You gave me a fright."

"I'm sorry."

He didn't look sorry in the least.

But he did look handsome. Confident. Charming.

Glory. When Beauregard O'Toole produced that particular smile, he had all the charisma and style of his rogue brother. With none of the cunning.

Hannah wondered if Beau knew how engaging he

was, in that masculine sort of way that made a woman want to rest in his strength. She wondered if he knew his charm was utterly irresistible. She wondered if he knew his smile was a powerful weapon, one that should never be misused.

She wondered if he knew she was getting very adept at wondering.

"Stealing from a helpless old woman?" he asked.

Caught in the act, Hannah grasped the tobacco pouch tighter in her fist. Then slowly, very, very slowly, she nodded.

"I'm shocked at you, Miss Southerland." His eyes crinkled at the edges.

Hannah caught his playful mood—at last—and returned his smile with one of her own. "I am what I am."

A single eyebrow arched toward his hairline. "Have you no shame, my dear?"

"Absolutely—" her smile widened "—*none.*"

He leaned in closer and lowered his voice to a conspiratorial whisper, creating a world all their own in the crowded railway car. "Can I get in on this brazen robbery of yours?"

"Only if you promise to dispose of…" She made a grand gesture of peering around him and then lifting her palm a bit higher. "The contraband."

"I'd consider it my personal duty."

Hannah's stomach performed a stunning flip, and then another, refusing to settle for even a moment. She didn't quite know what to do with Reverend O'Toole in this lighthearted mood.

She decided to take his lead and respond with a bit of comedy of her own. "You are a man after my own heart."

Unfortunately, her words escaped from her mouth in a far more serious tone than she'd intended. Mortified, she clamped her lips shut and waited.

She'd never been tongue-tied before. After all, she was Hannah Southerland. Esteemed actress in her own right. A woman who made a living donning roles and speaking words the greatest playwrights had penned. Yet this man, the son of one of her most valued and trusted friends, not only stole her breath, he stole the words right out of her mouth.

He must have noticed the change in her, because his eyes widened and then narrowed just enough to indicate his confusion. "Am I, Hannah?" he asked in an equally serious tone. "Am I a man after your own heart?"

Hard as she tried, she couldn't force her lips to form around a response. She had no idea how to answer such a question when her own emotions were in such turmoil. "I...I don't..." She swallowed. "I don't know."

"Then I have a bit of work to do," he said. The solemn glint in his eyes told her he wasn't teasing.

In that moment, she knew that she was in over her head with this man.

Nevertheless, she was an actress, a well-trained one at that.

Pretending they were still talking about the tobacco she'd confiscated, she jiggled the pouch in front of him and said, "You do indeed."

His gray eyes swept across her face, measuring, gauging.

She remained in character, standing mute under his scrutiny with a playful glint in her eyes.

Still, he made no move to retrieve the tobacco. Just

when the moment became uncomfortable, his smile relaxed. "Then I'd better get rid of that before our girl awakens."

"Right," Hannah said, thinking she was in the clear. But then he plucked the pouch from her palm, and his fingers brushed against hers. The instant warmth and comfort that braided through her should have surprised her. Especially after all they'd been through. Instead, she felt a sense of rightness.

A sense of homecoming.

The emotion scared her spitless and her pulse fluttered in response.

"Give me a five-minute head start, then go wake our little sneak." His tone was very businesslike now, the minister firmly back in place.

Hannah knew she should be grateful for the return of Reverend O'Toole. Yet she couldn't stop a sigh from slipping past her lips as he pivoted on his heel and left her to stare after his retreating back.

In her years on the stage, she'd met the most captivating, charismatic men of the world. She'd socialized with heads of state and crown princes. She'd had offers, some honorable, others dishonorable. And yet none had inspired her to consider anything more than friendship. Not one.

But now, when she needed to concentrate on her sister and then go forth with her own future plans, a rebel preacher with no place to call home had not only turned her head, he had captured her heart.

She placed a hand to her throat and breathed in slowly.

Hannah didn't know what to do with all the emotions rushing through her. She needed discernment to guide her.

She needed prayer, a lot of prayer. Because, when it came to her future, one thing was certain: Horatio Beauregard O'Toole had become an unexpected complication.

Chapter Fourteen

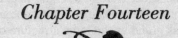

Beau knew Cheyenne well. Originally a rowdy home for railroad personnel, the Wyoming town had once boasted at least seventeen saloons providing three to five burlesque shows a night. But now, thanks to the completed railroad and the rise of cattle barons, the residents enjoyed a social life on par with larger cities back East.

Despite the limited population, the cultural advances and stylish set alone would entice Tyler to stay awhile.

Or so Beau surmised.

With the shocking turn of events of the last week, he couldn't pretend to know what had been in Tyler's mind when he'd run off with Rachel Southerland. Thus, Beau led his tiny group away from the railroad station in silence, while his mind worked overtime.

He wondered if Tyler would be performing in the new opera house, or the reputable playhouse, or if he'd dare subject himself to playing in one of the seedier saloons left over from the rowdy days. The information from the town marshal hadn't been clear on the matter.

And at this point, speculation was useless.

As Beau directed his party around a corner and onto
17th Street, he took a moment to study the familiar surroundings. Not much had changed in the year since his
last visit. Clean, stylish, rich—those were the words
that came to mind when he looked around. The sidewalks were free of debris. Even the tracks left by wagon
wheels in the street were in straight, neat rows. All in
all, the fashionable buildings outdid one another. But
none were as grand as the large structure on their left.
The famous Cheyenne Club.

"That's some building," he heard Mavis whisper in
awe.

"It is," Beau agreed.

He'd been inside a number of times. Much like the
gentlemen's clubs of London, the clientele was the
wealthiest and most influential of the community. Con-
structed mostly of red brick and sturdy wood, the
building made its own unique statement of style and impeccable social standing. A wide veranda and seven
chimney stacks surrounded the outside perimeter of the
first and second floors, respectively. On the main floor
alone, there were two large dining rooms, four billiards
rooms and three card rooms.

The club was top-notch, a spectacle to the eye, palate
and senses. If Beau was a betting man, he'd have said
Tyler was already a member.

The wind suddenly kicked up, bringing a chill to the
air and the scent of cold. A sly hint that winter was on
its way. Beau remembered how the weather bit hard and
left casualties in this harsh northern land.

During his stay, Beau had helped the community
grieve a mining accident where the snow had played a

nasty role. It had been a grim time for many, but not always so for Beau. Amelia Jane Nelson had caught his attention, and his admiration. Beau had thought himself in love. Yet the memory of that feeling was drowsy and uncertain now. Try as he might, he couldn't recall her face in his mind.

Lord, why can't I remember her? Help me. Help me to sort this out and move on if that is what You want for me.

In the next moment, Beau sensed he wasn't supposed to remember Amelia or the painful blow she'd dealt him with her rejection. Which made little sense. Thus, he forced his mind to drift back in time.

Daughter to a local cattle baron, Amelia had been kind, godly and well-spoken. Although not a great beauty, her behavior and manners had always been impeccable—unassuming and proper. In Beau's estimation, she'd represented the perfect choice for a minister's wife. He'd nurtured hopes that she might become his wife and move to Greeley with him.

She'd dashed those plans with her appalled refusal of his proposal, for equally appalling reasons. He was a son of an actor, after all, a man who ate with sinners. Amelia didn't want to be the woman to make him a better man, mostly because she thought the task would be impossible.

A sense of lingering dread came with the memory, making his stomach churn.

Would he see her again? Would the pain of her rejection still burn, especially now that she was married to a man who'd attended seminary with Beau? Had Beau's pride been hurt, or his heart?

Hannah chose that moment to laugh at something

Mavis said to her. Beau angled his head in time to watch the two link arms. Pulling Mavis closer, Hannah pointed at one of the buildings on their right and then another.

Mavis giggled and beamed at her new friend, clearly smitten with the beautiful young actress.

Hannah had that way about her, Beau realized as he watched her steer Mavis to the inside corner of the wooden sidewalk. She made the people around her feel special, as though they mattered more to her than anyone else. She was gracious, captivating, a fairy-tale princess come to life.

And watching her now, he was finally able to pinpoint what made her special.

Hannah Southerland accepted people. All people. She liked them, too, genuinely liked them. And they gravitated to her because of it.

It was no wonder Mavis cherished her.

Of course, the older woman hadn't discovered her missing tobacco yet, nor Hannah's role in the confiscation. There would surely be a bit of drama between the two at that point.

Then again...

Hannah would probably know exactly what to do and say to soothe the older woman's temper.

You're hooked, Beau.

Which he already knew. The question, of course, was what he planned to do about this unexpected turn of events. One woman had already spurned him because of his bad blood and unconventional ministry. He could never subject Hannah to that sort of prejudice. But what if she was the one for him?

Lord, I'm losing perspective.

Needing a moment to organize his thoughts, Beau

looked to the western sky. Puffs of cotton white drifted against the clear blue backdrop. Much like his life, the fluid clouds glided in random, unpredictable directions, colliding with one another and then bouncing aimlessly in a new direction.

"I'm gonna head over to the jail," Logan declared when they stopped in front of their destination.

The two-story hotel, with its clapboard front and unassuming entrance, wasn't grand by any stretch of the imagination, but it was respectable. And, like the rest of the town, clean.

When Beau didn't respond, Logan turned to address him directly. "I'll find out what I can about the fugitives while you get the women settled in their room."

Beau's gut clenched. Of course. This was not a time to be thinking about his past or his future. There was work yet to do in the present. "I'll speak with the hotel manager while you're gone. We'll meet in the restaurant on the ground floor in an hour."

Logan nodded, then shot a quick glance to the women. "I'll see you in a little while, Miss Southerland."

Hannah touched his arm. "Thank you, Deputy Mitchell. Thank you for accompanying us on this search."

The deputy's eyes stared into Hannah's—a little too long for Beau's way of thinking—but, eventually, Logan tipped his hat and said, "It's been my pleasure, ma'am."

Mavis snorted and then shot her nose into the air.

Logan sighed. His blue eyes flickered with annoyance, but he kept his tone mild. "Good day to you, too, Miss Tierney."

Without waiting for a response, he crammed his hat farther on his head and took off in the opposite direction.

Mavis stared after the young man with her jaw slack.

"Close your mouth, Mavis," Hannah said with a soft smile playing at the edges of her lips.

"Miss Tierney?" she said, still gaping after Logan. "Did that boy just call me *Miss Tierney?*"

Beau and Hannah shared an amused look. Snared in her gaze, Beau's heart hammered hard against his rib cage. He had a surprising urge, one that stunned him with its strength, to grab Hannah's hand and bring it to his lips.

Of course, now wasn't the right time or place for such an intimacy.

"That's what I heard him say," he said, turning his attention back to Mavis.

"I heard it, too," Hannah agreed, her voice a breathy whisper.

Was she as affected by Beau as he was by her?

"Humph." Mavis's lips pulled past a tight flash of crooked teeth. "We'll just see about that, now, won't we?"

She pivoted on her heel and started marching in the direction Logan had taken. Hannah's hand shot out and grabbed Mavis by the sleeve before the older woman took two full steps.

"You can give him a piece of your mind when he gets back," she said.

Mavis glared after the young deputy, but acquiesced without further physical resistance. However, she did mutter several epithets about young men who had the nerve to call her names. Some of the terms, if Beau heard her correctly, would have blistered the wallpaper off Charity House's parlor room.

Miss Mavis Tierney was certainly an interesting woman.

* * *

Two hours later, Hannah had made her own observations about her appointed chaperone. None of them were pretty.

"You cannot go to the theater dressed like that," Hannah said, dropping her gaze over the bold-colored, East Indian tunic that stopped midthigh on Mavis's scrawny *bare* legs.

The dress, and Hannah used that term loosely, was downright shocking.

"I can and I will."

Honestly, it was like trying to reason with a two-year-old. Yes, the term *theater* was stretching things a bit. In truth, Tyler's play wasn't in the new opera house or the playhouse Beau had told them about. Instead, Tyler had chosen to produce, direct and star in an untitled play in the back of a saloon on a makeshift stage.

Well, no matter where the play was performed, Hannah would not allow Mavis to step foot outside their room dressed so inappropriately, both for the weather as well as for propriety's sake.

"You'll catch your death," Hannah said in answer, thinking she deserved a medal for diplomacy when what she really wanted to say would have offended the poor dear.

Mavis crossed her spindly arms over her bird-thin chest. "It's September."

"I don't care what month it is, we're in Wyoming. The temperature has already dropped several degrees in the last hour. You need more clothes on your body." Hannah picked up the pair of men's denim pants the older woman had worn on the train. "At least put these on."

"I ain't wearing no man pants to the theater."

Right. That made sense. Since Mavis wore man pants everywhere else.

Hannah pawed through the pile of clothes strewn on top of Mavis's bed. She didn't have time to argue with the stubborn woman. Thanks to Deputy Mitchell's investigations, and Beau's persistence with the hotel manager, they'd discovered that Tyler and Rachel were most definitely in Cheyenne *and* staying in the same hotel as they were.

Unfortunately, the renegades had left for the saloon-turned-theater before the information had been conveyed and verified.

Perhaps that had been for the best. Hannah had needed the time to prepare. To pray. To ask God for the courage and wisdom to carry out the most important confrontation of her life.

Eventually she found what she was looking for. "Then wear this."

Hannah tossed the skirt to the other woman, then watched in frustration as the garment fluttered to the floor untouched.

"Put it on, Mavis, or I won't let you come with me."

Mavis stomped her foot. "No."

Hannah prayed for patience, a prayer that was becoming dangerously close to rote whenever she was in the older woman's company for longer than a few minutes.

"Why are you being so ornery?" she asked.

"If you'd give me back my tobacco, I'd do whatever you asked of me."

"Are you blackmailing me, Miss Tierney?"

"Absolutely."

Hannah shook her finger in her friend's face. "You are bad. Very, very bad."

"You don't let me have a smoke, then I don't wear no pants *or* no skirt. That's my deal. Take it or leave it."

Hannah sighed. "Right then. It's settled." Picking up her handbag, she added, "I don't expect I'll be back until late tonight. But I'll bring you something to eat when I do."

Mavis's face went dead white, the only sign of her shock. But she recovered quickly. "Sarcasm does not become you, missy."

"Who said I was being sarcastic?"

"You can't do this to me. I'm going. And that's the end of it." She puffed out her bird chest. "And before I go you're going to give me back my tobacco."

With one quick slash of her hand, Hannah dismissed the order. "No."

"No, I can't go? Or no I can't have my tobacco?"

"No to both."

As if time had slowed, both women took two very determined steps toward one another. Their gazes locked and held.

Mavis scrunched her face into a frown.

Hannah did the same.

Mavis jammed her hands on her hips.

Hannah did the same.

Frozen to the spot, Hannah waited, held firm, gauged her adversary and waited some more.

Five minutes later Hannah was close to losing the patience she'd prayed so hard for earlier.

Thankfully, Mavis cracked first. "I just want one—"

"No."

"But—"

"*No.*"

Mavis stomped her foot again. "You can't—"

"Oh, but I can."

Mavis cocked her head and studied Hannah for a long moment. "You ain't gonna budge, are you?"

"Not an inch."

"This stubborn side of you is not going to win many hearts."

Hannah gave her a quick, unrepentant grin. "Perhaps not, but I will win this argument."

With a snort, Mavis snatched up the skirt at her feet. "Fine. I'll wear this one."

"Wise decision." From the pile on the bed, Hannah plucked a light wool jacket and held it between her thumb and forefinger. "Add this to your ensemble and we'll call you stage-ready."

Frowning, Mavis yanked the jacket out of Hannah's hands and jammed her arms into the sleeves. "You can be downright mean when you want to, Hannah Southerland."

"So I've been told."

"You remind me a little too much of…" A smile slipped onto the corner of Mavis's lips. "Me."

"It's why you love me," Hannah said. Dragging Mavis into a tight hug, she kissed the top of her head as she would a child's. "And why I love you."

"Humph," Mavis said between suspicious-sounding sniffs. Was the woman crying?

Hannah released Mavis and touched the lone tear running down a weathered cheek. "Oh, Mavis."

Not to be outdone, Mavis lifted onto her toes and kissed Hannah smack on the forehead. "Take that."

"Well," Hannah said through watery eyes of her own.

Mavis just smiled at her, but then got that crafty look in her gaze that meant pure trouble. "Now that we're friends again, you wouldn't reconsider giving me back my toba—"

"No. Absolutely not."

Before Mavis could start the argument all over again, Hannah wrapped her own shawl around her shoulders and trod to the door leading into the hallway. As she passed the nightstand, she caught sight of the flyer that the deputy had brought to her less than an hour before.

Compelled, Hannah picked up the parchment and studied the drawing of her former friend turned traitor. At the sight of Tyler's smiling face, Hannah sank her teeth into her bottom lip.

The drawing was a near-perfect rendition of the man, all the way down to the jaunty angle of his head and the cocky half smile that had become as much his trademark as his outrageous talent had.

Mavis rested her chin on Hannah's shoulder and peered at the sketch along with her. "That boy sure does look like our Pastor Beau."

Hannah bit down harder on her lip, then took a slow breath. "No. Not at all." She traced her finger across Tyler's jaw. "Beau has a stronger chin, with just a hint of a cleft in the middle." She moved her finger upward. "And his eyebrows are more winged. His eyes more pale silver than green."

"Poor Hannah," Mavis said, snatching the flyer from her fingers and setting it back on the nightstand. "You got it bad for the preacher."

Why deny the truth, when it was so glaring, so obvious? "You have no idea."

The admission didn't bring much comfort, though. Instead, Hannah felt a sense of dread run across her spine, as though she was about to lose her solid, predictable future. The one she'd worked so hard to chart and organize ever since her father had banished her.

Did God have a bigger plan for her life, one that didn't include worldly security?

And if so, did she have enough faith? Enough to obey His design for her life, even if it went against her own plans?

She shook her head at the frightening prospect.

"Come on, Mavis. Let's go witness one of the most famous Shakespearean actors of our day perform on a stage set up in the back of a rowdy saloon."

Mavis let out a loud cackle. "Can't think of anything more absurd than that."

Hannah's sentiments exactly.

Chapter Fifteen

Beau had made his share of mistakes in life. But he didn't usually make them on such a colossal scale. A raucous saloon, even one turned into a temporary theater, was no place for a decent woman of good, moral, Christian upbringing like Hannah Southerland.

But they were here now. Close to the end of their journey. And he doubted Hannah would be willing to put off the confrontation with her sister any longer.

At least Logan had thought ahead and ordered box seating for their party of four. The deputy might be young, but he was smart. And Beau was glad the lawman had agreed to accompany them tonight.

With as little spectacle as possible, Beau escorted Hannah and Mavis toward the back stairwell leading to their private box. The steps were old, and creaky, but out of sight from most of the other patrons. Nevertheless, Beau had insisted Logan bring up the rear, sufficiently shielding the women against interested stares.

At the top of the landing, he waved his party into the curtained booth. Following closely behind Logan, Beau took a quick look around while the others settled into their seats.

His stomach dropped at the sight before him.

It was much worse than he'd anticipated, and he'd expected ghastly. The box's walls were adorned with the same red velvet as the cushioned chairs and balcony railing. In the center of the room sat a plate of fresh fruit and an empty silver bucket that would have chilled a bottle of champagne if they'd been any other group. Obviously, the management had attempted to create an illusion of upper-class elegance.

But it was only an illusion.

Even if he ignored the smell of stale whiskey and unwashed bodies, there wasn't much to hide the fact that the Bird Cage was nothing more than a saloon with chairs lined up in front of an empty stage.

There was no orchestra, just a bass drum set up next to an ancient piano. An equally ancient gentleman sorted through a pile of sheet music. But for now, the only melody came from the bawdy jokes yelled out across the general seating area. Every few seconds, the shouts were interrupted by the high-pitched ping, ping, ping of tobacco hitting spittoons.

As if determined to turn the experience into a Wild West cliché, a fight broke out over an empty seat. Beau couldn't tell which of the cowboys won the ridiculous match. Within moments, they both ended up passed out on the floor.

Speaking his thoughts for him, Hannah muttered, "What on earth was Tyler thinking?"

Beau took his seat next to her and said, "That's just it, my dear Hannah. He's *not* thinking."

Just then a bottle came sailing their way. Palm to nape, Beau forced Hannah's head forward and ducked, as well.

"Lovely," he mumbled. "First-rate."

Hannah didn't respond. She just raised her head and stared at the stage. Her sudden gasp had Beau following her gaze to an easel and placard. Squinting, he could just make out the words through the veil of cigar smoke. *Faust. A Tale of Damnation.*

"Love-ly," he muttered again.

At the precise stroke of ten, a man sauntered toward the oversize drum and began beating a rhythmic cadence. After a round of hooting and shouting, a dark-hooded figure glided onto the stage. A hush came over the crowd.

The drumming ceased.

The mysterious character continued to stand in silence.

A gun fired, its bullet hitting the ceiling and spraying plaster over the audience. Hannah jumped in her seat. "Oh!"

Beau reached out and took her hand.

She braided her fingers through his and held on tight. "What is this?" she whispered.

"I have no idea."

Using the thrill of suspense, the dark figure stretched its arms slowly overhead.

The audience leaned forward, paused and held its collective breath. The apparition reached down and, with a flick of a wrist, whipped off the cloak.

The crowd went wild.

A loud gasp escaped Hannah.

Logan muttered under his breath.

Mavis looked to Hannah, back to the stage, then to Hannah again. "It's...it's you."

Speechless with shock, Beau blinked at the woman standing in the center of the stage. Her eyes gleamed with impish delight as she accepted the bawdy roars as her due. Beau shifted in his seat, fighting the urge to mutter an expletive. Dressed in a red silk gown in the latest Parisian fashion, the woman *was* Hannah. Only... somehow...less.

Taking command of her audience, Rachel Southerland stretched out her arms again and the noise died down to a smattering of whistles and howls.

The man at the piano poised his fingers over the keys, then started banging out a happy melody.

Rachel sashayed across the stage, humming along to the tune. Her movements weren't elegant or even practiced, but rather coarse. Suggestive. Beau was ashamed for her. And disgusted with his brother. Tyler should have taught her better.

There was acting. And there was what Rachel Southerland was doing on that stage.

Even as anger gnawed at his shock, an ache clutched at his chest. Tyler *knew* better. But did Rachel?

Raise up a child in the way that he should go...

The Scripture said it all. Reverend Southerland had done Rachel a disservice by shutting his eyes to the truth all these years. By allowing Hannah to take the blame for her sister's transgressions, without once questioning the veracity of her stories, he'd failed both daughters. Rachel most of all.

Jesus had said a man's enemies would be members of his own household, but surely the cycle could yet be broken.

Lord, may redemption be at hand. May You shine

Your light into this darkness and bring healing to both women, bring peace to their family.

Flicking her hair over her shoulder, Rachel began to speak. "I present to you a story as old as time. A sad tale full of sin and ultimate damnation."

The male-dominated crowd went wild again, laughing and calling out promises to take a trip to hell as long as she joined them in the journey.

She stuck out her hip and parked her fist there. "Let this be a warning to you all."

Hannah buried her face in her hands—the safest place for her eyes in Beau's estimation. Unfortunately, she raised her head in time to catch Tyler's entrance.

Always the showman first, actor second, Tyler strolled toward Rachel with confidence and purpose in his steps. His slow, deliberate pace made him look almost predatory while the crafty light in his eyes made Beau bristle.

Whatever Tyler was about to do, it was not going to be proper.

With a bold wink to the audience, Tyler roped an arm around Rachel's waist and drew her slowly—very, very, *very* slowly—into his arms.

He dipped her low. Lower still. Then…

He kissed her. Right on the mouth.

The endearment had nothing to do with love, but possession. Ownership. Beau's gut twisted with a fresh surge of disgust.

"Oh, oh!" Hannah shook her head violently, as though she couldn't believe what she was witnessing.

Unfortunately, Beau wasn't quite so shocked. He'd seen worse in the brothels. He knew sin was rampant in the world, knew evil lurked in every man to some extent. Hence the need for a Savior.

But Beau hadn't expected to see such wickedness displayed so blatantly in a member of his own family. He found himself harboring a strong desire to wrap his fingers around his brother's throat and squeeze.

Humiliated for them all, Beau touched Hannah's arm in a show of sympathy. Even Mavis made a clicking noise with her tongue. And as the kiss turned into two, Logan pretended grave interest in his thumbnail.

Hannah jumped to her feet.

Beau followed suit.

Wild-eyed, she clutched at her throat. In a haphazard fashion, her gaze bounced off the far wall, to the stage and back to the wall again. "I can't watch any more of this."

Beau eased her around to face him. He placed a finger under her chin and pressed gently until her eyes met his. "Hannah, listen to me." He kept his tone low, but he could feel his own temper licking at the edges of his calm. He gulped. "It's all right. We'll wait outside. Together."

Hannah opened her mouth, shut it and then nodded. "Yes, yes. Thank you."

"I'll stay a bit longer, myself." Mavis snorted in dismay. "I ain't so easily shocked as you two. And someone had better find out what those two naughty children are up to."

Beau turned a questioning stare to Logan.

The deputy's expression was as bleak as Beau's mood. "What do you want me to do, Reverend? Just ask."

"Keep an eye on Mavis for me," Beau said. "Take her back to the hotel if we don't reappear shortly."

Neither Mavis nor Logan argued, which would have taken Beau by surprise if he'd been in a more lucid state.

Laying his palm on the small of Hannah's back, he led her into the empty hallway. Once they were alone, Hannah spun around. Beau reached to her, hoping to give her comfort, but she shrank back and collapsed against the wall.

Gasping for air, she closed her eyes on a shudder.

Beau shifted his body so that he shielded her from the view of any wandering patron. Guilt gnawed at him.

Lord, what have I done? Why did I bring her here? She shouldn't have witnessed that unseemliness.

"Hannah, I'm sorry. I shouldn't have—"

"I knew it was going to be bad," she choked out, wringing her hands together and blinking rapidly. "But I never thought..." She let her words trail off and gazed up at him.

The shock and helplessness in her eyes made him want to wrap her in his arms and protect her from the bad in the world. Even if that corruption was in her own family. And his.

Speechless with frustration, Beau drew in a sharp breath. Heart pounding, head reeling, one powerful thought arose.

There was going to be a reckoning tonight. And Tyler had better come bearing answers.

"It's all my fault," she said through clenched teeth. "All of it."

"Hannah," Beau began, but she cut him off with a finger to his lips.

"No. Let me say this." She dropped her hand. "If I hadn't always accepted the guilt for her transgressions, Rachel wouldn't think she could get away with such...such behavior."

Her words were so close to his earlier thoughts that Beau couldn't deny their veracity. Whether Thomas Southerland had believed her or not, Hannah had told untruths. She might have been motivated by her promise to her mother. Perhaps guilt had played a role, as well, but in the end she had chosen to claim acts she hadn't committed herself.

That had been wrong.

At least she was here now, in this ugly world where she didn't belong, accepting her share of the responsibility and attempting to break the destructive cycle at last.

He admired her courage, and would support her to the end. At this point, his loyalty belonged to Hannah alone.

Using a gentle touch, he brushed a strand of hair off her forehead. "This is your day, Hannah. You have the opportunity to undo the dangerous pattern once and for all."

"I know." Hannah sighed, then lifted her chin at a determined angle. "That's why I've traveled so far. It ends here. Tonight."

Beau doubted this would end clean and neat, nothing between families was ever that simple—especially when something as complicated as an estrangement was involved.

But Hannah was right about one thing. The end was near.

And once the performance was over, Beau would demand answers from his brother. Tyler's explanations had better be worthy of them all.

Hannah had never wanted to punch another human being. Never. She wasn't prone to violence. But Tyler

O'Toole was asking for a fist right in the middle of his nose.

Needing a moment to calm her distress, she let her gaze rest on Beau. He leaned against the wall on the other side of the room. His expression was unreadable, but she could see his tension in the rigid angle of his shoulders and the thin line of his lips. She could tell it cost him to remain silent. But he'd promised to let her handle this initial confrontation. So far, he'd held to that promise.

Hannah had never met a man with that much patience and strength of character. His presence alone brought her the courage to finish having her say.

Rising to her full height, she broke eye contact with Beau and ran her gaze across the jars of face paint to the dirty tissues strewn about the dressing table. The tools of her trade looked ugly in this cold, dank room. Mere items used to create deception, rather than entertainment.

If the saloon-turned-theater had seemed sordid from the box seating, this dressing room was far worse. The furniture was faded and threadbare. The scent of mold, stale cigars and rotting wool cloaked the damp interior.

Hannah couldn't understand why Tyler would choose to perform in such squalor, such filth. Not when he could have top billing at the most prestigious theaters in the world.

And to subject a woman he reportedly loved to this dark existence? Something didn't add up.

"I don't understand why you chose to stay here, when you could have escaped to New York. Or Europe. Or even San Francisco." She tasted the bitterness on her tongue, heard it in her voice and accepted it as her right.

Unwilling to see the seriousness of the situation, Tyler let out a jolly laugh and placed Rachel in the crook of his arm. Side by side, they made a ridiculously beautiful pair. Her dark to his light. And yet, something about the way they stood together was…ugly. Sordid.

Bile rose in Hannah's throat.

"Soon, Hannah darling," Tyler said, completely unaware of her growing dismay. "We will make our move in a few weeks. For now, this is our secret adventure."

Tyler smiled down at Rachel then, the look far too intimate for public viewing. Hannah's stomach rolled over itself, and again she sensed that she was missing something important.

As though hearing her thoughts, Tyler abruptly released Rachel and took Hannah's hands in his. She desperately wanted to pull free of his grip, but she refused to allow him to see her distress. Nevertheless, she found she couldn't look at him, couldn't force her eyes off the lapel of his jacket.

He'd once been a good friend, a surrogate brother of sorts and the son of her most trusted mentor. Their shared history alone had to be worth something. "What am I missing, Tyler? What aren't you telling me?"

"Hannah, darling, don't you understand?" Tyler gave her the kind of smile adults spared unruly children. "We are anonymous here. Free to do whatever we wish. No rules. Just Rachel and me. *Together.*"

Shocked at the lewd implications of his words, Hannah snatched her hands free. Men like Tyler were so predictable. She'd hoped for more from him.

He'd proven less.

"You mean share a room while remaining unwed,"

she said, then placed her gaze deliberately on Rachel. "How could you do this again? Didn't you learn anything from your disastrous affair with Mr. Beamer?"

There, she'd said it out loud. Perhaps now they could get to the heart of the matter.

Owl-eyed, Rachel's expression turned blank, placid even. And she completely ignored the question. "Can't you just be happy for me this *one* time?"

Happy? How could Rachel be so indifferent to all the people she was hurting by embarking on this indecent liaison with Tyler? How could she be so selfish?

Hannah opened her mouth to speak, but Tyler spoke over her.

"Happy doesn't begin to describe my feelings when I am with you, my darling," he said, pulling Rachel into an embrace more suitable for a brothel. "Blissful. Ecstatic. Delirious. Those are much better adjectives."

Rachel touched his cheek, ran her finger along his jaw.

Tyler kissed her on the nose.

Hannah averted her eyes.

Their bold, public intimacy was disconcerting, something that shouldn't be shared with anyone but each other.

With a loud hiss, Beau pushed abruptly from the wall. "Tyler! Enough. You can't—"

"No." Hannah stopped Beau's approach with a hard shake of her head. "Let me finish this. Please. You'll get your turn. For now, this is still *my* fight."

His face constricted with barely controlled emotion. And with that hard look in his eyes, Hannah expected him to deny her request, but he gave her one sharp nod and stepped back.

"Rachel," she said through her teeth. "You *cannot* share a room with a man you aren't married to. It's a sin."

Rachel snuggled up against Tyler and rolled her eyes to heaven. "You are such a prude, Hannah. Father never did understand how different we are, and that he had us mixed up from the start."

And here it was. The moment of truth. The reason Hannah had traveled all these miles. She struggled to hold on to her temper, but angry heat flushed into her cheeks. "Father never knew because *you* never told him."

Rachel cast a dark look in her direction. "Did you?"

Hannah staggered back as if slapped. "I... You..."

"Did you?" Rachel said.

"No," Hannah whispered, her heart dipping in her chest at the ugly realization of her own guilt.

Oh, Lord, forgive me. Forgive me. All this time, all these years, I've blamed Rachel for not speaking up. And resented her for it. But I never spoke up, either.

"No," she repeated. "I didn't say a word."

"Then mind your own business now."

Hannah's heart beat wildly at the prospect of her impending defeat. She'd traveled all this way, and once again a man was proving more important to Rachel than her own sister. "You can't hide like this forever."

"I know that," Rachel snapped.

"Good. Because I'm performing the marriage ceremony," Beau said, pushing from the wall. "This very night." His words were clipped, controlled and very, very angry.

Shocked at his forcefulness, Hannah swung around to stare at him. She drew slightly back at the intensity of emotion on his face. She'd never seen him that im-

placable, that righteously disgusted. And yet, his unbridled anger made him seem more vulnerable to her.
Even as his eyes blazed with resolve, she knew he was
ashamed and hurting.

Hannah understood his pain. Tyler had wounded him
as only one sibling could hurt another. Deep at the core.

Clearing his expression, Beau stepped between Tyler
and Rachel, sufficiently separating them with a hard
shove at Tyler's chest.

Tyler stumbled back, caught his balance and then
took a menacing step forward.

"Stop right there." Beau squared his shoulders.
"Neither of you will leave this room until you are wed."

"Is that so, *brother?*" Tyler spat, the first chink in
his perfectly polished armor sounding in the sour tone
of his voice.

"It will be done," Beau reiterated.

The two men stared into each other's eyes. The anger
between them was palpable. Hannah feared they would
come to blows any moment. With each beat of her heart,
the standoff turned more intense, more angry and bitter,
becoming a ruthless clash between brothers as old as
Cain and Abel.

Eventually, Tyler lowered his head and sighed in
defeat. "As you wish."

Beau placed his hand on Tyler's arm. "It's the right
thing to do."

"I know."

Recovering quickly, Tyler placed a careless grin on
his lips. With a challenge in his eyes, he held Beau's
stare as he tugged Rachel into his arms once again.

"Rachel Southerland, will you marry me?" he asked,

still glaring at Beau as he spoke. Eventually, he dropped his gaze to Rachel and cocked his head at a jaunty angle. "Will you be my wife, in name now as well as in deed? Will you—"

Beau cleared his throat, cutting off the rest of whatever improper request Tyler had been about to ask of her.

Hannah whispered a silent prayer of thanks that at least one O'Toole sibling was a gentleman.

Giggling, Rachel trailed a finger down Tyler's cheek. "I suppose it wouldn't hurt to make it official."

Hannah gasped. The realization of what marriage between the two would mean was finally sinking in. "Wait. What about Will? What about Father?"

Rachel flicked a speck of dust off Tyler's shoulder. "What about them?"

"You must tell them of your marriage to Tyler. They deserve to hear it from you."

"Me? No." She slid Hannah a bitter glare from under her lashes. "You tell them. Save the day like always. It's what you live for."

At Rachel's feral glance, Hannah's lips parted in shock. She'd never seen such revulsion in her sister's eyes before. "You must tell them yourself," Hannah insisted, but her voice shook at the realization she was losing the fight.

In response, Rachel twisted on her heels, lifted her chin in the air and turned her deaf ear toward Hannah.

With that one gesture the battle was complete.

Rachel had made up her mind. There would be no reasoning with her now. She had literally shut Hannah out.

Hannah shouldn't have been surprised. She shouldn't feel this devastating sense of defeat, this...*hurt*.

This was their pattern, after all. She had been naive to think anything would change between Rachel and her.

Hannah slowly set her hands on Rachel's shoulders and turned her sister to face her directly. "Write one letter to Father and another to your fiancé. I'll deliver them personally," she said with little expression in her voice. She turned to Beau. "It's the only way now."

He gave her an understanding nod.

Perhaps this had been part of God's plan for Hannah all along. *Thou shalt not bear false witness against thy neighbor.*

Hannah had lied all her life. But now she would make restitution. She would confess her sin to the one person she'd offended most. Her father.

"You won't face Reverend Southerland alone," Beau declared, closing his hand over hers in perfect understanding of the situation. "I won't allow it."

Even in her devastated state, Hannah felt a smile tug at her lips. For once, this man's arrogance brought her comfort. And a unique sense of safety. Beauregard O'Toole was a good man. By accepting his generous offer, she would make her own bold statement. Would he understand?

"I would consider myself fortunate, fortunate indeed, to have you stand by my side," she said.

Rachel snorted, ruining the moment. "Hannah? You? Traveling alone with a man? I'm shocked."

Hannah's entire body wanted to tremble again, but she would not give in to her anger now. "*I* have a chaperone."

Rachel rolled her gaze to the ceiling, looking as though Hannah's sense of propriety was anything but. "Of course you do."

Beau touched her arm. Needing his strength, she turned to him. His eyes crinkled at the edges, and he gave her hand an encouraging squeeze. "It'll be over soon. I promise."

Perhaps this wasn't the ending Hannah had hoped for when she'd set out in search of Rachel and Tyler. But a sense of peace filled her at the prospect of her imminent confession.

This was the right course of action. The web of lies would be broken at last.

Chapter Sixteen

An hour later, Beau completed the marriage ceremony with very little pomp. "I now pronounce you husband and wife."

He didn't bother telling Tyler to kiss the bride. The two had certainly done enough of that prior to the exchange of vows. Regardless of how uncomfortable it made Hannah or Beau—or anyone else, for that matter.

In truth, Beau had never met two more selfish people in his life. He didn't think either was inherently evil, just unaware of the pain they were causing others as they pursued their own ends. They were like children, entitled children who hadn't been told "no" enough. Or, rather, hadn't suffered the consequences of "no" enough.

Watching them now, with their heads bent toward one another, Beau didn't doubt they would be happy together—their love was easy enough to see—but now others would be hurt.

Hannah most of all.

Beau glanced over at her. She stood rigid, her shoulders stiff. She looked more fragile than the first time they'd met, more wounded. His heart weighed heavy in his chest because he knew there was nothing he could do for her now. Informing the venerable Thomas Southerland that his favorite daughter had run off and married an actor would not be an easy task.

Beau gulped back his rising concern, but only succeeded in wedging the lump of dread deeper in his chest. He walked over to Hannah and asked, "How are you faring?"

She lifted a shoulder, sighed. Her eyes held all the pain he knew she must be feeling. He'd seen the look of betrayal often enough to realize he was staring at it now.

That enigmatic blend of melancholy and defeat mocked him. He was a minister with no tools to erase her sorrow. He had a fierce, primitive need to rush her out of the room and fight off anyone who so much as looked at her oddly.

"What will I tell him?" she asked in a shaky breath. "And Will. Oh, poor Will."

Beau took her hand and threaded her fingers through his. He remembered her advice back at Charity House when he'd worried in a similar manner over Megan. "The Holy Spirit will give you the right words at the right time."

She turned large, round eyes toward him. Clearly, his words hadn't settled her nerves. Well, there was one worry he could remove. "I promise you this, Hannah, you aren't alone anymore. I will share this burden with you."

He knew he was pledging more than a solid presence during a hard conversation. By standing with her, by confronting Reverend Southerland, he would be jeopardizing his future with the Rocky Mountain Association. And yet, he didn't care as much as he should.

Hannah needed him. That was all that mattered at the moment.

There would be time to sort through what that meant to his future and his future ministry. He had to trust that God would provide, as the Heavenly Father always did.

"Oh, Beau." Tears wiggled along her eyelashes. She looked both relieved and bemused by his declaration. "Are you certain?"

His answer came without hesitation. "Yes."

"What if my father—"

"It doesn't matter." And he meant his words.

The risk to his future *didn't* matter anymore. He'd done the right thing by marrying Tyler and Rachel. Even if Reverend Southerland considered Beau the most culpable party for having officiated at the ceremony.

He had no regrets. "Hannah, fear not, we're in this together now."

She smiled then. And, oh, what a smile. It was the one that grabbed at his heart and twisted.

"You aren't going to relent on this, are you?" she asked.

"I treated you abominably the first time we met." He lifted her hand to his lips, forced himself not to linger. "Think of this as my way of saying I'm sorry."

"You don't owe me—"

"Yes, I do." He dropped her hand. "I cannot be swayed in my decision. You are stuck with me now."

Her smile turned watery, and Beau's heart dipped in his chest. He would have said more, but Hannah's twin shoved him out of the way with a nudge of her hip.

Eyes gleaming with female satisfaction, Rachel kissed Hannah on the cheek. "Be happy for me."

Hannah blinked, a contradictory look of pain and

hope flashing in her gaze. Beau understood the conflict-ing emotions all too well. As angry as he felt toward Tyler, the man was still his brother.

Of course, that didn't mean he wouldn't confront him. Alone. Now was as good a time as any. Before leaving the two to their conversation, Beau whispered in Hannah's ear that he would be close by.

She offered him a sweet smile and then turned her attention back to her sister. Beau motioned to Tyler to meet him on the other side of the room.

Tyler joined him and boomed out a laugh. "I'd say we're both fortunate in our choice of women. What say you, brother?"

Beau stiffened, fearing where this conversation was leading. He would not allow Tyler to sully his feelings for Hannah. They were private and pure and not up for discussion with his brother. "Say nothing more, Tyler."

Unaware of Beau's growing frustration, Tyler slapped him on the back. "There's something about those Southerland women, eh?"

Beau tensed like a tightened coil. "Don't."

"Perfect matches. Rachel and me." Tyler wiggled his eyebrows. "You and Hannah."

Tyler often surprised Beau with his perception. But there were times—times such as this one—when his brother used his unexpected insight to rile Beau. Beau, however, would not give him the satisfaction of taking the bait. And he certainly wouldn't discuss his feelings for Hannah with a man who had no sense of decency when it came to relations between men and women. "What you did was wrong, Tyler. Fornication is a sin. Worse, Rachel was engaged."

"Please, Beau." He blew out an exasperated breath. "If she wasn't married, she was fair game."

Shocked at his brother's callousness, Beau stared at Tyler with new eyes. Throughout their childhood, things had come easy for Tyler. His charm had been present from the start. And he'd learned to use the O'Toole good looks to full advantage. Never had Tyler been reined in. Well, certainly not enough. The youngest of five siblings, he'd been doted on by everyone. Beau included.

Was this egocentricity and self-centeredness the by-product of that indulgence?

"Tyler, this time what you've done has hurt people." Beau looked at Hannah and took note of her tenuous expression as she spoke softly with her sister. His heart ached for her.

As always, Tyler homed in on the wrong portion of Beau's argument. "*This* time? Are you saying I'm irresponsible by nature?"

"Yes, I am." Beau raised his hands to ward off Tyler's arguments. "Don't misunderstand. I love you. I always will. But life has been too easy for you."

Tyler narrowed his eyes to tiny slits. "And you hold it against me, is that it?"

"No."

Tyler continued to study him. "Yes, you do." He snorted. "But you're wrong."

Beau lifted his eyebrows but didn't respond. Tyler was being sarcastic, at any rate. It was part of his makeup, as much a part of him as the practiced smile and theatrical gestures.

"I wasn't born with natural acting talent like you, Beau. I've spent my life honing and practicing. While you—" Tyler pointed an accusing finger at him "—were born with the most natural talent of us all. Did you choose to pursue it? No. You went into the ministry."

Tyler's expression was a perfect mask of outrage, but there was a great deal more going on behind those eyes. Mostly resentment. And jealousy.

Beau held the odd stare for a long moment. "I chose to follow God's calling for my life," he said with conviction. "How is that wrong?"

"It's not, but you hold your family's profession against us every time you fail."

Beau had no intention of leaving that foul statement alone. "Now there you *are* wrong."

"Am I?" Tyler crossed his arms over his chest and gave Beau a haughty look. "What about when you got kicked out of the church in Laramie? *You* said it was because of us, because of the scandalous nature of your family's profession. Scotts Bluff, the same excuse. Kearney, again, the same. You were chased out of those churches, *according to you,* because of your family."

An ache squeezed around Beau's heart. "It's true."

"No."

Beau's head snapped up at the hostility in that one word.

Tyler leaned closer until his nose was an inch from touching Beau's. His pale green eyes were hard and un-relenting. "You were run out of those churches because of you. Not me, or our parents, or our family. You!"

A fleeting shadow of uneasiness passed through Beau, only to be replaced by white-hot fury. "You weren't there," he said. "You don't know."

"I know you." Tyler growled, and a flush came over

his face. "Take a good look into your own heart, Beauregard. Take a look at that dream of yours to have a traditional church and see where it comes from."

Beau looked into Tyler's face and knew the man's pride was hurt. That explained the attack. Didn't it? "Tyler, I—"

"You're the selfish one here. Not me. I've never pretended to be anything other than what I am, a hard-working actor who loves the stage and all the trappings that come from my success. You, on the other hand, have never been honest with yourself."

Beau clenched his hand into a tight fist. A muscle jerked in his jaw. He tried to hide his anger behind a wall of superiority. "This isn't about me. And you know it. You are the one who ran off with a woman already engaged, the daughter of the one man who could take away everything I've worked for."

"Aha!" Tyler snapped his fingers and smirked. "I knew it."

Beau glared at him.

"You're worried about losing your new church." The sound that came from Tyler's throat was a growl of distaste. "Where's your faith, Beau? Maybe you should listen to God for a change, instead of telling Him to bless your own plan for your future."

Beau's sense of outrage swelled. "Now you're a pastor, too? You stand there and tell me how hard you've worked. Well, so have I. I want this church in Greeley. It's a traditional church with a stable lifestyle attached."

"And then you'll get a boring, staid, unassuming wife who will bear you perfectly behaved children." Tyler sneered.

"What's wrong with wanting those things?" Beau asked. "What's wrong with not wanting to travel across continents, with wanting to live a settled life?"

His anger clearly spent, Tyler leaned against the nearby wall and gave Beau a pitying look. "Nothing is wrong with that. Nothing at all. In truth, it's a good goal, maybe even a noble one. But you're missing who *you* are in the scenario. You're a rebel, Beau."

"I am a man of God."

Tyler's lips twisted in sympathy. "Can I give you some advice?"

It was Beau's turn to sneer. "Can I stop you?"

"You'll die a slow death in that little church in the meadow, the one you seem to think you want."

Sweat broke out on Beau's skin. Panic crawled up his spine. "You're wrong."

"Beau. There are people who need you, just as you are, in all of your unconventional, eat-with-sinners glory."

"You don't know me or what I want," Beau said in frustrated anger.

"Ah, but you see, my dear brother, the problem isn't whether I know you. It's whether you know yourself."

Beau felt the blood draining from his face. He opened his mouth to speak, but Tyler slapped him on the back and dislodged the breath right out of him. "But I digress. Are we going to continue arguing, or are you going to congratulate me on my good fortune?"

Beau swallowed back a load of arguments and forced a smile onto his lips. Tyler was wrong. He was wrong about everything. His brother would never truly understand him, as *he* would probably never understand Tyler.

There was no reason to argue any further. "If you are as happy as you seem—"

"I am."

"Then congratulations. May you have a satisfying marriage filled with few regrets and many healthy years together."

Tyler laughed. "Count on it, because, dear brother, I plan to work harder at this than I have at anything else in my life."

Beau sighed. *Lord, may that be true.* "Then I give you my blessing."

Just by looking at Beau's intense expression, Hannah caught the seriousness of the brothers' conversation. Whatever they were discussing, she doubted it included joyful tidings.

She completely understood. Rachel hadn't stopped extolling Tyler's many virtues since she'd nudged Beau aside.

Hannah had quit paying attention some time ago.

Turning back to Rachel, she decided to stop pretending to listen and got straight to the point. "What were you thinking?" she demanded.

"What?" Rachel stopped in midsentence. "When?"

"You weren't going to let Will or Father know of your change of heart, were you?"

Rachel crossed her arms over her chest in a defensive, angry gesture. "They'd have figured it out when I didn't come home."

Hannah sighed at the antagonism in her sister's voice. "When did you get so callous, Rachel?"

"Isn't it a burden always making the right decisions?"

"Don't be snide. It's beneath us both."

Rachel snorted in disgust. "What do you know? All my life I've never had the chance of doing the right thing."

"Nobody told you to lie or cheat or have an affair with a married man," Hannah said, refusing to allow her sister to throw the full blame at her feet. "And when the deeds were found out, you never accepted the blame."

"You never gave me a chance. You always had to step into my business."

Hannah's teeth clenched. Her heart filled with frustration and regret. There was probably pity and disdain there, as well, but she chose not to sort through the rest.

It seemed unnatural for Rachel to blame Hannah like this, unreal even. Except it was real. It was very real. At least to Rachel.

Out of fairness to her sister, Hannah forced her mind to the past and thought over all the incidents and many transgressions throughout the years.

No, Hannah's memory was clear. Rachel had willingly committed the acts in the first place. When caught, she hadn't stepped forward. Not once.

Did you give her the chance?

Hannah didn't know for certain. However, there was one incident that ran firm in her mind, the one time when Rachel hadn't tried to step forward. The night of Hannah's banishment.

"Even if what you say is true, what about your affair with Mr. Beamer? That night, I waited for you to come forward. You never did."

"I know." Rachel's face contorted with annoyance but not remorse. "I miscalculated that one. I never thought Father would disown you. And once he had, I knew he wouldn't believe the truth."

Hannah stared at her sister. "How could he? By pretending to be me throughout the affair, you made it impossible for *anyone* to believe the truth. That was very badly done of you, Rachel."

"Perhaps." And yet, *still,* she didn't ask for forgiveness.

"Why didn't you at least warn me?" Hannah asked.

"Because I thought you would take it badly, or worse, lecture me." She blessed her with an ironic smile. "Good thing I was wrong."

Hannah ignored the sarcasm. "You could have confessed all this in Chicago."

"I met Tyler," Rachel said, as though that explained her lapse. As though finding her one true love erased her from any further blame.

Hannah stared at her in disbelief. Surely, she didn't think resolution came that easily. "Rachel—"

"Don't look at me like that, with that self-righteous snarl on your face. You played your own role, Hannah. If you hadn't set the precedents, I wouldn't have pulled it off."

"Maybe." All right. Yes. Hannah *had* played her role. She couldn't pretend otherwise. Regardless of the fact that Rachel had taken advantage of the situation, Hannah owed her sister an apology. "I'm sorry."

Rachel said nothing.

And in that moment, Hannah finally saw the truth for what it was. Rachel would never ask for forgiveness. Hannah could either love her as she was, flaws and all, or carry the burden of her own bitterness in her heart forever.

Hannah chose freedom.

She chose to give forgiveness where forgiveness wasn't earned. As her Lord and Savior had done for her.

It wasn't easy, and she would probably lapse, but wasn't that the point? Wasn't the path Christ asked His followers to walk a narrow one?

Lord, please fill me with Your forgiveness. I can't do it on my own power. It's too big for me.

"It's over, Rachel. I hold no ill will toward you." She wanted to mean her words. Perhaps one day she would. "I pray you and Tyler have a lifetime of happiness together."

Relief washed across Rachel's face, and she yanked Hannah into a hard, bone-rattling embrace. "Thank you, Hannah. Thank you."

Hannah knew it was as close to an apology as she would get from her sister. It was enough. It had to be enough.

Beau and Tyler joined them just as Hannah pulled out of the hug.

Ever the gentleman, Beau took Rachel's hand and kissed the knuckles with a theatrical O'Toole flair that had amusement beaming in Tyler's eyes.

"Be happy, my new sister," Beau said to Rachel.

"I already am," Rachel said.

Tyler bent at the waist before Hannah. "Thank you, my good friend, for bringing the love of my life to me."

At the genuine note of joy on Tyler's face, Hannah's heart softened toward the rogue. "It's the least I could do. After all, you taught me the finer points of my craft when I knew nothing."

He wrapped her hands in his and squeezed. "You deserve the best in life. And I think you know what I mean."

He slid a sly glance in his brother's direction, but, thankfully, Beau wasn't looking at him. He was looking at Hannah. Looking at her with his pastor face on, steady and unwavering, unrelenting strength in the set of his jaw.

Her heart thumped one strong, powerful knock against her ribs. The truth had been there from the start. God's hand in the process all along. All this time she'd thought this journey had been about her past. She'd been wrong.

Beauregard O'Toole was the man of her dreams. The man of her heart. The man of her future. He just didn't know it yet. But with God's help, and a little nudge from Hannah, he would.

Tyler lowered his voice to a stage whisper. "Don't let him blow it. He's just foolish enough to ruin it for you both."

"Don't worry, Tyler. I have a plan."

Well, not precisely. But Hannah had every intention of making sure Beau came around very soon. Very soon indeed.

Chapter Seventeen

The next morning, the sun shone brighter, the sky blazed bluer. Hannah's mood, however, failed to navigate the atmosphere quite so well. Unable to calm her sporadic thoughts, she'd spent a sleepless night sorting through all the mistakes she'd made with Rachel over the years.

By dawn, she'd been completely worn out. Thus, it was with leaden feet that she followed the others to the local church for Sunday meeting. Wanting to file away every detail in her mind of the town where her life had taken a dramatic turn, she scanned the streets and buildings. But she found her eyes focusing on the townspeople instead.

They seemed as unfriendly as she herself felt. They stared. Unashamedly. Their eyes filled with open curiosity tempered with...disdain?

Hannah shook the ugly thought aside and continued watching them watch her.

Their strange attitudes notwithstanding, what struck Hannah as most odd was their homogeneous nature. The men were dressed identically in clean black suits of understated fashion. The woman wore nondescript dresses in pale, lifeless colors, buttoned tightly to their necks. Their bonnets were tied snugly around their chins.

On the surface, they were typical churchgoers. Yet there was something different about them, a definite note of scorn in their stares that put Hannah on edge.

Surely she was seeing disdain where there wasn't any. She was simply feeling vulnerable after her encounter with Rachel and Tyler from the night before. Yes, that must be it.

Then again...

She took a quick survey of her companions. They certainly stood out. Hannah was considerably overdressed in her favorite blue silk dress. While Mavis was underdressed in her men's pants worn under a homemade dress. *Burlap,* no less.

And then there were the two men. Logan wore a suit identical to most of the men in the city, but his cowboy hat, tin star and pair of six-shooters set him apart. Beau, smooth, slick and neat in his brown suit and gold brocade vest, could pass for a man of distinction in any large city.

Hannah couldn't help but notice how he caught the eye of every woman that passed by.

Most probably focused on his physical beauty. Hannah, however, saw his reliability. His strength of character. And his... All right, yes, his outward appeal, as well.

Just looking at him now, her throat went dry, turning her speechless. Following the others a full step behind, she silently mulled over how she would approach her father after all these years.

As much as she wanted to blame Rachel for putting her in such an unpleasant predicament, Hannah also knew it was long past time she confronted Thomas Southerland with the truth.

The truth shall set you free...

Yes, in truth there was power. The power of Christ.

Shooting a quick glance over his shoulder, Beau slowed his pace until he came alongside her.

Logan took the lead without question.

Beau didn't speak right away, and so they walked in companionable silence side by side for several minutes.

A cloud crossed over the sun, deadening the light at the precise moment he broke the hush between them. "I have something to tell you before we get to the church."

At his serious tone, her heart stumbled. "You do?"

As they drew closer to the church, people nodded at Beau. He smiled and nodded back. A few times he responded with a personal greeting.

Waiting until they were alone again, Hannah asked, "Did you give a sermon here before? Is that what you wanted to tell me?"

Beau stopped walking.

She stopped, as well.

A grimness passed over his features. For the first time in their acquaintance, Beauregard O'Toole looked unsure of himself. "You could say that."

There was an odd note to his voice, and an apology in his eyes. Hannah had to work hard to keep her throat from slamming shut. "You don't have to join us this morning," she offered. "If you—"

"I wouldn't miss this opportunity to worship. But I

wanted you to know there might be a woman here, a woman from my past."

She concentrated on his voice, on his words, anything but the implication of what his declaration meant.

"I asked her to marry me."

Hannah's heart took a tumble at the news.

"She said no."

The muscles in Hannah's stomach quivered out of control. Oh, but she was glad. Glad, glad, glad the woman had turned him down. But her joy came from purely selfish reasons. So she made herself respond, made herself speak with sincerity. "I'm sorry, Beau."

He cast a look to the darkening sky, frowned, then gave a short laugh. "I'm not."

Although his tone was mild, he held his shoulders tense and unmoving. No matter what he claimed, the woman's rejection had hurt him.

"I just wanted you to know," he said, lowering his gaze back to hers.

"Why?" she asked. "Why are you telling me this now?"

He planted considerable O'Toole charm in his expression. "Because I wanted you to know about my past. All of it."

He kept his eyes on hers as he spoke—*directly* on hers. And then his gaze filled with a quiet intensity that sent a promise of the future dancing along her skin.

"I don't want any secrets between us," he said.

She laid her hand on his arm. "Thank you for telling me."

Before she could comment any further, Logan stopped short of joining the queue entering the church and stepped slightly back from the crowd.

"Are you two joining us?" he called out.

"Of course." Beau took Hannah's arm and steered her forward.

"Please, go ahead Miss Southerland," Logan said. "You too, Miss Tierney." He offered a smile that encompassed both women.

Mavis hesitated.

Logan held his smile.

Mavis cocked her head at him.

"Ma'am." He winked at her, and then removed his hat. "Ladies first."

At last, she smiled. Sort of. Perhaps it was a baring of teeth; one could never be sure with Mavis.

Before climbing the steps, Hannah slid a final glance toward Beau. His face was a cool mask of indifference, but she could feel that he was wound tighter than before. Wondering at the cause, she followed his gaze to the top of the stairs.

At the threshold of the church stood a young man and woman greeting each person as they walked in.

Looking respectable, yet somehow hard, the man wore a black suit, black tie and crisp, white shirt. His dark hair was cut meticulously close to his head. And his eyes held a severe, hawklike expression.

Hannah ignored the little flutter of uneasiness in her stomach and turned her attention to the woman standing next to the serious man in black.

She looked irritable, and not at all welcoming. Her dark blond hair was pulled into a tight bun, and her face held a pinched expression. She was thin, also perfectly groomed, and yet the most uninviting woman Hannah had ever seen.

They couldn't be the pastor and his wife. And yet, who else would they be?

The young woman's gaze widened as she caught sight of Beau. Her eyes held just a hint of joy at the sight of him but then just as quickly flashed with anger before becoming a blank slate.

Taking an audible breath of air, Beau moved in front of Logan and led their group up the steps himself.

"Why, Reverend O'Toole, we didn't expect you to grace our humble little church with your presence again so soon." The woman's voice came out colder than Hannah would have expected of someone standing outside a church.

Nonetheless, Beau smiled at her. "Amelia, you are looking well."

Amelia fiddled with one of the buttons at the neck of her dress.

Was this the woman Beau had once wanted to marry? The woman who had turned him down?

Beau shifted to look at the stern-looking gentleman and offered his hand. "Jim, that is, Reverend Smith, I understand congratulations are in order."

"Amelia and I were married two months ago." There was a flash of derision in Reverend Smith's eyes as he pumped Beau's hand. Behind the contempt was a challenge, as if he were saying, *Ha, the better man won after all.*

"I bet you could build a mighty large snowman in that bedroom," Mavis whispered through her teeth.

Hannah shushed her.

Taking notice, Amelia's gaze shifted to Hannah. Her

eyes turned flat and her nose went up. "And who is this?" she asked.

Beau boldly took Hannah's hand and gently drew her forward to join him. "This is Miss Hannah Souther-land. She is a dear friend of my family's." Still holding her hand, he gave Hannah a smile that spread warmth all the way through her. "And of mine."

Amelia didn't seem impressed. In fact, her eyes bulged and then narrowed. "A family friend, you say?"

"Yes," Beau said, with a flick of iron in his tone. "She tours with the same acting company as my brother."

"I see."

Hannah had a strong urge to slap the smirk off Amelia's face. But she held back. She had experienced this sort of petty reaction before, especially once her profession was revealed. She wasn't here to start an argument. And after the turmoil of the past week, she just wanted to forget about herself and focus on praising the Lord.

Obviously finished with Hannah, Amelia's eyes searched the rest of their group. The moment her gaze landed on Mavis, she gasped, blinked hard and then whispered to her husband in a furious manner.

Hannah's heart dropped to her toes when she heard the words "prostitute" and "how dare he bring that person here."

Mouth thin, Reverend Smith stuck out his chest. "Reverend O'Toole," he said in a haughty tone that carried halfway down the block. "You cannot bring that woman in here." He pointed directly at Mavis.

Hannah tugged her hand free of Beau's and rushed to Mavis, shifting her slightly behind her. "Mavis is a remark-able woman and I'm honored to call her friend," she said.

Amelia lifted her chin higher still. "I know for a fact that *woman* worked in the brothel at Laramie. I did charity work there once. One doesn't forget a woman like that."

Reverend Smith clicked his tongue in disapproval. "That makes her a—"

"Don't say another word, Jim," Beau warned. There was a quick flash of rage on his face, and almost as quickly it was banked.

His control was impressive.

Just then, a bell tolled the top of the hour. People continued to rush past them as they made their way inside the building. Most looked at their unhappy little group, but none stopped to speak to them.

"Service is starting. We must get inside, Amelia," Reverend Smith said, pivoting on his heel.

Amelia followed suit.

"Not so fast," Beau said. "You would deny us access into the Lord's house on a mere impression from years ago?"

Reverend Smith spun back around. His unsmiling face looked harsh under the bright morning sun. "That woman is a sinner, O'Toole. And thus is not welcome in my church."

"*Your* church? Jesus came to call sinners into His church, Jim, not the righteous," Beau said, his eyes hard. Clearly, he wasn't bothering to hide his anger from them now.

Reverend Smith's gaze was just as unrelenting. "You know we have a covenant. Sinners who have failed to repent publicly are not allowed inside our church. It's how we protect our congregation from evil."

Hannah actually saw the pulse jump in Beau's throat. "How do you know she hasn't repented?" he asked.

"I...*know*."

"You can see into another's heart?" Beau asked, stepping in front of both Mavis and Hannah and easing them behind him. "And here I thought only God could do that."

Amelia snorted. "We all know what she is. Just look at her. It's obvious she's a harlot."

Beau lowered his voice to a dangerous whisper. "She is a child of God."

Hannah had never seen Beau so angry. She reached out and touched his forearm. "I think it's time we left."

Beau's gaze still burned, but he covered her hand with his and leaned slightly toward her.

Wide-eyed, Amelia blinked at Hannah's hand on Beau's arm, clearly shocked at the public intimacy.

Hannah quickly dropped her hand. The woman could easily spew poison over the innocent gesture. Beau deserved better. "I don't much care for your brand of Christianity," Hannah blurted out.

"Nor I," Beau agreed.

Amelia gurgled in indignation.

"You cannot bring that woman in my church," the pastor boomed. His face a study in scorn.

At the unconcealed insult, Logan joined in Mavis's defense. "I don't care if you are a minister. Nobody talks to Miss Tierney like that. *Nobody*."

He pushed all three of their party aside and stood toe-to-toe with the pastor, prepared to do bodily harm to the man.

Beau nudged Logan back. "Let me handle this,

Deputy." He looked at Hannah. "Take Mavis back to the hotel. I'll rejoin you in the lobby and escort you to the depot before our train leaves."

Nodding, Hannah pulled gently on Mavis's arm. Mavis turned to look at her then. Devastation wavered in the other woman's eyes.

Hannah blinked back tears of her own. "Let's go, sweetie," she said.

Mavis shook her head. "We leave together." She twined her other arm with Logan's. "Isn't that right, boy?"

"That's right, Miss Tierney."

"You may call me old woman, if you like."

Logan leaned over and kissed Mavis on the cheek. "I'd be honored."

Amelia snorted at the show of affection between the two.

Beau's eyes narrowed coldly. "I don't know how you both got so hard of heart. You've read the same Bible as I have. If we are to follow Christ's example, that means we should bring up a person's past only so that we may point to the future with love, not condemnation."

Tossing his shoulders back, Reverend Smith glared. "You dare lecture me?"

Beau sighed, and although his eyes still blazed with anger he lowered his voice. "You're right. It's not my place." He turned on his heel and looked at the rest of their group. "Let's go."

Hannah, still linked with Mavis, waited for Beau to pass them and then lead their group down the street. He walked at a clipped, angry pace. Compelled, she released Mavis's arm and trotted to catch up with him.

"I only have one thing to say to you," she said.

He looked at her. Fury, anger and sadness shimmered in his gaze. She had a sudden urge to hug away his pain.

Instead, she said, "Amelia didn't deserve you."

His expression didn't change, but his eyes softened with an emotion she couldn't quite define. "Thank you," he said.

And with those two simple words, her future turned a little clearer.

Beau wasn't a man who liked being wrong. It went against his nature. Yet, he had been wrong on so many points.

Tyler, of all people, had been right.

For years, Beau had thought he'd wanted what Jim and Amelia had. But he'd forgotten about the Rocky Mountain Association's required covenant for all its member churches. The covenant stated that known sinners were not allowed inside the building without having publicly confessed their sins in front of the congregation the week before.

Although the covenant was designed to prevent its members from living in unapologetic sin, it also made it impossible for a pastor to shepherd those in his flock still questioning their salvation. Certainly, none of the people Beau had ministered to in the last five years would be allowed to enter his church in Greeley.

He would not be allowed to minister to women like Jane Goodwin on their deathbed, for fear their sin would rub off on others. There were so many other restrictions, as well.

Too many.

Tyler had claimed that Beau would die a slow death in a church like Jim's.

Tyler had been spot-on with his assessment.

But Beau didn't want to keep traveling forever. There had to be a way to reconcile his dream of a stable church home with his unique calling to the lost.

There is, Beau. Look deeper in your heart. The answer is there.

Still confused, Beau shook his head. He knew God guided his life. Nothing happened to him by chance. Perhaps this upcoming journey to Reverend Southerland's home would reveal the answers he sought. Perhaps this bump in the road had been part of God's plan all along. Perhaps Beau needed to listen to God more, and talk less.

On more matters than starting his own church.

As he sat on a bench outside the train station, Beau watched Hannah's gentle treatment of Mavis. The older woman was still sad and hurt over Amelia's abominable treatment of her. No wonder. Amelia had claimed to see inside Mavis's heart.

Beau had done the same with Hannah.

The dangerous combination of impulse, pride and temper had colored his initial judgment of her. He was no better than the very people he criticized.

"Don't let that nasty young woman get to you," Hannah said, her soft voice cutting across his thoughts. "She was *wrong* to say those things about you."

"She spoke the truth." Mavis's eyes filled with tears of shame. The kind of shame the enemy used to keep God's children separated from Him. "I am a former prostitute with sins a mile long that can never be taken back."

Beau moved closer, prepared to boldly speak of God's love, but Hannah continued. "No, Mavis. Your sins are in the past. You're a godly woman now."

A lone tear rolled down Mavis's cheek.

Hannah gripped one of the older woman's hands.

"What I did is the worst sin of them all," Mavis said.

Beau had heard a similar argument from Jane. No longer able to keep silent, he said, "There's no hierarchy of sin in God's eyes. Sin is sin. But God can *and* does forgive all. You just have to ask for His forgiveness."

Beau took Mavis's other hand and nodded for Hannah to continue.

She gave him a grateful smile. "You are a beautiful, kindhearted woman, my friend. The children of Charity House love you. And we all know children are excellent judges of character."

Mavis gave them both a watery smile. "Don't forget small animals. I have a way with them small animals, too."

Hannah laughed. "There you go."

"You're a good girl, Hannah Southerland."

"Yes," Beau agreed. "Yes, she is."

He shared a look with Hannah before he released Mavis's hand and the two women hugged. He couldn't believe he'd once considered Amelia his ideal image of a wife, while he'd considered this beautiful, softhearted actress inappropriate in all ways.

Forgive me, Lord.

Boot heels clicked in rapid succession along the platform. "Sorry I'm late. I got detained at the jail." Logan deposited the last of the luggage on the platform. "I've received an urgent telegram from Marshal Scott. I have to pick up a prisoner in Laramie and escort him back to Denver for trial. I've already hired a horse for my journey."

The way Logan refused to make eye contact with him alerted Beau that trouble brewed.

Taking Logan by the arm, he led the young deputy out of earshot of the women. "Did you truly get a telegraph from Marshal Scott?"

Clearly offended, Logan glared at him. But instead of responding, he yanked a piece of paper from the inner pocket of his jacket and shoved it under Beau's nose.

"That's not what I meant." Beau lowered the man's hand by applying pressure to his wrist. "Are you using this as an excuse to go back to that church and defend Mavis before you head out of town?"

Logan made a noncommittal grunt that could have meant either yes or no.

Beau pressed for an answer. "I want a firm response out of you."

Logan's gaze darted all around, bounced off Mavis then back to the platform. "Maybe."

"Don't do it, Logan. Violence won't solve anything."

"It couldn't hurt to try."

Beau blew out a slow breath. "You know that's not true. You're not thinking rationally. Now, give me your word you won't do something stupid. Stupid, as in defending Mavis's honor with a fist to Reverend Smith's face."

"And here I thought that oily pastor needed a little rearranging of those pretty, girlish features."

"I'm picking up the sarcasm."

"Gee, truly?"

Beau felt a line of annoyance carve its way into his forehead. "I want your word you're finished with Smith."

Logan scowled. "You're as relentless as Marc Dupree. Especially when you know a well-placed right hook would give you just as much satisfaction as it would me."

Beau looked away, just for a moment, so Logan wouldn't see his amusement and consider it silent agreement. "I won't condone violence."

"Fine." Logan gave him a frustrated sigh. "I won't go back to the church before I head out of town."

"And?"

"And." Logan grinned in a wolfish, arrogant pull of lips over teeth. "I won't hit the pastor so hard in his nose it'll mess up his pretty face forever."

Beau rubbed a hand down his face. "Can I trust you're a man of your word?"

Logan snorted at him. "I said I wouldn't go back, and I won't. But, you gotta admit, it's certainly a tempting idea—"

"*Logan.*"

Logan held up his hand. "You have my word."

Beau finally allowed the smile tugging at his lips free rein. "That's enough for me."

"Can I go tell Mavis and Miss Southerland goodbye now, or do you need to yell at me some more?"

Beau waved him off with a flick of his wrist. "Go on. Say your farewells."

Logan swung around, stopped and looked back over his shoulder. "For the record, you handled that pastor and his wife real well. You're a far better man than I am."

Beau had his doubts. Serious doubts. After all, now that Logan had given him the idea, he wasn't sure he wouldn't head back to the church himself and—how did the lawman put it?—rearrange Reverend Smith's pretty face.

Apparently, Beau needed to work on a few of his anger issues. But at the moment, he had other matters on his mind. Matters concerning his future.

Tyler had planted a seed. So had Marc Dupree.

Jim and Amelia, unbeknownst to them, had watered them both.

Now, with the Lord's help, Beau needed to figure out the particulars.

Chapter Eighteen

The train ride to Colorado Springs had gone far too quickly, Hannah thought as she stood on the platform of the train depot just outside town. Five years. Five full years had passed since she'd left home. Nothing had changed.

Everything had changed.

She had changed.

The early-morning air slapped her in the nose and stung her throat. Pike's Peak, purple in color under the soft dawn light, rose high above the land, lifting its mighty face past the clouds as if to say *I'm larger than the earth can handle.*

The welcoming smell of fresh pine filled her nostrils.

She had returned.

But was she home?

Time would tell.

One thing was certain: Hannah had matured in the last five years. She was twenty-six years old, a fully grown woman with a large amount of money saved. Would it make a difference? Would she be strong enough to face her father as the confident woman she'd become? Or would she fall back into old patterns and turn into the surly, arrogant, young girl with a boulder-size chip on her shoulder?

Reviewing the past with an adult perspective, she now understood her father's disapproval of her. She'd been a willful child. Hard to handle. But, in her defense, she'd been missing her mother. And with her father choosing to favor Rachel, Hannah had felt abandoned.

Well, she was here now. Prepared to the reveal the truth and ask for her father's forgiveness.

The rest would be up to him.

Glancing around, she wondered why he wasn't at the depot. She'd sent a telegraph ahead to warn him of her impending arrival. That small courtesy had been Beau's suggestion, one Hannah had initially fought. She'd relented because she'd known he'd been right.

As usual.

She looked over at him standing next to Mavis, who was guarding their baggage as though she expected some miscreant to steal their valuables. Hannah could only smile at the silly, adorable picture the old woman made sitting perched on top of the pile of bags. Laced up in Hannah's fancy boots, Mavis's feet dangled near the ground without quite reaching the wooden platform.

Hannah's heart clenched. Mavis was a grown woman, nearing the end of her life, with a childlike joy for living. Hannah loved the old dear as if she'd been her own grandmother.

Beau shifted his stance, drawing Hannah's attention back to him. She worried for him, more than she probably should. He'd been quiet on the journey from Wyoming to Colorado. Was he mourning the loss of Amelia?

Why did that thought steal her breath?

He turned slightly to consider the mountains. She took the opportunity to study him. She cataloged his handsome features, one by one, starting with the aristocratic sweep of his nose that was so much like his mother's. And the strong jawline that came straight from his father and proclaimed his O'Toole heritage.

Her heart stumbled at the sight of all that masculine strength of character. For a brief moment she couldn't gulp in enough air. She couldn't think. It was just a moment, but her world tilted, her head grew light and she knew. Oh, she knew.

She loved him.

She loved Beauregard O'Toole.

But instead of bringing fear, she felt an inner peace she'd never known before. And then a soft voice whispered from deep within her. *Everything will work for the best for both of you, together.*

The thought brought some comfort. But they had a long way to go to become a "both of you, together." For one, Beau wasn't on board with the "both of you, together" part. But he would be. And she would be.

And, together, they would be—

A hard clearing of a throat jolted her out of her thoughts. "The prodigal daughter returns."

Hannah froze.

With panic clawing at her throat, she pivoted around to stare at the man who had banished her from his home five years ago.

There was no mistaking this was her father. The harsh features and unyielding expression in his eyes were the same as always.

He still judged her.

After all these years.

Why, Lord? Why?

Numb from too many emotions surging through her blood, she blinked up at him.

He looked older. Thinner. More haggard.

And so very, very sad. She'd never noticed that sadness before. It made him seem more approachable. Yet all the more distant.

"Hello, Father."

He didn't acknowledge her greeting, merely cast his gaze around the platform. "Where is your sister?"

"She—"

"What's happened? What have you done to her? What—"

"Reverend Southerland?" Beau cut him off in mid-sentence.

Hannah didn't know where Beau had come from. Or when he had joined them. She hadn't realized he could move so quickly and without any sound.

Then again, she couldn't hear anything over the pounding of her pulse rushing in her ears.

"Reverend O'Toole." Her father's gaze collided with Beau's and his eyes sharpened to thin slits. "What, may I ask, are you doing here?"

"I am escorting your daughter, sir."

Beau held the other man's gaze, but he didn't explain any further.

Why not? Hannah wondered.

Her father's chin rose a mere fraction of an inch, but it was enough to indicate his genuine displeasure. His brow scrunched into a disapproving frown. Hannah was familiar with the look. She'd been on the receiving end far too often.

"You traveled with Hannah?"

Beau nodded, but still he kept silent on the particulars. "Alone?"

Beau lifted a shoulder.

In that moment, Hannah realized this was some sort of standoff between the two men, a masculine battle of wills she didn't understand.

"You're not helping matters," she whispered to Beau. "Tell him the rest."

Beau kept his gaze locked with her father's.

"Beau, please."

He didn't budge. Not one single inch.

Nor did her father.

Hannah sniffed her impatience at them both.

Did they have to be such…men?

"Father," she said. "Reverend O'Toole was good enough to accompany *both* Mavis and me on our journey."

Her father's quick eyebrow flick was the only measure of his surprise. "And who might this Mavis be?"

Hannah resisted the urge to tug on her collar and straighten her skirt. She ran her tongue across her teeth and pointed to Mavis, who chose that moment to adjust her chamois strap and shoot out a stream of spit between her front teeth.

Sensing inspection, she looked up and gave them her trademark gap-toothed grin. The gesture was pure Mavis Tierney, with a bit of an imp thrown in for good measure.

"Ah." Reverend Southerland dismissed Mavis with a grunt and returned his attention to Beau. "I would have expected you to be in Greeley by now, working with the committee on the plans for the new church building."

Beau's shoulders relaxed. With a hard blink, he wiped his features of all expression. "I was called to Denver on a personal matter, sir. A family friend was in need."

"That's where I met Reverend Southerland," Hannah said. "In Denver."

She wanted to say more, but she was jostled by someone walking by, reminding her they weren't alone on the platform.

When she stumbled, Beau rushed to her aid. He steadied her with one hand on her back and the other on her arm.

Her father frowned at them both, but Beau didn't release her until she found her balance.

"Where is your sister, Hannah?" His gaze traveled across the platform, then darted back to her. "What have you done with her?"

"That's why we're here," she said. "To tell you of Rachel's...fate."

Shock and worry traced a hard line along his forehead. "Is she hurt? Ill?"

His concern was so familiar, so painfully genuine, that it broke Hannah's heart. Her father had never, *never,* worried about her like that. "She is well."

"I don't understand."

Hannah sighed. "I know. And that's my fault. I—"

"So you haven't changed."

At the disappointment she heard in her father's tone, her stomach knotted. She wanted to toss Rachel's letters at him and run. But Hannah wasn't that impetuous, angry little girl anymore. She was a woman, a mature woman of independent means. God had brought her to this point in her life to end the lies of the past.

She would not cower now.

"No, Father, in that you're wrong. I *have* changed." She lifted her head and stared Thomas Southerland in the eyes. "In more ways than one."

But whether the change was for good or evil was all a matter of perspective.

Beau could not stand the pain on Hannah's face any longer. But he had to show respect to her father, for her sake. Starting an argument now would only hurt her more. He'd already made matters worse with that silent battle of wills of a few moments ago. Yet how could he show respect when all he wanted to do was slam his fist into the other man's nose?

Didn't Thomas Southerland see how much pain he was causing his daughter? It was one thing to threaten Beau with his future in Greeley. That was man-to-man. But what sort of parent had such little regard for his own child as to treat her so coldly and with such lack of affection?

"Reverend Southerland," Beau said, clearing his throat of the resentment he heard in his own tone. "I think we should find another, less populated spot to speak further. I assure you, we will explain everything." Beau didn't add that the explanation would not be to the reverend's satisfaction.

As though yanked out of a trance, Reverend Southerland shook his head and began moving toward Mavis and the baggage.

Mavis stood, winked and then offered her hand.

"I'm Mavis. And I say any father of Hannah's is a friend of mine."

He gave a noncommittal grunt and completely ignored her outstretched hand.

She sighed, rolled her eyes to heaven and stepped aside so he could lift the largest of the pieces of luggage off the top of the pile.

Beau followed his lead and began hoisting bags, as well.

They were a silent group as they left the train depot and loaded their belongings into the reverend's smart carriage. It wasn't until they were in the heart of town and stopping in front of a hotel that Beau realized the good reverend was not going to open his home to any of them.

As healing old wounds went, it was a vile start. For Hannah's sake, Beau hoped this obvious slight was merely a temporary show of distrust on the reverend's part and not the start of worse things to come.

Chapter Nineteen

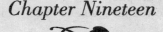

"I respectfully disagree, Reverend Southerland," Beau said, lowering his voice so the other diners in the hotel restaurant wouldn't hear the angry edge in his tone. He was glad Hannah was still up in her room, changing into fresh clothing. She didn't need to hear this conversation. "You don't know either of your daughters very well."

"Might I remind you exactly who you are talking to?" The older man leaned forward. He kept his voice equally low, but his anger was just as evident as Beau's. "I have the power to pull the Rocky Mountain Association's support from your new church. One word in the right ear is all it would take."

Beau acknowledged the threat with a low growl. He held back from open defiance. Giving in to his temper now would be nothing more than a dangerous indulgence, so he forced a bland expression on his face. "Nevertheless, you have misjudged both women."

With predatory slowness, Reverend Southerland sat back, rested his elbows on the arms of his chair and then steepled his fingers under his chin. "You dare judge me?"

Beau blew out a tense breath that scalded his throat. He wanted to give his anger free rein, wanted to let it spread, but that would only hurt Hannah in the end. So he rubbed a hand down his face and relaxed his shoulders. "I'm only speaking the truth as I see it."

"Ah, truth." The reverend spoke with a perfect mix of challenge and scorn. "You sit there, with your youthful arrogance and bold words of truth, yet who are you to speak of such matters? You, who spends his time in brothels, mining camps and saloons. You once came to me and said you wanted out of that life, yet I wonder. Do you enjoy living amongst sinners, Reverend O'Toole?"

Beau bristled. How many times had Beau heard this same accusation from men who should know better?

Jesus himself had lived and eaten among tax collectors and sinners. Beau was only trying to model his life after his Lord and Savior. "Sinners are in need of the love of Christ as well as the righteous, perhaps more."

The older man's cold, black eyes swept over him. Hesitation flickered over his harsh features, softening them for a tense moment. He looked as if he fought an internal battle. And lost. "What you say is true enough, to a certain extent. But our association has a strict doctrine that must be obeyed. Without exception, members are to be excluded from the church for the sins of intoxication, disorderly conduct and living in adultery, to name only a few."

Beau felt the other man's annoyance. And wondered at it. Yet he couldn't stop himself from defending the Jane Goodwins, the Megans and even the Matties of the world. "The covenant also states that exclusion can be rescinded if the sinner appears at the next church service, confesses and asks for forgiveness."

"Which they never do."

The clear sign of defeat in the other man's eyes took Beau by surprise. Determined to have his say, he placed his palms on the table and pressed forward. "What of those excluded? Do we just let them live damned forever? What of the parable of the lost sheep?"

"A pretty ideal, O'Toole, but in my experience most are happy in their sin."

Beau should have been outraged at the observations, but he saw the genuine disappointment in other man's eyes, the lost hope that the world could never be different. Sadly, Reverend Southerland had given up and taken the easier path of excluding those who needed him most.

Beau couldn't let such a tragedy pass without comment. "Perhaps it's time for a change in how the Association ministers to the lost," he ventured.

Reverend Southerland's expression instantly closed. "Young people put too much emphasis on change."

In that moment, Beau's confusion disappeared. Right then. Right there. The answer he'd been seeking had been there, waiting for him, in Isaiah 1:17. *Learn to do right! Seek justice, encourage the oppressed. Defend the cause of the fatherless...*

Yes. Beau would go where God was leading him, right to the spot where the Heavenly Father was already working.

"It's time for a *real* change," Beau whispered aloud.

A snort was the reverend's immediate response. "When young people say *change* what they mean is rebellion. Take my Hannah, for example." The lack of grief and defeat in his eyes was as unexpected as it was unbearable.

Beau shifted in his seat. "You're wrong, Reverend Southerland. Hannah doesn't need to change. She is the most kindhearted, Christian woman I have had the pleasure of knowing."

"She is an actress." And with those four simple words, the angry, closed-minded pastor returned.

"She is so much more." A sense of urgency swam through Beau's mind, thundered in his chest. "Yes, she is an actress, but one who follows the same Almighty God you introduced her to when she was a child."

A tiny spark of hope lit in Reverend Southerland's eyes, right before it was doused with a bold slash of skepticism. "You know this about her? How?"

Beau took a deep breath and began regaling Reverend Southerland with every glorious detail of the daughter he never knew, starting with her work at Charity House.

At precisely an hour after arriving in Colorado Springs, Hannah went in search of her father and Beau. She'd left Mavis with strict orders to stay in their hotel room and consequently out of trouble.

Mavis had responded with the same saucy wink she'd tossed at Hannah's father on the train platform. But then she'd given Hannah her word and a swift, bone-rattling hug of encouragement.

Mavis had become a genuine friend.

The thought gave Hannah comfort as she made her way across the lobby. With nerves fluttering in her stomach, she barely took note of the expensive decor, hardly eyed the rose-patterned wallpaper.

The only sound she heard over the beat of her heart

was her heels clicking along the marble-tiled floor.
Click, click, click. Like a clock marking time.

This would be the hardest meeting in her life, far
harder than that first night backstage of the theater. Unpleasant memories assailed her. She let them come.
Desperate, alone and full of shame from her father's
words of condemnation, she'd joined a traveling troupe
headed to New York the very night of her banishment.

Instead of punishing her for her sins, God had protected her on that initial journey toward independence.
Her outer beauty had opened the door to an immediate
position in the troupe. Once in New York, God had led
her straight into the loving world of Patience and
Reginald O'Toole.

Thank you, Lord.

As prayers went, it was one of her shortest. As passionate intent went, it was one of her most fervent.

Click. Click. Click.

Her heels hammered against the marble, echoing
through the cavernous lobby. Each step took Hannah
closer to her father and one final confrontation. This
time, however, she would face him as an adult. She
would tell him about Rachel, hand over the two letters
and then confess her own sins. No matter his reaction,
Hannah would be free.

It is for freedom that Christ has set us free.

This was it, then. Her chance to stand firm.

A quick burst of fear stole her breath. The resulting
pain was repulsive, like sharp, needle-thin icicles
stabbing in her chest.

Lord Jesus, please fill me with Your courage.

Drawing in a tight breath, she stuffed her gloved hands

in the pocket of her skirt. Her fingers connected with Rachel's letters, and the air hitched in her throat again.

Almost there.

Pasting a smile on her lips, Hannah negotiated the final corner then circled her gaze around the dining room. At the height of the noon-hour rush, most of the tables were full. She continued searching for her father.

There he was, in the back left corner. Sitting at a table with Beau.

Her smile slipped.

From their body language, she could tell that they were in a heated discussion. Even from this distance she could see that they each kept their voices in check.

However, both had an identical look of intensity in their eyes. Both leaned forward, neither backing down from the other's heated words.

They were so similar. Why hadn't she noticed that before? Why hadn't she acknowledged the parallel?

She waited for the rush of antagonism from the sudden insight. It never came. And then she knew. She wasn't angry at her father, had never been so.

She was hurt. She was sad. And yet, she was...hopeful.

Oh, Lord, do I need his approval that badly? Am I that weak?

Maybe she was. Maybe when it came to her father, she *was* that weak.

Shattered. Everything in her felt like it was shattering into tiny pieces.

Is this what it feels like to have a heart break, Lord? I love my father and I need his love in return, but he doesn't love me. Not enough.

As if sensing her presence, Beau glanced up and quickly rose from his seat to gesture for her to come closer. As she wove a path between the tables, the drone of the other diners drummed in her ears. Her head grew dizzy from the effort to focus on Beau. Only Beau.

So much strength there.

With each step she took, her pulse slowed, while everyone around her seemed to speak and move at a quickened pace.

At last she drew alongside the table, and her father finally rose, as well.

Beau touched her arm and smiled at her. The support in his gaze made her want to smile in return, but she couldn't make her trembling lips obey.

For courage, she retrieved Rachel's letters and clutched them in her fist.

Still smiling, Beau held out his chair for her then dropped his head close to her ear. "Remember, you aren't alone. I'm with you. God is with you." He straightened and then spoke loud enough for her father's ears. "I'll leave you two to speak privately."

Her hand shot out and gripped his arm. "No, please stay."

Gently pulling her hand free, he pressed on her shoulder until she sat down in the empty chair. "It will be all right, Hannah. Your father is willing to listen to the truth now."

"I—"

"I'll be across the room if you need me." He leaned forward and kissed her on the cheek.

Her father's gasp alerted Hannah to his opinion of Beau's public display. She refused to cringe.

"I'll wait for you," Beau said. His eyes told her he meant more than merely waiting for the end of this conversation.

Did he return her feelings, then? Was there a chance for them to be together?

Her father cleared his throat. In a single sweep, Beau lifted his hand off her shoulder and walked away.

Needing a moment to gather her courage, she watched him go.

"That young man certainly thinks highly of you. If half of what he said is true, I've misjudged you."

Unsure what he meant, Hannah turned her attention back to her father. "I...I'm sorry, what did you say?"

Watching her with a speculative look in his eyes, he lifted a glass of water to his lips, sipped slowly, then set the glass back on the table. "I see it's mutual."

"It is?" Her stomach twisted in a frightening mix of hope and dread. "What is?"

And what an odd conversation to have with her father after so many years had passed.

"You both wear your hearts in your eyes." His tone was not unkind. Rather, it was a bit wistful, as was the expression in his gaze.

"It's the same way I used to look at your mother."

There was sadness in his words. An emotion she knew all too well. The mention of her mother brought back so many memories. Too many to sort through all at once. "I still miss her," Hannah said.

Her father merely nodded. Took another sip of his water.

Couldn't he say more? Couldn't he make this easier for them both? Hannah balled her hands into fists, the sound of crumpling paper reminding her why he couldn't give her the benefit of the doubt.

Rachel stood between them.

"I have a letter for you from my sister." Her voice broke. She couldn't stop it, didn't even try.

The expression in his eyes turned unreadable as he stretched out his palm.

She handed him the two letters. "The top one is for you. The other is for Will."

His mouth thinned as he examined the folded pages in his hand. The waiter chose that moment to ask for Hannah's order. "I'm not eating," she said. "Thank you, though."

Clearly baffled, his eyes shifted to her father. He dismissed the young man with a flick of his wrist. "We'll let you know if we need anything else."

"Very well, sir."

By the time the waiter scurried off, her father was bent over Rachel's letter. His gaze ran furiously across the page. His abrupt gasp was the most emotion Hannah had seen him display in her entire life. There was such fury in the sound. Such anger. And pain. So. Much. Pain.

At last, he folded the letter with agonizing slowness and said, "To run off with an *actor.*" His voice cracked. "I don't understand why she would do such a thing."

Hannah crossed her arms around her waist and tried to hug away the cold. "I'm sorry, Father," she whispered. "But it's true."

He looked at her with tears in his eyes. At the obvious sign of his vulnerability, a fist of ice clutched around her heart and squeezed. She didn't know what to say in the face of such raw emotion. He'd always been a rock. A stone-faced rock.

"It makes no sense," he said. "This is so unlike her."

With awkward movements, Hannah reached out and touched his hand but he flinched away from her.

Shaking his head, he blinked away the tears and then narrowed his eyes. "Did you have something to do with this?"

Determined to be truthful, Hannah sat back and folded all emotion deep inside her and nodded. "I introduced them."

"That's not what I meant. Did you talk her into marrying him?"

"No." She forced herself to sit still under his penetrating stare. "I *insisted.*"

"And Reverend O'Toole? Am I to assume he performed the ceremony?"

"Yes." She held up her hand before he could speak over her. "Rachel ran off with Tyler. Beau married them once they were found. Those are the facts, but not the entire truth. For that, let me start at the beginning."

And she did. At the very beginning, at the scene of her mother's deathbed. She explained about her promise to care for Rachel, and all the subsequent lies Hannah had told to protect her sister ever since.

As she spoke, her father never once interrupted, but he looked at her with devastated eyes. When she got to the part about the affair with Mr. Beamer, another, equally horrified change came over him. And his eyes widened with alarm. "Weeks later, she tried to tell me *she* had the affair, not you."

The muscles in Hannah's stomach shook. Perhaps Rachel had tried to explain. But it had been too little, too late. "You didn't believe her, did you?"

He shut his eyes and released a shudder. "Of course not."

"No, why would you?" For a moment, a tiny one, everything seemed to slow down while Hannah's thinking sped up. A tiny trickle of apprehension slid between her shoulder blades as one thought surfaced. In her own way, Hannah had been as guilty as Rachel.

"Can you forgive me, Father?"

"But you said you didn't commit any of the...sins." The merciless look in his eyes would have made a brave woman quiver. Hannah was not a brave woman.

Nevertheless, she had come this far. "No. I've sinned, as well. In my own way. I bore false witness," she whispered. "All these years, I allowed you to believe one lie after another. Thinking I owed it to Mama, I played my role."

And all these years she'd thought of herself as the victim, the tragic heroine in the story of her life. But the reality was nothing so glamorous. How could she not have seen her own ugly role? How could she have lied to herself?

"I was ready to believe the stories. I never questioned them. Not once. I wanted to believe you were the bad sister." His eyes turned haunted. "For that, I owe you my own apology."

Hannah held her breath. A little crack in her heart opened, begging him to fill it with fatherly love. "Father? Are you saying you believe me now?"

"You were so close to your mother. She relied on you

because you were strong, like her. You are so much like her." He shook his head, blinked. "Even now, I see her in you, in the way you hold your head high, in the way you look me straight in the eyes." He released a shaky sigh, his sorrow stripping away the hard exterior. "When she died, I saw too much of her in you. Perhaps I resented you for that."

In spite of the pain and anger she'd harbored all these years, a portion of her own resentment washed away with his confession. "Perhaps you were grieving in your own way."

"That was no excuse." For once, the hard tone of judgment was centered on himself.

Hannah reached out and gripped his hand. This time he didn't pull away. But even through her glove, his fingers were ice-cold. "We were both wrong," she said.

"Yes, we were."

The ragged shake of his breath was identical to hers. But then his gaze fell to the other letter, and he abruptly released her hand to grip it in his fist. "Will," he whispered. "This will devastate him."

With a sinking heart, Hannah lowered her gaze to her lap. Her hands were shaking. She couldn't deny that his obvious devotion to Will Turner hurt. "I know you love Will like the son you never had."

"I must be the one to tell him." He motioned to the waiter and took care of the bill in a frenzy of orders and money tossed to the table.

Watching her father's agitated movements, Hannah tried not to feel abandoned. "Of course." She allowed herself a tight smile. "You should go to him at once."

He rose. "Yes."

Hannah stood, as well, and caught sight of Beau heading quickly toward them.

Her father shut his eyes a moment and took a deep breath. "Hannah, we have much yet to discuss, but I fear Will must be told of Rachel's marriage. Would you and your friends do me the honor of coming to my home for supper this evening?"

Beau arrived before she could respond. It was a comfort to have him standing next to her. Like an anchor in turbulent seas.

His gaze searched hers, a question raising his eyebrows. "Is everything all right here?" he asked.

"Yes, everything is fine," Hannah said to him. Then she turned to her father. "Thank you for the invitation. We would be pleased to dine with you this evening."

He nodded. "Be at my home promptly at six-thirty."

His tone was gruff, demanding, and, as always, he refused to accept any argument on the matter.

What had she expected? A complete change in the course of a single conversation?

"We'll be there on time."

No, Hannah would make sure they arrived a full five minutes ahead of schedule. Just to be safe. Just to be respectable. Just to be…contrary. A smile tugged at her lips.

Apparently, a single conversation hadn't completely changed her, either.

Chapter Twenty

Beau took Hannah's hand as he led her down Monument Street. With a brief smile, he tightened his grip and pulled her a little closer. The smell of pine was strong in the air tonight. Crickets clicked out their evening song. The city gas lamps provided a golden glow at their feet, making the world seem a little softer, a little more welcoming.

With each step away from her childhood home, Beau could feel the tension leaving Hannah. They'd had a pleasant enough evening with her father, all things considered, but Beau had sensed the conflicting emotions rushing through her. By the end of the meal, she'd been trembling with nerves and bravely hiding that fact behind a serene smile and gracious manners.

Her acting abilities were good. But not that good. No one, not even his glorious mother, was *that* good.

Consequently, Beau's protective instincts had reared, and he'd invited her for this walk. Right now he wanted a moment alone with her, to enjoy her company and discuss anything other than her sister, his brother and painful childhood memories.

"Hannah, I—"

"Beau, I—"

They laughed together, their voices uniting in flawless harmony. A surge of satisfaction filled him. Tonight,
everything felt right. "You first," he said.

She paused, turned to look him in the eyes. The big
silver moon cast its pale light across her face, making
her look ethereal and fragile. A storybook heroine come
to life. A surge of affection jammed the breath in his
throat. Beau would not risk losing the gift that stood
right in front of him by focusing on what he didn't yet
have and certainly couldn't control.

No matter where his ministry took him in the future,
no matter where he settled, he wanted to spend a lifetime comforting and protecting this woman. If she
would have him.

"I just wanted to thank you," she said, her eyes
burning with silent gratitude. "I don't know what you
said to my father at the hotel, but by the time I sat down
he was willing to listen to me, actually listen. More so
than he's done since my mother passed away."

Beau lifted her hand to his lips, forgetting everything
but how soft her skin felt against his palm. "I merely told
him you are the most amazing woman of my acquaintance
and that he'd regret losing an opportunity to know you."

"Oh, Beau." Tears spiked along her lashes.

Like most men, Beau was helpless around feminine
tears. But Hannah's slaughtered him. The reflex to hold
her came so fast, so powerful, he had to shut his eyes
and pray for strength. He silently counted his heartbeats—one, two, three—until he had control over his
baser impulses.

"Hannah, my beautiful Hannah, I can't tell you how sorry I am for the way I treated you at our first meeting." He pressed a finger to her lips to prevent her from interrupting him. "I know you've already forgiven me," he began. "I know we've moved beyond this, but I still feel the need to make it up to you."

"You already have." She smiled at him, that soft lifting of lips that punched him straight in the heart. "You came here with me, knowing my father could take away your new church."

"That no longer matters." He was startled by the surge of peace that came with the declaration. "I've been fooling myself for so many years, chasing a dream I only *thought* I wanted. Tyler was the first to help me see the truth."

"Of all people." But her eyes told him she didn't doubt that his brother had helped him. That was part of Hannah's appeal—her ability to see the good in others, even when no one else could.

It was why he loved her. And, oh yes, he loved her. With all his heart.

And that was why he had to confess all. "I thought if I could settle in a nice church in the meadow, I could win the good people's support. Their approval. And then, once I'd earned their trust, I would open the doors to others, the outcasts."

"Oh, Beau, don't you know how courageous you are?" She patted his cheek.

Such pretty eyes. Such softness.

His stomach did a quick pitch.

When had this woman's approval become so important to him? Far more important than a shaky dream surrounding an elusive brick and mortar building.

"I've always thought I was too stubborn, too arrogant, to be a good preacher," he said. "I thought if I could find a calm, sedate wife, she would help smooth my rough edges and take the flamboyant son of an actor out of me."

Her gaze softened with understanding. "You would die in a life like that."

Home. Family. Permanence. Those were the things he'd always wanted. Still did. He hadn't realized God would give them to him in an unexpected way. But God had made him wait for his perfect match. In the process, Beau had learned patience. And now, he understood that the best things in life were worth a little delay now and then.

"All this time, I thought I had to prove I was a man of God by fitting into the usual image of what that looks like."

"Oh, Beau." She sighed. "You serve so many just as you are—the kind of people who would never learn of God's mercy if you didn't teach them." She cupped his cheek. There was acceptance in her gaze, a quiet understanding that eased his concerns. Hannah Southerland drew feelings out of him no one else ever had.

It was a heady sensation. One he rather enjoyed. And hoped to continue enjoying the rest of his life.

"Did I ever tell you how proud your parents are of you?" she asked. "They speak of you with such love. It would break their hearts if they thought you were unhappy because of them."

A quick flash of guilt kicked in his gut. He tried to talk and coughed out air instead. Gulping, he tried again. "All this time, I've thought of my childhood as a curse. But now I see that the constant travel and inconsistencies, all my dealings with crazy characters on and off the stage, were equipping me to do the work God had planned specifically for my life."

"You've found out who you are."

"Yes."

"I'm happy for you, Beau."

Her gentle tone affected him far more than her words. "There's only one thing missing." The hope in her eyes gave him the courage to continue. "Hannah, I want you to be... No." He stopped himself.

What was he thinking?

After what Tyler and Rachel had done, he couldn't let impulse drive his actions. Hannah deserved better.

Their future demanded more.

He looked over his shoulder, back toward her father's house. The lights were still blazing. There was time yet tonight. If he hurried.

"I want to do this right," he said and touched her cheek. With gentle fingers, he pushed her hair aside and studied her face. "No mistakes. No selfish acts. I must speak with your father first."

Her eyebrows slammed together, and she tilted her head at a confused angle. "Now? You need to speak to my father at this hour?"

His mouth curved at the sign of her bafflement, and he dropped his hand. "I don't want to wait until morning." Surely, she understood what he meant. Surely, she understood why he had to ask her father for her hand in marriage before he asked her. Tyler and Rachel had made propriety all the more necessary.

She took a shaky breath. "But why tonight? I don't understand the rush."

"Because I have to…" Fearing time was running out, he stabbed a glance toward her father's house. Urgency sent his blood screaming through his veins. "We have to go quickly, before he retires for the evening."

He spun on his heel and made his way back toward the house at a hurried pace.

"Beau, wait."

She trotted after him.

He slowed his gait to accommodate hers.

"Have you gone mad?" she asked when she caught up.

With a quick flash of teeth, he grinned down at her. "Mad? No. In fact, I'm the sanest I've ever been."

Hannah couldn't imagine what was taking so long. Her father and Beau had been holed up in the church's office for well over an hour. What could they possibly be discussing that couldn't have waited until morning?

Beau had been so agitated earlier.

Weariness swamped her suddenly, made her want to collapse in a puddle of shivers. If only she had someone to help her sort out the confusing facts. But for all intents and purposes, she was alone with her worry.

Mavis had long since abandoned the vigil and had fallen asleep in a chair in the far corner of the parlor, snoring and muttering in her sleep.

Hannah didn't have the heart to wake the older woman.

When she looked over at her chaperone-turned-friend, a flutter of affection shifted in her stomach. Mavis was a part of her family now. Would Beau be a part of it, as well?

A rush of excitement surged through her at the thought.

Beau had mentioned he wanted to do things right. With Tyler and Rachel running off the way they had, she could understand that desire. But surely Beau wouldn't ask her father for her hand without speaking with her first. He couldn't be that dense, that heavy-handed. That...male.

Please, Lord, let me be wrong about this.

But when another handful of minutes passed by, and the door remained firmly shut, Hannah's fears increased.

She paced.

She worried.

She paced some more.

Looking around the parlor, she took more than a cursory inventory of the room this time. Nothing had changed in the last five years of her absence. The room was still clean. Neat. Unpretentious. Much like her father.

And yet, it had her mother's stamp on it, as well, left over from all these years. The rose and peony wallpaper had been hung on Hannah's seventh birthday. The memory of the day when her mother had allowed her to help pick out the pattern still burned in Hannah's mind. But just as quickly, it skipped away.

Hannah sighed and continued her inspection.

Although the pattern was unique, the brocade upholstery on the furniture matched the colors on the walls seamlessly. The sturdy mahogany chairs and tables, brushed golden from the firelight, brought to mind permanence. Stability. Reminding her of—

The door to the office swung open, and Hannah jumped.

As both men approached, Hannah desperately tried to calm her nerves. She looked from Beau to her father and back to Beau again.

Although they were smiling, there was something in their expressions, something a little too arrogant and a little too masculine, that sent trepidation hovering at the back of her throat.

Beau's eyes danced with an unreadable look as he took her hands in his. She hated that he was so inscrutable all of a sudden. Something deep inside her, something inherently female, warned her that the ensuing conversation was not going to go well. "Beau? What is it? What's happened?"

His expression transformed, and he gave her the lazy O'Toole smile that should have warmed her heart. Dread settled hot in her chest instead.

"As soon as I can make the arrangements, we'll break ground on my new church."

Hannah's stomach pitched at the news.

No, Lord, please no. Not this.

She stole a glance at her father, who was watching them with an air of satisfaction.

Oh, Lord, no.

Beau had settled. In spite of what he'd said earlier tonight, he'd settled for a life that would eventually suck his passion for the Lord dry. And yet, his eyes gleamed with joy. She tried to be happy for him, tried to understand. "I... That's wonderful."

But it wasn't wonderful. It was awful.

She loved Beauregard O'Toole, and silently wept over the mistake he was making. Her heart broke a little and she selfishly mourned the loss of her own dream.

Because, no matter what words came out of his mouth next, that new church of his would not include her. Beau might be able to settle. She, however, could not.

"And now, Hannah, your future will be safe, as well," her father said.

Switching her attention to him, Hannah pulled free of Beau's grip. "*My* future?"

She tried to sound haughty, but her voice held a hollow edge even to her own ears. Her world had just turned crooked and off balance, and she had no idea how to set it right again.

Clearly unaware of her disappointment, Beau continued smiling. "What your father is trying to say is that you don't have to worry about your future ever again. You'll never be scared and alone." The look in his eyes was possessive.

And broke her heart a little more.

"But I'm not alone now." She glanced toward her loyal chaperone, who was stretching and blinking herself awake. "I have Mavis."

Mavis smiled at her. "That's right, dearie." She pounded her birdlike chest with a fist, then released a round of harsh coughs. "You'll always have me," she declared once she had herself under control again.

Beau touched Hannah's arm, and she turned to look at him again. "That's not what I meant. With me, you'll never end up like Jane."

Of course she wouldn't end up like Jane. She'd already taken care of that herself. But the inflexible look in Beau's eyes hiked her chin a little higher, and the first threads of despair roped through her blood. Beau looked as though he'd just given her the greatest gift in life—male protection.

Her heart pounded thick with fear.

It wasn't that she didn't want his protection. She

didn't *need* it. Why didn't he understand that essential truth? After everything they'd been through, Beau didn't know her. He didn't know her at all.

Her father cleared his throat and gave her the smile he usually reserved for Rachel. In fact, he looked like the happy patriarch presiding over his brood. "And best of all, you're going to be a minister's wife."

"That's right," Beau said. "We're getting married."

She opened her mouth, closed it and then said, "Who's getting married?"

But she knew what he meant. How could he believe all was settled when he hadn't even asked her the question?

As though she hadn't spoken, her father added, "Of course you have my blessing." He turned to Beau. "I think you will make my daughter a fine husband."

Mavis gasped. Loudly. Then she snorted. *Then* she mumbled something that sounded like "idiot men."

At least one other person in the room understood.

Beau couldn't be doing this to her. He respected her too much not to properly ask for her hand in marriage.

Too stunned to do much more than stare at them both, Hannah responded with a growl in her throat, a furious shake of her head and a narrowing of her eyes.

Still, the idiot men forged ahead.

"Your father will perform the ceremony, of course."

She gawked at him, terrified of how easy it would be to break down and cry. But the vicious stirrings of pride began weaving through her, and she promised herself she would never cry in front of Beauregard O'Toole. *Never.*

As though sensing her mood at last, Beau's shoulders stiffened in alarm. "Hannah?"

She tried to speak, she could even feel her jaw working, but discernible words eluded her. Finally, she said, "Let me see if I have this straight. We're getting married." She pointed to her and Beau. "And he's performing the ceremony." She pointed to her father.

She held the pause, praying, wishing, hoping either Beau or her father would redeem themselves at any moment.

Which, of course, they didn't. They both stared at her, eyes blinking in identical displays of confusion.

The ticking of the mantel clock mocked her. Tick, tick, tick went the pendulum. No, no, no went her heart. Wrapping her dignity around her like a shield of armor, she set her chin and held to her silence.

When Beau scrunched his forehead, indicating he was deep in thought, Hannah prayed for a miracle.

Mavis came up next to her and clutched her hand. Hannah held on for dear life. Tears pricked in her eyes. The tears were more from loss of pride than pain, or so she told herself, and that made controlling them so much harder.

In slow, clipped tones that would have sent a sane man running for cover, Hannah broke the silence. "And you two have planned all of this so I won't end up like Jane."

Beau's eyes narrowed, and she saw the exact moment when understanding dawned. His face instantly fell and he raked a shaky hand through his hair. "Hannah, I didn't mean—"

"Oh, but you did." Seething anger replaced the hurt. His apology had come too late. The damage had been done. "I thought you said you were sorry for the way you treated me at our first meeting. But I see you truly believe that I will fall into a life of sin without you guarding me against that terrible fate."

Oh, but this time, *this* time, he'd hurt her deep at the core—where she trusted most.

"I *am* sorry. You are a kind, compassionate, Christian woman. You are—"

"A woman who will end up like Jane if left to her own devices?"

Obviously stunned by her vehemence, he blinked. Then blinked again.

Didn't he understand? "There is no shame in what I am, in what I do. I am a successful *actress,*" she shouted. "Do you hear me? An actress."

Mavis snorted. "*I* certainly heard you." She clutched Hannah's hand tighter. "And I don't blame you for being angry. Not one bit." She glared at Beau with disappointment in her eyes. "You should know better, boy."

"You stay out of this," Reverend Southerland said.

"*You* stay out of this, as well." Hannah jabbed a finger in his direction. "This isn't about you, either."

Her father lifted himself to his full height. "You are my daughter. And that makes this my business. I've turned my back on you for five years. I was wrong to abandon you. You could have been hurt—" he shuddered "—or worse. I can't allow you to walk out of this house unprotected again."

"Oh, Father."

His eyes looked so somber, so full of pain and regret. "Beauregard can protect you as I never did," he said.

Hannah stared at her father in awe. Wisps of childhood memories flitted across her mind. But tonight, she didn't see the unforgiving preacher who'd condemned her for her sins. No, tonight, she saw the grieving widower unprepared to care for two young daughters. One too wild for him to handle, the other too weak and needy. She saw a man who had escaped in the safety of the rules and rituals of his religion.

He hadn't been a bad man. Just a hurting one.

He'd done the best he could. And now, in his own, arrogant way, he was trying to make up for his mistake.

She took a deep breath. And forgave.

"Father, I understand your concern."

She stopped, shook her head, suddenly very tired, and frightened, and confused. But then, she did something she never thought she'd do in this lifetime. She rushed to her father and hugged her arms around his waist.

He stood rigid at first. With awkward movements, he finally returned her embrace. "I'm so sorry, Hannah." His voice hitched with emotion.

"Me, too. But, Father, you don't have to worry about me. I have money. Lots of it. And I own property. And stocks and bonds, too."

She swung around to glare at Beau, pinpointing all of her turbulent emotions into one seething spark of anger. "When your mother took me in, do you think she only taught me about acting?"

"I—"

"No." She cut him off. "Patience taught me how to save and invest and manage my money properly, once I started making more than I knew what to do with."

"I don't understand." There was such male confusion in his eyes that Hannah almost felt sorry for him. *Almost.*

His arrogance had cut her too deeply to stifle her pride now.

"I am a wealthy woman in my own right, Beau. So, you see, I don't need you."

Oh, but she lied. She lied, lied, lied. She did need him, needed him like air. But stubborn pride, that evil, evil character flaw that ran deep and wide within her, wouldn't let her take back her words.

His face collapsed and he reached out his hand to her. All facades were gone. He wore no mask. And no O'Toole charm softened his features. All that was left was raw exposure. "But, Hannah, I need you."

She lowered her head, unable to bear the pain in his eyes. Her pride wouldn't release her enough to give him the words he wanted. "Maybe you do need me," she whispered. "But not enough to ask me to marry you."

"I did."

"No." She sighed. "You *told* me."

When he stared back at her and didn't declare his love for her right away, Hannah knew she'd lost him. No, she thought, she couldn't lose something she'd never had.

He might think he needed her. But it wasn't her he needed. It was some ideal woman who would smooth his rough edges.

"Come on, Mavis," she said, her tone flat. "Let's go."

Beau found his voice then. "That's it?" he asked, a hard steel of anger edging his words. "That's how this ends? You just walk out on me? Don't you want to know the particulars of my new church?"

"No." She turned her back on him, felt his hand hover near her shoulder but then drop without making contact. She desperately wanted to swing around to face him, but she was too proud to let him see the helplessness in her eyes. "It would break my heart."

Chapter Twenty-One

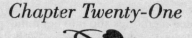

The Grand Opera House, Chicago, Illinois
Six weeks later

Shakespeare's *Hamlet* progressed toward its dramatic conclusion. Crimes were exposed with the perfect blend of shock and retribution. Schemes and false loyalties were revealed at a precise, well-rehearsed pace.

Unfortunately, Hannah no longer found joy translating every nuance found on paper into a memorable performance onstage. The irony of playing Ophelia, an obedient young woman dependent on men to tell her how to behave, brought back poignant memories of her last meeting with Beau.

If only that night had been a dress rehearsal, she would have played her role differently in the final performance.

After tonight there would be no more performances for her. Fitting, perhaps, that her last play was a tragedy.

With nothing left to do but take her bows, Hannah stood poised in the shadows offstage. She tried to contain her nerves, but she was impatient to move on to the next chapter of her life.

At first, when Hannah had returned to Chicago with Mavis in tow she had craved the escape of her profession. Needed it as much as breath itself. In the end, she'd only found loneliness. Guilt.

Regret.

Unwanted memories slid into her mind, playing out as strangely real as the last moments of the play. She'd been so angry at Beau for his high-handed treatment of her. All because he'd chosen to ally himself with her father. Looking back now, she realized she'd felt betrayed by them both. Yet it had been easier to forgive her father than Beau.

Why was that?

Because she'd allowed fear and pride to dictate her actions. She'd overreacted, jumped to conclusions and had cowardly disappeared before the final act.

Well, Hannah would make it right. All she had to do was find Beau and then ask for his forgiveness.

With that thought, Hannah leaned slightly forward, her eyes searching for the woman positioned in the wings off the opposite end of the stage. Mavis waggled her fingers at her, and then pointed to their packed trunks behind her.

Tonight they would leave the theater forever.

Hannah's hands started to shake again, threatening her outward calm. A deep, driving urge to leave now, before the play was complete, washed through her. Hannah roped her fingers together and clutched her palms tightly against one another. In this mood, her mind wandered back in time, back to that dismal night in her father's parlor.

Why hadn't she asked Beau about his church? Why hadn't she loved him enough to support his dream?

Because she'd been afraid. Afraid she'd turn into an Amelia. And because of that fear, she'd allowed pride to rule her heart.

Unable to bear her own emotions, she shifted her gaze toward the audience. Hannah squinted deep into the shadows until her gaze focused. Countless faces stared at the stage with their usual rapt attention.

Tonight, however, their willingness to accept the lie grated. Why were so many hungry for an illusion? Hannah no longer wanted the deception herself.

From this day forward, she wanted nothing but truth in her life.

Taking a deep breath, Hannah turned her attention back to the stage. The actor playing the Norwegian prince, Fortinbras, had just demanded Hamlet be carried away in a manner befitting a fallen soldier.

Hannah sighed in relief. A few more minutes and she would be free.

At last, Hamlet's body was carried offstage.

A hushed pause filled the theater.

Then…

The audience surged to its feet. Applause thundered. And the curtain began its slow descent. Chaos instantly erupted behind the delicate veil between audience and actor.

"Places, everyone," yelled the director. He turned to Hannah and motioned her forward.

Hannah wove her way through the labyrinth of rushing humanity, gliding toward her spot on the far edge of the troupe.

Once in place, Hannah rubbed her tongue across her teeth before turning her head to seek out Mavis once more.

Hannah's breath backed up in her lungs.

Mavis was gone.

In her place stood...

Beau.

With greedy eyes, Hannah looked at him. He'd grown thinner, a bit worn, but was still the most beautiful man she'd ever seen. For once in her life, she ignored pride. She ignored obligation. And broke formation in a run.

"Hannah," said the director. "Where are you going?"

She flicked her wrist at him. "I'm through."

"You can't do this," he called after her. "You must take your bows."

Speechless with frustration, she turned back. One step, two, and then she hesitated, poised between her past and her future.

She chose the future.

Shooting the director an apologetic shake of her head, she swung her back to the stage and rushed toward Beau.

Eyes focused on him, and him alone, she ignored the director's howl of outrage.

With each step, Hannah noted the conflicting emotions on Beau's face, love overriding everything else.

She picked up the pace, but was suddenly jostled by an actor on her left. Beau's eyes filled with alarm, but Hannah caught her balance and continued forward.

At last, he smiled at her.

Fear gripped her in response. She couldn't lose him again.

Lord, fill me with a humble heart, she prayed. *Fill me with the courage to ask his forgiveness.*

How easy it would be to allow pride to keep her from admitting her share of the guilt.

Hannah pressed her lips together, realizing she'd missed the point all along. What did it matter if they lived in a church in the meadow or in a mining camp or a saloon? Life with Beauregard O'Toole, wherever it took them, would hold the perfect blend of Christian grace, charity and hope.

With a shake of her head, Hannah smiled at her astonishingly handsome costar in life.

Golden, spectacular, filled with charm, Beauregard O'Toole was everything she wanted in a man. Three priorities ruled his actions. God. Family. Ministry.

She stopped in front of him, suddenly unsure where to begin. She looked at his chiseled, handsome face. What if he didn't want her? What if she'd misread the love in his eyes?

A knot of anxiety twisted in her stomach. The noise of the theater became a dull drumming in her ears.

He reached for her hand, bent at the waist and dropped a kiss onto her knuckles. The gesture brought tears to her eyes.

Everything would be all right. As long as they were together.

"You were breathtaking tonight, my dear." His voice was a little shaky, and the most beautiful sound Hannah had heard in the last six weeks.

He rose slowly, deliberately, and then sent her a suave half smile. "How I've missed you."

Pressure built in her chest and stole her breath. "Oh, Beau, can you forgive me?"

"It is I who needs to be forgiven." The sorrow in his

eyes was real. "I've been a stupid, stupid man, ignoring the blessing right in front of me. Well, I see you now. And I see my mistakes. I should have asked you to marry me before I spoke to your father."

"I should have given you the chance to tell me about your church."

He shook his head.

She gave him a wobbly smile.

The noise increased, making it hard to speak without shouting. Hannah looked around, tugged him farther away from the stage and into a private nook under the rigging.

"I'm leaving the company tonight," she told him once they were nestled in the quiet alcove.

His eyes met hers, and in them she saw what she'd missed in her father's parlor. Beau was prepared to treat her as his equal. "Mavis told me."

She made a watery sound in her throat. "Did Mavis also tell you we were starting our search for you?"

"She did."

Ah, Mavis. The dear old woman was better than any godmother in a Grimm's fairy tale.

"You never let me explain about my new church."

His gray eyes blazed so brightly with conviction, the heat of shame warmed her face.

Hannah lowered her head. "I'm sorry," she whispered.

He placed his finger under her chin and applied pressure. As her chin rose, Hannah had to fight the urge to look away from his face. But she forced herself to keep her gaze locked with his.

"I didn't accept the position in Greeley," he said. "I turned your father down that night in his office."

In the face of his declaration, it was remarkable

Hannah's knees didn't give out. As Beau had once done to her, she'd judged him without knowing the complete facts. Yet he didn't hold her mistake against her. He'd come to find her, with love shining in his eyes.

Oh, Lord, thank you.

"I… You're going to continue traveling as before?" she asked.

"No." He smiled. "God has a different plan for me, for us."

Hannah blinked. "Oh?"

"I'm starting a new church, outside of Denver, right next to—"

"Charity House."

"Precisely."

A sense of rightness filled her. "That's wonderful."

"Marc planted a seed months ago," Beau said. "One I nearly let die. The orphans at Charity House need a spiritual shepherd, as do their mothers and others like them."

"It makes perfect sense."

"Although the Rocky Mountain Association won't offer any support or assistance, your father will. Actually, he's been giving me advice in the initial planning stages."

Her father giving Beau advice on a church designed to open its doors to all people? Oh, how far they'd all come.

"I would have been here sooner, but I wanted to have some stability to offer you first."

"Oh, Beau, my home will be wherever you are. I will follow wherever you go. So, you see, I don't need stability."

"Maybe I do. Maybe I need to know I can give you more than a vagabond life."

She cocked her head. "What if God uproots us?"

"Then we go. Together." His eyes glittered, and he tugged her hand against his heart. "You said you were coming in search of me? Where did you plan to start that search?"

"In Greeley. I wanted you to know I would support you wherever God leads."

He stared at her with awe and love in his eyes. "Will you consider coming back to Denver and assisting me in my new adventure?"

Her heart dropped to her toes, bounced, then hung suspended for a split second before settling back in place. "*Assist* you?"

His eyes never left her face, but a charming O'Toole grin slid on his lips. "I need your help."

"My help?"

"Starting a new church is too big a job for one man to accomplish alone."

"Too big a job?"

His grin turned into a full, heart-stopping smile. It was a weapon against which she had no defense.

"Are you going to keep repeating my words?" he asked.

She cocked her head at him, searched his eyes. Beauregard O'Toole was up to something. "Are you going to ask me the right question?"

"I'll need a helpmate to start my church."

"A helpmate."

"A wife," he blurted out. "I need a wife." He shook his head. "That had to be the worst proposal ever. Second only to the last one, when I *told* you we were getting married. Hannah, I—"

She placed her finger against his lips. "I kind of like this most recent proposal of yours. In fact, I think it's going rather well."

"Do you like it enough to say yes?"

"How can I? You haven't actually asked me a question."

He lowered to one knee. Threads of light from the stage cascaded in his hair. Her golden knight. No, better, her rebel preacher.

"Hannah, will you marry me?" His voice came out grave. "Will you assist me in doing God's work? Will you stand by me, no matter where life takes us, even when I'm an arrogant son of an actor?"

"How could I refuse such a lovely offer?"

He slowly rose to his feet and placed both hands on her shoulders. "Is *that* a yes?"

"No."

His face fell. Apparently, he wasn't in the mood for teasing.

"It's an ab-so-lutely."

He abandoned restraint and pulled her into his arms. "That's more like it." He pulled back and gave her an arrogant wink. "We'll get married right away. No arguments. I'm not going to risk losing you again."

"You know, Beau." She turned her head at a saucy angle. "Sometimes your arrogance is really rather appealing."

"I'll remember you said that."

"Well, remember this. I'll marry you, yes. Under two conditions."

"Two?" He set her away from him and studied her face for a long moment. Then he smiled. "Only two?"

Apparently, he *was* in the mood for teasing now.

"One." She pointed her finger toward the ceiling. "We get married right away."

"Makes sense to me." He regarded her with a triumphant look. "Since I already said that."

Enjoying herself immensely, she pursed her lips. "You scoundrel."

He gave her a careless shrug. "I'm working on my arrogant streak."

Hannah rolled her eyes and tried not to smile. "You still have a ways to go."

Ignoring her comment, he touched a strand of her hair, twirled it around his fingertip, then looked back into her eyes. "What's your other condition?"

She took a deep breath and forced a serious expression onto her features. "We adopt Mavis."

He stared at her. Blinked. Stared at her awhile longer. "Isn't she a little old for adoption?"

Up went her chin. "I think she's the perfect age."

"Hannah Southerland, you are an eccentric woman, and I love you with all my heart." He punctuated his words with a soft kiss to her lips.

"I love you, too, Beau." This time she didn't have to feign her serious expression.

He cupped her cheek in his hand and smiled.

"So, what do you say about adopting Mavis?" she asked on a wispy sigh.

He kissed her on the nose. "Done."

"I knew you'd see things my way."

A single eyebrow shot up. "Now who needs to work on their arrogant streak?"

"We'll work on them together."

He laughed and pulled her into a tight hug. "It'll probably take us a lifetime."

"I have the stomach for it, if you do."

He laughed again.

"I love you, Beauregard O'Toole," she whispered in his ear.

"I love you, too, Mrs. O'Toole."

"Mrs. O'Toole?" She pulled slightly away and lifted her head.

"Just checking to see how it sounds."

Mavis chose that moment to join their happy twosome. With a gnarled finger, she poked Beau on the shoulder.

He released Hannah and looked down at the scowling woman. "May I help you?"

"Are we getting married or not? Yes or no, boy?"

Beau pivoted and kissed Mavis on the cheek. "I say, yes!"

Mavis snorted. "'Bout time."

Beau reached out a hand to both women and pulled them against him. "What say we make our final exit and start our life together right away?" He looked down at Hannah with love shining in his eyes. "Yes or no, woman?"

A lone tear slipped from her eye. "I say, yes!"

Epilogue

Hannah and Beau's wedding day arrived on a snow-filled morning in late November. Beau had requested the ceremony take place at Charity House. Hannah had immediately agreed.

Of course, once her friends at the orphanage took over, the simple ceremony in Marc's study had turned into an elaborate affair that required an additional three weeks to organize.

Beau, being Beau, hadn't complained.

Hannah, being Hannah, had resolved to make the celebration well worth the many delays.

With that silent promise in mind, Hannah spent all morning preparing for the big event. Determined to impress her groom, she took special care dressing, paying particular attention to her hair. Confident she'd done her best, she pinned the last ribbon in place, brushed a barely noticeable wrinkle from her skirt and strolled to the window overlooking Charity House's backyard.

The cold mountain air seeped past the window casing

and whispered across her face. Taking a moment to settle her nerves, Hannah dragged the coolness into her lungs and took in God's splendor before her.

The sun shone in a cloudless sky, soaring over a world washed clean with snow. A gentle breeze swirled a transparent, frosty mist along the top layer of flakes. Off in the distance, the western peaks wore a heavy blanket of glossy white.

Hannah squeezed her eyes shut and prayed for her future with Beau.

Heavenly Father, I pray You mold me into a good and decent wife. Bless my marriage to this wonderful man and make us better together than we could ever be apart. I pray this in Your Son's name, Amen.

Opening her eyes, she returned her attention to the yard. She traced the perimeter with her gaze, noting with joy how it backed into the empty lot where they'd soon break ground on their new church. She would always remember the look of admiration in Beau's eyes when she'd told him she'd sold some of her Chicago property to buy the land and materials needed for the building.

If she squinted, Hannah could almost see the church in her mind. God's house would be sturdy and tall, with an impressive white steeple and a long line of eclectic members seeking refuge. A—

The door swung open and hit the wall with a thud. She jumped away from the window and spun quickly around. Her shock turned to pleasure as she caught sight of Laney entering the room.

"Oh, *Hannah.*" Laney gasped, her words coming out in a rush of pleasure. "You're beautiful."

There was no time for a response. One breath, two, and Hannah was pulled into Laney's tight embrace.

Overwhelmed with joy, Hannah clung to her new friend, her sister in Christ.

One more solid squeeze and Laney released her. "The guests are all assembled in the parlor. We just need—" she stretched out her hand "—the bride."

Smiling, Hannah reached out, as well, but a deep-pitched clearing of a throat had her dropping her hand and peering toward the masculine sound.

"Father," she said in surprise. "I thought you were waiting with Beau."

"I was." He moved deeper into the room with his usual air of authority. "I would like to speak with you first."

He sounded so formal. So distant. So like the father she'd always feared. But then he smiled, revealing a dimple in his left cheek, and Hannah immediately relaxed. Praise God, the cold man of her childhood no longer existed.

"I'll leave you two to talk." Laney squeezed Hannah's hand and quickly left the room.

Alone with her father, Hannah stood very still, very attentive. What had he come to say? Would she know how to answer?

Seeming in no hurry to speak, he scanned the room and then flicked a glance out the window. Moving closer, he rocked back on his heels and studied the pristine scenery with a blank, unreadable expression.

Anxiety churned in her stomach. Had the venerable reverend changed his mind about supporting her marriage to Beau?

She held her breath as he turned to face her again. But when their eyes met, Hannah saw nothing more than nervousness staring back at her. Not judgment. Not second thoughts. Merely the genuine unease of a father releasing his daughter to another man.

That knowledge gave Hannah the courage to break the silence herself. "I'm grateful you agreed to perform the ceremony, Father. It means a lot to Beau and me."

"I wouldn't have missed it." He pulled in a deep breath, released it slowly. "You make a beautiful bride, my dear. Just like your mother on our wedding day." Tears formed in his eyes.

Love and hope blossomed in her heart. "I…thank you."

"I have something for you." He stuck his hand into one of the inner pockets of his coat and pulled out a small velvet-coated box.

At the sight of the familiar container, Hannah willed her own tears into submission with a hard swallow.

"Oh, Father," she said, curling her fingers into the soft velvet. "You don't have to do this."

"I want to."

The look in his eyes stole her breath. It was the look of fatherly love. The look she'd craved all her life but feared would never come.

"Go on, Hannah. Open my gift."

With trembling fingers, she flipped back the lid, and gasped at the emerald pendant winking up at her.

"It was your mother's," he said, his voice storming with emotion.

Blinking rapidly, Hannah concentrated on the necklace. On the black velvet box. On anything but the fresh ache in her chest. "I remember," she whispered. "She only wore it once a year, on Easter Sunday."

He smiled. "The stone reminded her of spring, renewed life and—"

"The Resurrection."

"She would want you to have it." He cleared his throat. "*I* want you to have it."

His softly uttered words staggered her, and the muscles in her throat quivered, making a response impossible.

Silently, she handed him the necklace and turned to face the mirror. "Will you help me with the clasp?" she choked out.

"Of…course."

She lowered her head and waited.

He hesitated. Then, with unsteady fingers, he fastened the pendant around her neck.

When she lifted her head, she caught his gaze in their shared reflection.

A lone tear slid down his cheek.

"I'm forever grateful the Lord brought you back to me," he said on a shallow breath.

Hannah squeezed her eyes shut and then faced him directly. It was time she set aside the last of her foolish pride. There could be no more excuses now. After years of deception and misplaced loyalties, Rachel no longer stood between them.

Lifting her chin, Hannah gave her father a shaky smile. "I love you…*Daddy.*"

A strangled sound whipped from his throat, and he roped her tightly against him.

"And I you, my beloved daughter."

The hug was short. But when he stepped back, another tear trailed down his cheek.

The reflex to scrub at her own eyes came fast, but he lifted his hand and wiped her face with the pad of his thumb.

"Our time is up, Hannah," he said softly. "Your groom is waiting."

As if on cue, Laney reappeared in the doorway. "Is the bride ready?"

Hannah inhaled deeply, touched her fingertip to the emerald pendant growing warm against her skin. "Yes."

Her father pivoted on his heel.

"Father, wait."

He turned, a question in his gaze.

Lifting to her toes, she placed a kiss on his cheek. "Thank you."

With pure delight in his eyes, he gave her shoulder a quick pat and then headed down the hallway that led to the back entrance of the parlor.

Arm in arm, Laney and Hannah made their way to the front of the house. At the sound of voices lowered to muted whispers, Hannah stopped midstride. Much to her surprise, a surge of nervousness swept through her. She hadn't been this anxious before, not even the first time she'd graced the stage as a leading lady.

Happiness overwhelmed her to think her life would now be guided by the Master Director, the Ancient of Days—her Heavenly Father.

Laney gently unwound their arms. "This is where I leave you, my friend."

Swallowing, Hannah nodded.

With a quick smile and a backward glance over her shoulder, the other woman disappeared into the room. Stomach twisting into a dozen knots, Hannah peeked around the corner after her.

Every orphan was in attendance, grinning from ear to ear and, of course, fidgeting. She counted at least ten adults lined against the outer wall. Thankfully, it didn't take Hannah long to locate Mavis sitting on the floor amidst a group of the younger children. Several had managed to climb onto her lap.

As though she sensed Hannah's eyes on her, Mavis looked up and winked.

Hannah winked back, and just like that her nervousness melted away. She was among friends. People who loved her. People she loved in return.

Feeling more confident, Hannah moved into the center of the threshold and met her father's gaze. His tenderness, his quiet acceptance silenced her remaining apprehension.

Chin up, Hannah finally turned her attention to her groom. Their gazes locked. A low buzz filled her ears, and everyone else in the room faded.

In the span of a single heartbeat, a thousand words passed between them.

Beau. *Her Beau.*

So handsome, so upright. With him, her life had found its pulse.

In pure O'Toole fashion, he sent her a quick, captivating smile. And the breath backed up in her throat.

With his charming brand of arrogance firmly in place, he stretched out his hand and summoned her to him.

Her heart took a quick tumble.

And then…

She simply…

Sighed.

Notching her head a fraction higher, Hannah squared her shoulders and began her ascent toward the man of her dreams. Her best friend.

No matter what hardships arose, no matter what challenges God brought their way, they would face them together. Two cords linked as one.

Bucking tradition, Beau abandoned his post next to the reverend and hastened down the makeshift aisle to meet Hannah halfway across the room.

Surrounded by the adults and children of Charity House, he took her hand and cupped it protectively in his. A dozen happy thoughts ran through Hannah's mind as Beau swept in a low bow and touched his lips to her knuckles.

When he rose, his eyes locked with hers again. "I'm yours, Hannah Southerland. Heart and soul, forever."

She had to gulp several times in order to regain her voice.

"I'm yours, Beauregard O'Toole," she pledged. "No matter the place, the circumstance or the season, I will always stand by your side."

Grinning, he lowered his forehead to hers. For a long moment they simply stood unmoving, neither speaking, both breathing deeply.

A hush filled the room. Hannah heard a rustle of clothing as everyone leaned forward in anticipation.

Finally, Beau stepped away and aimed his beautiful, silver gaze at her. "Then I say we get married *right now*."

Forty-some voices lifted in a cheer of agreement.

Twining his fingers with hers, Beau led Hannah down the last half of the aisle toward her father and the place where they would pledge their lives to one another.

Sealed in marriage, Hannah and Beau would no longer be two transient people drifting from place to place, waiting to hear God's clear direction for their lives.

Secure in His plan, they were home. Home, at last.

* * * * *

Dear Reader,

When I graduated college, one of my beloved mentors sat me down for a little one-on-one preparation for the real world. At one point in the conversation, she said, "Remember, Renee, you never get a second chance to make a first impression." Now, I'd call that sound advice for a young woman entering the workforce for the first time.

But as I've matured, I've come to realize a major flaw in those sage words—the inability we often have to see past the outward appearance to the person underneath. After all, no one can truly know another person's heart. No one, that is, except God. Hannah and Beau had to learn this lesson the hard way. I truly hope you enjoyed their journey past wrong first impressions to the discovery of redeeming love, hope and acceptance.

Hannah is special to me in another way. I, too, am a twin. For the record, I'm far more fortunate in my wonderful sister than Hannah is in Rachel. There's nothing quite like the close bond I share with my twin. In fact, my sister was the inspiration for Hannah. So, hmm, does that make me Rachel? I certainly hope not. Unfortunately, there were times when I found myself understanding the woman a bit too well.

I love hearing from readers. Do you have a sibling story of your own to share? Please do so through my Web site, www.reneeryan.com, where you can also read about my upcoming releases in the CHARITY HOUSE series.
Blessings,
Renee Ryan

QUESTIONS FOR DISCUSSION

1. We learn in the opening scene that Hannah has an identical twin. What sort of complications has this added to her life? What role has she herself played? Could she have done anything differently? What could she have done?

2. Have you ever wanted to be a twin? Why or why not? Under what circumstances would it be hard to have an identical twin? If you parented twins, would you dress them alike? Why or why not?

3. Although Beau is an ordained minister who graduated from a respectable seminary, in what way is he considered a rebel preacher? Why would other preachers find him a threat? Why would they admire him?

4. When Beau first meets Hannah, he draws several erroneous conclusions about her, merely from the way she's dressed. Have you ever made a snap judgment, only to regret it later? How did you handle that? What would you have done differently?

5. Have you ever been on the receiving end of a false first impression? How did that make you feel? What, if anything, did you do to change the person's mind?

6. Charity House is a unique orphanage, set up to care for children that more respectable orphanages have

refused. Why do you think Hannah feels instant camaraderie with Laney, the orphanage's proprietress? Why do you think she feels at home with these special children?

7. What do you think drives Beau's dream of shepherding a flock in his own "church on the meadow"? Why do you think he holds on to his dream so tightly, even when he's gifted in a completely different area? Have you had something in your own life that you held on to that tightly?

8. Beau's brother Tyler gives him sage advice about his dream church. Do you think God can use unlikely vessels such as Tyler? Why or why not? Have you ever received advice from an unlikely source that changed your entire way of thinking?

9. When Beau runs into the woman who turned down his marriage proposal, what insight does he get into her true character? Why do you think he was so nervous to tell Hannah about Amelia? Have you ever run into someone from your past and wondered why they ever held so much power over you? How did that encounter affect you?

10. Hannah returns home to confront her father for the first time in five years. Why do you think Beau encouraged her to ask for forgiveness, even when she was the one wrongfully cast out? Is her father's reaction what you expected? Why or why not?

11. If you had to choose between Hannah and Rachel, or Beau and Tyler, which character did you identify with most? Why?

12. In the end, do you think Beau and Hannah compromise their individual dreams in order to be together, or does God change the desires of their hearts? Has God ever changed the desires of your heart? If so, how did that change your dreams and future plans?

Dumped via certified letter days before her wedding, Haley Scott sees her dreams of happily ever after crushed. But could it turn out to be the best thing that's ever happened to her?

Turn the page for a sneak preview of
AN UNEXPECTED MATCH
by Dana Corbit,
book 1 in the new WEDDING BELLS BLESSINGS
trilogy,
available beginning August 2009
from Love Inspired®.

"Is there a Haley Scott here?"

Haley glanced through the storm door at the package carrier before opening the latch and letting in some of the frigid March wind.

"That's me, but not for long."

The blank stare the man gave her as he stood on the porch of her mother's new house only made Haley smile. In fifty-one hours and twenty-nine minutes, her name would be changing. Her life, as well, but she couldn't allow herself to think about that now.

She wouldn't attribute her sudden shiver to anything but the cold, either. Not with a bridal fitting to endure, embossed napkins to pick up and a caterer to call. Too many details, too little time and certainly no time for her to entertain her silly cold feet.

"Then this is for you."

Practiced at this procedure after two days back in her Markston, Indiana, hometown, Haley reached out both arms to accept a bridal gift, but the carrier turned and deposited an overnight letter package in just one of her hands. Haley stared down at the Michigan return address of her fiancé, Tom Jeffries.

"Strange way to send a wedding present," she murmured.

The man grunted and shoved an electronic signature device at her, waiting until she scrawled her name.

As soon as she closed the door, Haley returned to the living room and yanked the tab on the paperboard. From it, she withdrew a single sheet of folded notebook paper.

Something inside her suggested that she should sit down to read it, so she lowered herself into a floral side chair. Hesitating, she glanced at the far wall where wedding gifts in pastel-colored paper were stacked, then she unfolded the note. Her stomach tightened as she read each handwritten word.

"Best? He signed it *best?"* Her voice cracked as the paper fluttered to the floor. She was sure she should be sobbing or collapsing in a heap, but she felt only numb as she stared down at the offending piece of paper.

The letter that had changed everything.

"Best what?" Trina Scott asked as she padded into the room with fuzzy striped socks on her feet. "Sweetie?"

Haley lifted her gaze to meet her mother's and could see concern etched between her carefully tweezed brows.

"What's the matter?" Trina shot a glance toward the foyer, her chin-length brown hair swinging past her ear as she did it. "Did I just hear someone at the door?"

Haley tilted her head to indicate the sheet of paper on the floor. "It's from Tom. He called off the wedding."

"What? Why?" Trina began, but then brushed her hand through the air twice as if to erase the question. "That's not the most important thing right now, is it?"

Haley stared at her mother. A little pity wouldn't have been out of place here. Instead of offering any, Trina snapped up the letter and began to read. When she finished, she sat on the cream-colored sofa opposite Haley's chair.

"I don't approve of his methods." She shook the letter to emphasize her point. "And I always thought the boy didn't have enough good sense to come out of the rain, but I have to agree with him on this one. You two aren't right for each other."

Haley couldn't believe her ears. Okay, Tom wouldn't have been the partner Trina Scott would have chosen for her youngest daughter if Trina's grand matchmaking scheme hadn't gone belly-up. Still, Haley hadn't realized how strongly her mother disapproved of her choice.

"No sense being upset about my opinion now," Trina told her. "I kept praying that you'd make the right decision, but I guess Tom made it for you. Now we have to get busy. There are a lot of calls to make. I'll call Amy." Trina dug the cell phone from her purse and hit one of the speed-dial numbers.

Haley winced. In any situation, it shouldn't have surprised her that her mother's first reaction was to phone her best friend, but Trina had more than knee-jerk reasons to make this call. Not only had Amy Warren been asked to join them downtown this afternoon for Haley's final bridal fitting, but she also was scheduled to make the wedding cake at her bakery, Amy's Elite Treats.

Haley asked herself again why she'd agreed to plan the wedding in her hometown. Now her humiliation would double as she shared it with family friends. One in particular.

"May I speak to Amy?" Trina began as someone answered the line. "Oh, Matthew, is that you?"

That's the one. Haley squeezed her eyes shut.

* * * * *

*Will her former crush be the one
to mend Haley's broken heart?
Find out in AN UNEXPECTED MATCH,
available in August 2009
only from Love Inspired®.*

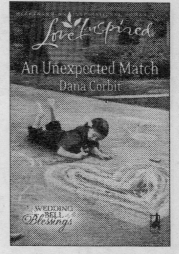

Love Inspired

Even their meddling mothers don't think practical single dad Matthew Warren and free-spirited nanny Haley Scott are right for each other. But they surprise everyone— including themselves— by proving that opposites do attract!

Look for

An Unexpected Match

by

Dana Corbit

WEDDING BELL *Blessings*

Available August wherever books are sold.

www.SteepleHill.com

Love Inspired
HISTORICAL
INSPIRATIONAL HISTORICAL ROMANCE

Mary Randolph is determined to help the orphans of St. Louis, even if that means battling with by-the-book police captain Samuel Benton. Sam had a rough childhood, but Mary's feistiness is reigniting his faith—and showing him how true love can fulfill dreams.

Look for

The Law and Miss Mary

by

DOROTHY CLARK

Available in August wherever books are sold.

www.SteepleHill.com

Steeple
Hill®

REQUEST YOUR FREE BOOKS!

2 FREE INSPIRATIONAL NOVELS
PLUS 2
FREE
MYSTERY GIFTS

Love Inspired
HISTORICAL
INSPIRATIONAL HISTORICAL ROMANCE

YES! Please send me 2 FREE Love Inspired® Historical novels and my 2 FREE mystery gifts (gifts are worth about $10). After receiving them, if I don't wish to receive any more books, I can return the shipping statement marked "cancel". If I don't cancel, I will receive 4 brand-new novels every other month and be billed just $4.24 per book in the U.S. or $4.74 per book in Canada. That's a savings of over 20% off the cover price. It's quite a bargain! Shipping and handling is just 50¢ per book.* I understand that accepting the 2 free books and gifts places me under no obligation to buy anything. I can always return a shipment and cancel at any time. Even if I never buy another book, the two free books and gifts are mine to keep forever. 102 IDN EYPS 302 IDN EYP4

Name	(PLEASE PRINT)	
Address		Apt. #
City	State/Prov.	Zip/Postal Code

Signature (if under 18, a parent or guardian must sign)

Mail to Steeple Hill Reader Service:
IN U.S.A.: P.O. Box 1867, Buffalo, NY 14240-1867
IN CANADA: P.O. Box 609, Fort Erie, Ontario L2A 5X3

Not valid to current subscribers of Love Inspired Historical books.

Want to try two free books from another series?
Call 1-800-873-8635 or visit www.morefreebooks.com

LIH09

Love Inspired HISTORICAL

TITLES AVAILABLE NEXT MONTH

Available August 11, 2009

THE LAW AND MISS MARY by Dorothy Clark
It's disgraceful how St. Louis's orphans are treated.
Mary Randolph is determined to help them, even if she has
to battle by-the-book police captain Samuel Benton every
step of the way. A poverty-stricken childhood left Sam
hungry for the social acceptance now within his reach. Then
Miss Randolph's feisty perseverance begins to give him
second thoughts, reigniting his faith—and showing him how
true love can fulfill all their dreams....

THE OUTLAW'S LADY by Laurie Kingery
Rebellious rancher's daughter Tess Hennessy seeks
adventure—and finds herself abducted by the Delgado gang!
Gang member Sandoval Parrish captured her as a means to
an end, seeking retribution for the sister Delgado ruined. Yet
when his plan puts Tess in danger, Sandoval must choose
between the drive for revenge and a newfound love.

LIHCNMBPA0709